ADIB KHORRAM

DIAL BOOKS
An imprint of Penguin Random House LLC, New York

First published in the United States of America by Dial Books,
an imprint of Penguin Random House LLC, 2022
Copyright © 2022 by Adib Khorram

Visit us online at penguinrandomhouse.com.

Library of Congress Cataloging-in-Publication Data
Names: Khorram, Adib, author.
Title: Kiss & tell / Adib Khorram.
Other titles: Kiss and tell
Description: New York : Dial Books, 2022. | Audience: Ages 14 and up |
Audience: Grades 10-12. | Summary: On boy band Kiss & Tell's first major tour,
lead singer Hunter Drake grapples with a painful breakup with his first boyfriend,
his first rebound, and the stress of what it means to be queer in the public eye.
Identifiers: LCCN 2021048423 | ISBN 9780593325261 (hardcover) |
ISBN 9780593325285 (epub) | Subjects: CYAC: Dating (Social customs)—Fiction. |
Gays—Fiction. | Boy bands—Fiction. | LCGFT: Novels.
Classification: LCC PZ7.1.K5362 Ki 2022 | DDC [Fic]—dc23
LC record available at https://lccn.loc.gov/2021048423

Book manufactured in Canada
ISBN 9780593325261 • 10 9 8 7 6 5 4 3 2 1

FRI

ISBN 9780593463116 (INTERNATIONAL EDITION)

1 3 5 7 9 10 8 6 4 2

Design by Jason Henry • Text set in Neutraface Slab

FOR EVERYONE WHO'S
EVER BEEN AFRAID TO SING
ALONG TO BOY BANDS—
BUT SECRETLY WANTED TO

COME SAY HELLO: KISS & TELL'S NEW STADIUM TOUR SELLS OVER A MILLION SEATS IN SECONDS

NewzList
Date: February 12, 2022

With stops at stadiums and arenas across North America, Canadian sensation Kiss & Tell's *Come Say Hello* tour promises spectacle and song for their legions of tween fans. Tickets went on sale at 8:00 A.M. Pacific Standard Time, and within minutes, heartbroken fans were getting error messages and sold-out notifications; by 10:30, the entire tour had sold out. Estimates put the number of tickets sold at upwards of 1,000,000 seats.

Kiss & Tell member Hunter Drake, who is openly gay, has promised that fifty front-row seats at each concert will be given free of charge to local LGBTQ+ youth, and a portion of each concert's proceeds will benefit local LGBTQ+ shelters.

CHECK OUT THE FULL TOUR SCHEDULE BELOW

March 25–27: Vancouver, BC

March 28: Seattle, WA

March 29: Portland, OR

March 31–April 2:
Los Angeles, CA

April 3: Las Vegas, NV

April 4: Phoenix, AZ

April 5: Salt Lake City, UT

April 6: Denver, CO

April 7: Albuquerque, NM

April 8: Austin, TX

April 9: Houston, TX

April 12: Dallas, TX

April 13: Oklahoma City, OK

April 14: Kansas City, MO

April 15: St. Paul, MN

April 16–17: Chicago, IL

April 19–21: New York, NY

April 22: Boston, MA

April 23: Philadelphia, PA

April 24: Hershey, PA

April 26: Montreal, QC

April 28: Baltimore, MD

April 29-30: Washington, DC

May 1: Raleigh, NC

May 2: Charleston, SC

May 3: Atlanta, GA

May 4: Orlando, FL

May 5: Miami, FL

May 7: Nashville, TN

May 8: Louisville, KY

May 9: Columbus, OH

May 10: Detroit, MI

May 12–14: Toronto, ON

May 17–19: Mexico City, MX

Kiss & Tell's Ian Souza Rates Cheese Bread Recipes

Build a Poutine Order and We'll Tell You Who Your Kiss & Tell Soulmate Is

HUNTER DRAKE & AIDAN NIGHTINGALE
CALL IT QUITS

TRS (The Real Scoop)
Date: March 5, 2022

BREAKING 11:15 A.M.: Kiss & Tell singer Hunter Drake and his boyfriend Aidan Nightingale (twin brother of Hunter's bandmate Ashton) have broken up after two years, a source close to the band has confirmed.

Fans got to know the couple—called Haidan by their shippers—in a series of candid videos posted last year during rehearsals for Kiss & Tell's first tour. The couple met while playing youth hockey and started dating while Hunter was recovering from a career-ending injury and subsequent knee reconstruction.

Though rumors of unhappiness have followed the pair for the last six months, they were spotted together at Granville Island Public Market on Valentine's Day, sharing artisanal doughnuts. Posts on Nightingale's social media showed what seemed to be a happy couple.

The news comes just weeks before Kiss & Tell's *Come Say Hello* tour is set to kick off with three nights in Vancouver, BC.

UPDATE 7:05 P.M.: Hunter has confirmed the breakup via Instagram. In a brief post, he said he will "always love" Aidan but that their lives were taking them in different directions.

Ashton Nightingale Surprises Fans with Shirtless Jog Around Kits Beach

Singer Kelly K Comes Out as Bisexual

SET LIST

Heartbreak Fever

Found You First

Young & Free

By Ourselves

Find Me Waiting

Competition

No Restraint

Kiss & Tell

INTERMISSION

Come Say Hello

Missing You

Wish You Were Here

My Prize

Chances

Prodigy

Your Room

ENCORE

Poutine

1

I can hear them out there: the buzz of excitement, the occasional whistle or shout. The electric anticipation, humming against my skin, as 36,000 people wait for us to take the stage.

I used to feel this way before games, too, and that was only a few hundred people at best: parents and grandparents, friends if they're not too busy, siblings if they're not pissed off that day.

But this is the home game to end all home games. This is BC Place. We've never played a stadium before.

Owen's bouncing on his feet in front of me, rolling his mic back and forth between his hands. I can't see the rest of the guys in the dim blue backstage light, but I'm sure they're just as anxious.

The vibration of the audience makes its usual preshow shift, like they can tell we're about to start. Shaz, our stage manager, says something into her radio. The brim of her cap casts her face in shadow.

The preshow video starts, a bass drum beating out a low heartbeat. Slow-motion video of us laughing, singing, goofing off fills the screens on stage, not that we can see them from back here. The audience goes wild, clapping and screaming so loud I can't hear anything else. I pop my in-ear monitors in, make sure they're snug. At the front of the line, Shaz taps Ashton on the shoulder, and we take our places in darkness. Haze condenses against my eyelashes and I blink the moisture away.

Drumsticks click. The guitars kick in, and then the keyboards, for the first chords of "Heartbreak Fever." The audience cheers even louder.

I find my mark, a little spot of glow tape, and glance offstage out of habit. Last time we played a show at home, Aidan was watching from the wings, cheering me on. Not this time.

I stare out into the audience. A constellation of mobile phones and exit signs twinkle through the dark.

I get that urge to vom, but it's swallowed by adrenaline as a spotlight picks up Ashton at center stage. He shakes his hair off his face as the crowd screams. He waves, struts downstage, brings his mic to his mouth and sings.

He ain't got no game
Just a dimple in his chin,
A twinkle in his eye,
A gentle laugh, and then

Stage right, another spotlight picks up Ethan, who gives a cheesy grin. He's trying out a new hairstyle, sort of swoopy, and the stage lights turn his inky black hair almost blue.

He whispers "Are you listening?
I wanna see you smile."
He promises a dance but then
He leaves with no goodbye

Ian's next, with his shy smile, hand over his heart; across the stage, Owen jumps as his light finds him, and they sing in harmony.

Oh

I can't shake this feeling,
I just can't believe, no,
I've just got to sweat it out,
This heartbreak fever—

The bridge hits, and my body crackles with electricity. This feeling, at least, is familiar. It's the same thing I used to feel at the starting buzzer, when I knew the puck was mine.

It's euphoria. There's no other word for it.

The spotlight blinds me as I lift my mic and sing.

I'm still floating as the last chord of "Poutine" rings and the lights cut to black. The crowd is still screaming, crying, even throwing a few flowers toward the stage as the lights come up for our last bow, but the barricade is far enough back they can't actually reach us.

No underwear this time, which is a relief, because gross.

We wave and smile and exit stage right, duck between two pieces of scenery (a stylized Lions Gate Bridge and a huge maple leaf, which both double as video walls) and head to our dressing rooms. We've only got five minutes before the meet and greet.

Ahead of me, Ashton spins around to walk backward. He's breathing hard. We all are.

"That was awesome!" His canines show when he smiles, and I can't stop myself from grinning back. "Do you think every night's going to be like this?"

Next to me, Owen says, "I hope so."

Ashton smiles wider and turns around, nearly skipping to his dressing room door.

Ethan grabs my shoulders from behind, almost hanging off me, as he laughs in my ear. "It's only gonna get better." He gives me a shake and turns toward his own dressing room.

Mine is the last one on the right. I duck inside and peel my black T-shirt off, wipe my chest and armpits with the towels on the little table, and put on some fresh deodorant. I tug at the waistband of my jeans to try to get some airflow down there, because I have terrible swampass, and my underwear's giving me a wedgie.

I pull on an identical dry T-shirt, pop in a couple breath mints, and try to salvage my sweat-soaked hair as best I can. It's not as bad as helmet hair, but then again, I wasn't getting photographed after games.

I wash my hands, take a deep breath, and step back out into the hallway. Ashton's already done and waiting, leaning against his door. His eyes brighten, blue turned nearly gray in the fluorescent lights. He looks so much like Aidan, it makes me ache.

We broke up over a month ago. When is it going to stop hurting?

"Hunter?"

"Yeah?" I fix my face and put my smile back on. "Tonight was great, eh?"

"It was fucking amazing."

Ashton says it like we've never done a concert before.

Then again, this is the biggest by far. Last tour we were in theaters and smaller arenas, not stadiums.

Not BC Place.

"It was pretty fucking cool," I agree. "Come on. Let's go meet your adoring fans."

"You mean yours!"

"Ours, then." I smack his shoulder and lead him into the hall toward the Reception Suite.

The meet and greet is packed. Ashton's line is the longest (like usual), but the rest of us have pretty respectable lines too. For some reason, my line has a weirdly high proportion of moms.

I don't know why moms like the gay boy so much.

Some of the people in line are crying as they meet me. I thank them for coming, sign their posters, pose for pictures.

"I came out because of you," one kid says.

"You're such a good role model," their mom says.

"I'm sorry about Aidan."

"Your music got me through some tough times."

"I want to be like you when I grow up."

"Do you think you and Aidan are going to get back together?"

"Is it okay if I hug you?"

There's a crew shooting footage for our documentary, and one of the camera guys is hovering over my shoulder. I think his name is Brett. All the camera guys so far have had the same full beards and worn the same black Henleys and black cargo pants, so it's hard to tell.

When the shelter kids come through, I drop my fake smile and put on my real one.

It's really overwhelming sometimes, to be honest, meeting people my age who got kicked out of their homes, disowned, hurt by the people that are supposed to love them the most.

And it makes me feel kind of shitty, too, because I'm a rich white gay cis boy and so many of them are poor and brown and trans.

I thought they'd be sad. I thought they'd be mad at the world for the way it never cares enough for queer kids unless they look like me. But they're laughing and smiling and telling each other jokes, accepting my hugs and thanking me for the tickets.

The lines finally start to dwindle. I'm the last one done, after thanking the shelter director for bringing her kids out tonight. I'm a terrible person because I've already forgotten her name, but she's wearing rose-tinted glasses and a huge, dimpled smile.

"Thank you for making this happen," she says. "I haven't seen our kids this happy in a long time."

I shake my head and fiddle with the cap of my empty water bottle. "I'm glad we could do it."

"These kids are lucky to have you to look up to."

My freckles itch as she shakes my hand and walks away. Once she's out of the room, I collapse back into my seat and sigh. I'm a wrung-out towel.

"Hey," a low voice says to my side. I start and turn to find Kaivan Parvani leaning against the wall behind me.

Kaivan and his brothers are our opener—PAR-K. (I still can't believe we get to have an opener this tour.) I've seen them around, during sound check and stuff, but haven't really gotten to talk to any of them.

Kaivan's my age, with short cropped black hair, thick eyebrows, and dark brown eyes. He's PAR-K's drummer, which means he's got drummer's forearms, which I have to admit I find kind of sexy. They're brown and corded and crossed over his black tank top.

I take a sip from my water bottle but then remember it's empty.

"That was awesome," Kaivan says.

"Thanks. You guys were great too." I only heard the first bit of their set, but they've got a good sound, edgy yet somehow nostalgic.

"I meant what you did, here. Like, with the queer kids. That was really cool."

I start to blush, because Kaivan is looking at me with his big brown eyes like I'm some sort of hero, and I'm not.

"Cheers. I mean, I try."

"Well, it means a lot to all of us queer kids, seeing you out there doing this."

I blink at Kaivan, and now it's his turn to blush.

"I guess I'm gay too," he says softly. "I came out a couple months ago."

"Oh. Wow. Congrats, dude."

I can't believe I missed that. But there's this lightness in my chest, like the ringing of a celeste.

I'm not the only gay boy on this tour.

Kaivan shrugs. "It was easier, you know? Seeing you out there? Made it less scary."

"Wow. I mean, I'm glad. I mean, does The Label know?"

"They do now," Kaivan laughs. "Our manager was kind of hesitant about it, but I told him if they were fine with you, they'd have to be fine with me."

"That's awesome." I'm smiling like a goof, and he probably thinks I'm a weirdo, so I ask, "What's your story, eh? No one ever tells us anything."

"The usual story? Wrote some songs, got picked up by The Label, got lucky I guess?"

"Nah, you guys sound good."

"Thanks. But it's still luck. Lots of bands sound good."

"It helps that you're good-looking too," I say before I can stop myself.

But he is good-looking. He's got the kind of face that demands attention, a smile that deserves to have songs written about it.

I clear my throat and look at my hands. "Sorry. That was super awkward."

"It's cool. You are too."

I bite my lip to stop myself from smiling, but I'm sure he can see my blush. I'm a ginger: When I blush, you can see it from space.

"It's all a clever ruse," I say, because he's looking me in the eye and there's this weird tension between us.

But Kaivan laughs, and the tension seems to relax, though it doesn't go away entirely. I take the chance to scan the room. The other guys are gone, except for Ashton. He hangs by the door, head cocked to the side in a question. I wave him off and stand, running a hand through my hair.

"I guess we're the last ones out. Where's The Label putting you guys up?" I ask.

"The Fairmont?"

"Oh wow. I've never stayed there." It's this super fancy hotel downtown. "I'm kind of jealous."

"You're not there too?"

"Nah, Mom wanted me to stay home until we hit the road."

"Aww." Kaivan opens the door for me and follows me down the hall. The back of my neck tingles from his proximity. I think I've got butterflies in my stomach. Actual butterflies.

It's been over a month since Aidan and I broke up, and some days I still wake up missing him. I promised myself I wouldn't like anyone new until after this tour. That I'd focus on myself.

I can't be into a new guy. Even if he is cute. Even if he does have those little dimples in his shoulders, and the kind of collarbone I want to press my lips against.

I take a deep breath, try to think about something else, but instead I get a whiff of his scent. He's wearing some sort of inky cologne, vetiver maybe, but underneath is sweat and warm skin.

I don't let myself wonder what he tastes like.

I'm just pent up, that's all. I'll be fine once I get back home and take care of myself.

Kaivan and I are going to be friends—I desperately need queer friends, especially on tour—but that's it.

KISS & TELL'S HUNTER DRAKE
ON LIFE, LOVE, HOCKEY, AND MUSIC

Profile in Perception Magazine,
January 21, 2022 issue

It started as a joke: five Vancouver teenagers singing a funny song about poutine, the Canadian fast-food favorite. No one could've predicted the explosion that followed. The teens' viral music video quickly caught the attention of manager Janet Lundgren. Lundgren, in turn, connected the boys—Ashton Nightingale, Ethan Nguyen, Ian Souza, Owen Jogia, and Hunter Drake—with executive Bill Holt at The Label, which released their debut album.

Kiss & Tell's fans have embraced the ethnically diverse band's impressive harmonies, charming musicality, and lyrics (largely penned by Drake) that alternate between wry and heartfelt.

A former youth hockey player, Hunter wrote "Poutine" while recovering from a knee injury, and convinced his friends to record it in their school's cafeteria using their iPhones. *Perception* caught up with him at a tea shop in Vancouver's Kerrisdale neighborhood.

PM: Your second studio album just came out. How are you feeling about it? Nervous? Excited?

HD: All of those things. Also tired and a little nauseated. There's a lot of pressure on us to make sure this album is even better than our first one.

PM: You were a driving force behind that album, and *Come Say Hello* as well. Where do you get your ideas?

HD: I mean, it's a team effort. Did you know Owen's a classically trained pianist? So he wrote some of the songs, and helped produce both albums too. Some of my favorites are the ones where he did the music and I did the lyrics. And on this new one, we convinced Ian to contribute some lyrics too. I guess maybe we bullied him after we saw him writing poetry one day. But they're really good.

I don't know, I really enjoy the whole collaborative process. It's like being on a team again. I miss that about hockey.

PM: You were on track for a career in hockey, weren't you?

HD: Yeah, I was the top scorer in our league. Me and Aidan and Ashton were unstoppable on the ice. I thought I'd get a scholarship to play for UBC or something, maybe study sports medicine and become a physical therapist. Either that or make it to the NHL, but everyone hopes that'll happen and the statistics aren't great, right? Especially for gay guys.

PM: That didn't stop you from coming out while you were playing, though?

HD: No. I thought about it a lot, but me being gay was kind of obvious, if you know what I mean. But it was cool. The team was cool. And, you know, Aidan came out a couple years later, and we know how that turned out.

PM: Indeed. It's safe to say you're everyone's favorite gay couple.

HD: I don't know about that.

PM: Why do you say that?

HD: I don't know. We're two middle-class white boys. I don't think we're supposed to be, like, the face of queer liberation or anything. We're both still figuring all this out, and now there's this spot-light on us. And I want to do good—we want to do good—but it's not always easy to figure out what good looks like. On this new tour, we're giving out tickets to local queer youth, and donating to shelters and stuff. The Label was really cool about helping me set that up.

PM: That's amazing. I'm sure it'll make a difference.

HD: Cheers. I think that's giving me too much credit, but it feels like a start.

KISS & TELL DOCUMENTARY

Footage transcription
003/04:12:57;00

IAN: So, we've just finished our first night at BC Place.

ASHTON (O/S): B! C! PLACE!

IAN: It's strange. Usually we'd all get on the bus to our next stop, or get in a car and go to a hotel if we're staying in one. But tonight we're just going back home.

ETHAN (O/S): I need a shower, dude, I've got BO like you wouldn't believe.

OWEN (O/S): We believe it.

IAN: And I got a text from my stepdad asking me to start the dishwasher before I go to bed. It's weird, like, we've just started this big tour, but I've still got chores for a few days.

OWEN: My mom's getting weird.

IAN: Oh yeah?

OWEN: Yeah, I caught her crying yesterday looking at photos from last tour. She'll be fine though.

IAN: Yeah. Like I was saying, it's weird, but it's good. We'll be on the road for almost three months. I'm gonna be stuck with these guys. Hey, where's Hunter?

ETHAN: I think he was talking to one of the PAR-K guys.

IAN: Really? Ashton, you see him?

ASHTON: Huh? Oh. Yeah.

IAN: Cool.

2

I'm not sure how it happens, but Kaivan and I keep talking as I head to my dressing room to pack up, and since he's in the middle of a story, he follows me right in.

"So The Label decided that since we were PAR-K, we should do parkour for our music video."

I shake my head. The Label can be truly ridiculous.

"What happened? I'm listening," I say as I step into the washroom in the corner. I grab my Invisaligns out of their case and give them a rinse before popping them in, then stuff everything into my backpack.

Kaivan's half sitting on the armrest of the beige pleather couch. "Well, Kamran used to run track, so he wasn't super awful, but Karim tried a somersault and managed to sprain his wrist and bruise his tailbone."

"Ouch."

"Yeah, The Label freaked out about it, so then they tried to make it into a super-choreographed dance video."

"Oh yeah? You got any sweet moves?"

"No way, I don't dance. And we didn't want it to be like all those other bands, you know?"

I shake my head. I mean, me and the guys do lots of choreo, for our videos and for our shows. It's hard work, but it's a lot of fun.

"Just, you know what they say, people only dance if they can't actually sing."

"Wow." I must pull a face, because Kaivan holds up his hands.

"Sorry, I didn't mean it that way. You guys can do it all. But you know, me and my brothers . . . we were going for a certain look, and The Label kept trying to push us in a different direction, to be what they wanted instead of what we wanted."

"Okay, I get that. So what happened?"

"Well, we finally got them to scrap the idea and let us do a concert video instead. Kind of basic but at least it felt like us."

I rest my hip against the other end of the couch, but my knee is starting to ache, so I let myself slide down onto the seat. Kaivan slides down to sit next to me.

"Okay, I told you mine, what's your best horror story?"

"Oh man. There are so many." Like our first video, for "Kiss & Tell," where no one got the memo I was gay and they tried to have me kiss a girl, before Janet finally got it sorted out.

Or the one for "No Restraint," where they tried to make it look like Ashton was hooking up with his schoolteacher.

Or even all the stuff with Aidan, like when one of Bill's assistants asked if I was "really sure" Aidan and I were never getting back together.

"Okay. Got it. So, we did a cover of this song called 'Don't Speak' for an AIDS charity, and we did a whole video too."

Kaivan nods.

"We were shooting on the beach, standing in the surf, and I heard this weird *ting* sound, and one of the cables on the jib camera broke, and it sideswiped me."

Kaivan's eyes bug out. "Oh my god, really?"

"Yeah, got me right here," I say, pointing to the right side of my rib cage. "Sent me tumbling under the water. Thankfully Ian fished me out. But I ended up with this huge bruise." I splay out my hands to demonstrate.

"Holy shit."

"And after, we did a whole press conference, and I had my ribs wrapped up, and they had flown in a bunch of kids who had HIV, from Africa I think, and we had to do all these photos and the whole time I was grimacing because my everything hurt."

"Dude . . . that's kind of messed up."

"I know, but they couldn't reschedule."

"No, I mean . . . flying kids in. Couldn't they have just spent that money on more research or something?"

"Oh. Yeah."

He's right.

"But you know how The Label is. They like good press." I clear my throat. "Besides, we raised over a million dollars. And me and the guys did a matching thing."

"That's cool," Kaivan says. "What did you do after, though, with your ribs?"

"Thankfully they were just bruised. We were mostly in the studio at that point, so I got to let them rest. Healed up fine." I pull up my shirt to show him.

"Ahh!" He acts like I've blinded him.

"Come on, I'm not that pasty."

He laughs. "Nah, you're fine."

I let my shirt fall and shift a little. The pleather couch cushions have slowly sunk, and my knee rests lightly against his, but it's weird. It feels warm, but in a comfortable way, not a sexy way. I smile.

"What?" he asks.

"Nothing. It's just nice. Talking to another gay guy for a change."

"Dude, you just talked to a whole line of queer kids."

"It's not the same. That's, like . . . it's not work, it's awesome, but it's kind of exhausting too. Hearing all their stories and stuff, it can be really heavy sometimes." I shake my head. "I mean, they're our age. That's . . ."

Kaivan nods.

"Anyway, that's not really a conversation. Not like this. Us just talking."

"I feel that."

"Yeah."

He studies my mouth for a second, which I only notice because I might be studying his eyes. They're dark brown, but the lighting in here highlights the flecks of amber in them.

"What?" I ask.

"Are you wearing Invisaligns?"

I close my mouth.

"Hey, it's cool, I had braces too. Mine had this thing in the roof of my mouth, and I had this key I had to crank every so often to expand my palette. It was awful."

It sounds truly heinous, but it paid off, because Kaivan's smile is luminous.

I should really stop looking at his mouth.

I can't tell if he's leaning in toward me or I'm leaning in toward him. And I honestly couldn't say what I want to happen. Because he's really attractive. But also, it just feels so nice to talk to someone like me. Ever since I got pulled out of school, I don't really have gay friends to talk to.

Kaivan's lips part, and I can't tell if he's going to say something or go in for a kiss, but a knock on my door startles me.

"Hunter? You in there?" Nazeer's low voice asks.

Nazeer is our security lead. He's like an escort/driver/sort-of-bodyguard when we need it.

I clear my throat. "Yeah. Sorry." I glance at the clock on

the wall. I was supposed to be outside ten minutes ago. "I got distracted. I'm ready."

I turn back to Kaivan. "Sorry. My car . . ."

Kaivan stands. "It's cool, my brothers are probably wondering where I am."

He offers me his hand and I take it. It's warm and callused, except for the meat of his palm, which is surprisingly smooth. He pulls me up.

"Thanks."

He grins. "Anytime."

I open the door, and Nazeer's black eyes immediately shift to Kaivan behind me.

"Sorry," I say again. "We were talking and lost track of time." I hoist my backpack over my shoulder and grab my guitar case. "All set."

Kaivan follows us out to the loading dock.

"Well," he says.

"Yeah." It feels weird, just saying bye. Not like this was a date or anything, but still.

Maybe it's just that I'm tired, but I step close and give Kaivan an awkward one-armed hug and a quick peck on the cheek. It's totally platonic.

But I'm not as careful as I should be and my guitar case smacks him in the face.

"Sorry!"

He just laughs and rubs the spot I kissed (and hit) with his fingers.

"All good. See you, Hunter."

"Yeah. See you."

I watch him head toward an idling SUV, then turn back to find Nazeer studying me.

"We really were just talking."

Nazeer smirks at me, his thin lips twitching. "Come on. Better get you home."

There's still a crowd of fans lining Pacific Boulevard, headed toward the SkyTrain station. A few wave, like they know it's me (or one of us at least), and I wave back even though no one can see me through the tinted windows.

A soft drizzle coats the windshield as Nazeer heads toward the Cambie Bridge.

"Good show?"

I catch his eyes in the rearview mirror and smile.

"The best."

Mom's already gone when I get home, working a night shift at the hospital. The apartment is dark and quiet, but I'm still too antsy to sleep, so I change out of my show clothes into a faded Canucks T-shirt and a pair of ocean-print leggings I bought off an Instagram ad a while back.

I used to be a sweatpants guy, but it turns out leggings are super comfy, plus I like the way my ass looks in them. I don't really have a hockey butt anymore, but it's still pretty good. Aidan always liked it.

There's a text from him. I must've missed it while I was in the car.

show okay?

I sigh and ignore it. I'm not in the mood to deal with him tonight.

Instead, I post a couple backstage photos from tonight, along with a thanks to everyone for coming and a link for people to donate to the shelters we're supporting. I plug my phone in to charge, brush my teeth, moisturize, and then curl up in bed with my notebook.

The Label's been on us to start recording our third album, but *Come Say Hello* only came out a couple months ago, and we've barely had time to breathe since then, with rehearsals and the documentary. Plus there's the tour. It's not that bad working on the road when we've got the bus, but once we're abroad and flying all around the world it'll be a lot more hectic.

And we have to make this one our best yet. Everyone knows a band's third album is what makes or breaks them.

Owen's already put together three demos that he wants me to write lyrics for. They're really good, a perfect evolution of our sound, but every time I pick up my notebook my mind goes blank.

I try free-writing some poetry, but it ends up getting really dark really quick, my thoughts bouncing between Aidan and the new album. And then I think about the shelter kids, and how happy the all were, despite what they've been through.

And here I am, whining about writer's block and a breakup. I try really hard not to cry in front of them, but I want to. They're my age, and they've been kicked out of their homes; and here I am, safe and secure, whining about writer's block.

This knot of guilt spreads its coils through my stomach, but that just makes me angry at myself, because that's a useless, shitty feeling.

I just wish I knew how to make things better. Something that would make a difference.

"Damn it." I wipe my eyes, grab my phone to check the time. It's filled with notifications already—comments and questions and likes on my post about the concert—but there's a follow notification too. From Kaivan.

I follow him back. Should I send him a message?

I type out a couple different ones, but they all sound either way too formal or way too sappy, so finally I just send him a 👋 Totally cool and neutral.

I'm still too antsy to sleep, so I slide my leggings down to jerk off, which always makes me sleepy. I imagine all the things me and Aidan used to do. Even when everything else was bad, the sex was good. But it's not Aidan I imagine; it's Kaivan. The way he smelled, the rumble of his voice, the strength of his shoulders when I hugged him, the way his stubble scratched against my lips when I kissed his cheek . . .

I run to the washroom to clean off, then find a cool spot on my pillow and finally fall asleep.

AIDAN NIGHTINGALE TURNED OFF INSTAGRAM COMMENTS AFTER THE END OF HAIDAN

NewzList Canada
Date: March 6, 2022

It's been less than 24 hours since Hunter Drake and Aidan Nightingale announced their breakup, and while most fans have been united in their mourning, some have settled in the "anger" stage of grief. While no reason has been given for the split, a small but vocal segment of fans have decided that Nightingale was at fault, flooding him with messages accusing him of "breaking Hunter's heart," calling him "a loser" and "an embarrassment."

Nightingale (and Drake) are no strangers to online harassment: The pair have faced homophobic abuse separately and as a couple, but this time the invective has taken on a much more personal note.

"You were never good enough for him!" one angry comment (since deleted) read; "Hunter deserves better!" another commenter wrote; "i'll never forgive you" wrote a third.

One user (since banned for terms-of-service violation) even suggested Nightingale should kill himself.

Nightingale has since turned off comments on his posts. In his last post before locking down, he stated that people "don't know the whole story."

Drake, who unfollowed Nightingale in the wake of the split, has remained mum, except for a request for fans to "give [them] both space."

__Masha Patriarki Is Not Your Magical Negro__

__Pick a Pho Order and We'll Tell You Which Ethan Nguyen Solo You Are__

3

My alarm goes off at 6:30, which is pure homophobia, but Ashton's picking me up at 7:00. I cram a protein bar in my mouth as I pull on my sweats and pack my skate bag.

Mom gets home as I'm tying my shoes. Her green eyes have dark circles under them, but they crinkle up when she sees me.

"Hey, Hunter," she says, and pulls me into a hug. Her red hair's in a messy bun, and the stray strands tickle my cheeks. "Going skating?"

"Yeah." She kisses me on the cheek and pushes my messy hair off my forehead.

"Good show last night?"

"It was."

"Sorry I missed it."

"Don't be. How was work?"

Mom doesn't really have to work anymore, with the money I make. I told her so. But she insists she likes her job as a neonatal nurse, and she won't let me support her financially.

"Good," she says. "Long."

"Get some sleep," I say. "Love you."

"Love you." She gives me another hug. I putter around in the kitchen, doing a couple dishes I should've done last night, until I get a text from Ashton that he's here. I grab my bag, pull on my tuque, and head down.

"Okay," Jill Nightingale says into her Bluetooth. "Okay. Uh-huh."

She's on the phone with Anthony, her ex-husband, Ashton and Aidan's dad. Ashton turns around in his seat and gives me a sympathetic look.

Me and him and Aidan used to skate every day, before and after school. I've barely clocked any ice time lately, though. Rehearsals kept me too busy, and my knee wouldn't take skating on top of the hours of choreography.

Plus, the rink reminded me of Aidan.

But we're going to be on the road for three months, and who knows if we'll have time or opportunity to go skating, so Ashton made me promise to come skate with him before we leave.

"No, he's got to keep a C average, you know that." Jill lets out an exasperated sigh. "You'll have to, we leave Sunday right after the show."

Jill's going with us as our chaperone and tutor. Our parents wouldn't let us leave school unless we got tutored to pass our Dogwoods.

"Well then, ground him, I guess."

I wonder what Aidan's done. I know I shouldn't care. Ashton turns toward his mom and opens his mouth, but he doesn't get a chance to speak.

"I don't know what else to tell you, Anthony. I told you that was a bad idea in the first place."

We finally pull up to the rink, and I get out of Jill's Prius as fast as I can, because otherwise I'm going to suffocate.

"Thanks!" I call as I close the door.

Ashton takes a little longer to get out, but when he does his shoulders slump.

"Sorry you had to hear that."

Growing up around the Nightingales, I got used to Jill and Anthony arguing. "It's fine."

As soon as we step into the rink, though, Ashton transforms. He stands up straighter, and a smile dawns across his face.

I take a deep breath and enjoy the smell of fresh ice. There's nothing like it.

We're the first ones. It's pristine, freshly Zamboni'd, and the air in the rink is crisp and cool.

As soon as my blades hit the ice, I'm wide-awake. It's the best feeling in the world. I don't know who it was that woke up one day and decided to strap knives to their feet, but I'm glad they did.

I come alive. It's different from performing, more primal.

It's euphoria.

Ashton's right behind me, watching like always, but I'm not going to fall. I take it slow, warming up my knees as I do some easy laps, working my crossovers. Ashton passes me and turns around to glide backward.

"So." He narrows his eyes at me.

"So?"

"Kaivan Parvani, huh?"

"We were just talking."

"Yeah?" Ashton gives me a toothy smile, the same one Aidan used to give, and my heart does this weird twinge because most of the time I'm still pretty pissed at Aidan but sometimes I just miss him. I'm never sure which feeling I'm going to get, but being here, on the ice, is making it worse.

Sometimes it really sucks, being best friends with your ex's twin brother. Sometimes Ashton will smile or laugh or something, and it'll remind me so much of Aidan it aches.

"It's totally platonic," I explain. "In case you haven't noticed, I don't have a lot of queer people around to talk to."

I mean, we've got a few queer people on our crew, but that's not the same. They're all older, for one thing. And they're all guarded around me, for another, which I guess makes sense since I'm "the talent," but it still sucks. The only one I ever really talk to is Patricia, my guitar tech, this cool lesbian from Kamloops.

"Okay, fair point." He does a quick loop around me. "How're the new songs coming?"

I groan.

"That bad? Still got writer's block?"

"It's not writer's block." I can't have writer's block. We've got to get this album written.

"You know Bill said we could bring on other writers if we want."

"We don't need other writers."

That's always been our thing: We write all our own stuff. We're not going to change that on my account. I've just got to focus.

"Hunt, if it's too much pressure, it's okay to ask for help."

"It's fine, really." It's going to be fine. I definitely don't have writer's block.

We skate in silence for a while, the only noise the music of steel edges against smooth ice.

"Aidan said he texted you last night," Ashton says after a while.

"He did?"

From the moment we started dating, me and Aidan made a rule: We wouldn't talk about the other to Ashton, because it wasn't fair to put him in the middle of our stuff, whether it was good or bad.

There were lots of other rules, too, though The Label liked to call them "branding" while we were dating and "crisis management" after we broke up.

"Yeah," Ashton says. "You didn't get it?"

"No, I got it," I say. "I meant, he told you that?"

"Oh. Yeah."

I still haven't answered the text. I'm probably not going to.

"I'm sorry. I didn't want you to get stuck in the middle of us." His parents always played tug-of-war with him and Aidan, and I won't let that happen with me.

"I know." He sighs. I wonder exactly how much Aidan has told him. I wonder what percent of it is true. "I'm okay, Hunt. Really. And I can still love you both even if you don't love each other."

"Thanks, Ash."

"Now, you warmed up? Wanna race?"

There's no way I'll win, but that doesn't matter. "You're on."

I'm sweaty but happy when the buzzer sounds the end of public skate. Ashton and I head back to the bleachers to take our skates off.

As I massage my right arch, which has been cramping a little, my phone buzzes. Kaivan's finally answered my

Hey

                                        Hey!

Know any good lunch spots near me?
Hotel keeps suggesting fancy places.

"Hunt?"

"Huh?"

Ashton's studying me with the hint of a grin. "You're
smiling."

"Am not."

But to Kaivan I send:

                              You like sandwiches?

KISS & TELL: THE BOYBAND OF THE FUTURE?

VAN ART
December 16, 2021

On paper, Kiss & Tell seems like just another group of good-looking baritones hoping to make money off a coveted demographic—but the group has quickly proved themselves anything but. A delightful mosaic of ethnicities (with Vietnamese-, Brazilian-, and Indian-Canadian members) and an out gay member (Hunter Drake) make the band feel refreshingly representative of Canada today. That diversity is paying dividends in fans' imaginations, especially Drake's high-profile romance with bandmate Ashton Nightingale's twin brother Aidan. The two first started dating shortly before Kiss & Tell broke out with a self-produced YouTube music video shot on iPhones in and around the members' Kerrisdale secondary school.

Drake and both Nightingale brothers got to know each other playing youth hockey before an accident ended Drake's hopes for a hockey career, but Drake spent the time in recovery writing songs that he eventually convinced Ashton—plus their classmates Ethan Nguyen, Ian Souza, and Owen Jogia—to help record.

"It started as kind of a joke," Drake recalled in an early interview. "We were all in choir together. Our teacher always called us the Back Row Boys, because we were always laughing and joking and stuff. And we just started making little videos for fun."

After the viral success of "Poutine," the boys quickly signed with The Label.

"It took us a long time to pick a name," Drake said. "I got voted down when I suggested 'Queerly Canadian.' It was actually Aidan who came up with Kiss & Tell, and everyone liked the sound of it."

Though Aidan Nightingale didn't join the band, he was never far from the action: As the band Kiss & Tell geared up for their first tour, cameras caught Hunter and Aiden cuddling during downtime at rehearsals, playing hockey in the hallways, and sharing kisses when they thought no one was looking.

A shaky, poorly lit video of Hunter serenading Aidan with one of the band's new songs immediately went viral, with over five million views to date.

Describing the start of their relationship, Drake recalled, "Aidan and Ashton have been my best friends since I was like ten and we ended up in Atom-league together. And then when I came out, and later Aidan came out, things just kind of happened. When Kiss & Tell started looking like maybe it was going to be a real thing, he was always super supportive and sweet."

That has certainly resonated with the band's fans.

"I love Haidan," Cam, a young person from Burnaby, said, referring to the "ship name" fans have assigned Drake and Nightingale. "They're so pure!"

Linda, Cam's mom, agreed. "Even though it's two boys, they're respectful and showing what a healthy relationship looks like for their fans. I hope my child will date someone like that."

4

I shower at home, then catch the bus to meet Kaivan in Gastown. With a tuque covering my hair and a pair of aviators that take up half my face, no one notices as I sit in the back and play on my phone, reporting dick pics.

I get sent a lot of dick pics. And buttholes too. I don't know what's wrong with people.

I get off outside Harbour Centre and make my way to Sammies. Kaivan's waiting outside, in a plain gray jacket and black jeans.

"Hey," I say.

He looks up from his phone. "Hey! This place smells amazing."

I get the door for him. "Wait until you taste."

Sammies is this little hole-in-the-wall that makes the best

44

sandwiches in Vancouver, if not the world. They serve them on fresh-baked rosemary focaccia, and they use this olive tapenade instead of mayo or mustard.

I pull off my shades as we get in line.

"What's good?" Kaivan asks.

"Everything."

"What's your favorite?"

"Smoked turkey."

We order two of them. Kaivan insists on paying, since The Label's giving him a per diem for food, but when I point out I get one too, he just says, "Never argue with an Iranian over a bill. There's no future in it."

So I smile and let him buy me a sandwich.

The other thing that makes Sammies amazing: The sandwiches are huge. Like, as big as my head, wrapped in white-and-red-checked paper that's already soaking up the olive oil oozing from the bread.

"Oh no," Kaivan says when he beholds his sandwich. "This looks amazing."

We grab a corner of the dark wood counter running along the windows, and I grab a handful of brown paper napkins for us, because things tend to get messy.

As we eat, Kaivan asks me about growing up here: what school was like, what I do for fun, where I like to eat.

"There used to be this macaroni-and-cheese bar in Kerrisdale," I tell him. "Real close to the rink where I skate.

You'd pick your noodle and your cheese and your toppings and they'd make it in a little cast-iron skillet for you. It closed a couple years ago, though."

Kaivan tells me about growing up in Columbus, Ohio. About his family, and his brothers.

"You guys have been to North Van, right?" I ask. "Where all the Iranian shops and restaurants are?"

Kaivan's eyebrows furrow for a second before he laughs. "Yeah, we went there for Nowruz."

"Nowruz?"

"Persian New Year. Couple days ago."

"Oh," I say, and my freckles itch. "Sorry."

"It's cool," he says. He leans in toward me. "You've got . . ."

He gestures at my mouth, and I wipe at it with a napkin.

"Did I get it?"

"No. Here." He uses his own napkin to wipe at my lip. My skin tingles where his thumb brushes my jaw, and my freckles burn.

"Thanks."

We talk for hours: about the music industry, songwriting, touring.

"Make sure to eat lots of vegetables," I tell him. "That's the hardest thing to get on tour."

"You brought me to a sandwich shop!"

"I mean, it had lettuce on it."

He balls up a napkin and bounces it off my chest.

He's genuinely easy to talk to. I didn't realize how much I missed having gay friends. Back in school, I was in the QSA, but I haven't had a real queer community since then.

"Shit," Kaivan says, looking at his phone. "Thirty minutes until sound check."

"Oh! We'd better go." I bus our trash and hold the door for Kaivan. The sun came out while we were talking, and downtown is bathed in the golden afternoon. "You need to go back to your hotel?"

"Nah." Kaivan hikes up his backpack. "All good."

"Cool." I pull my hat back on, but not before I get spotted by a couple girls across the street. I smile and wave as they snap a photo of me, then head toward Cambie. "Come on."

HUNTER DRAKE REBOUNDS
WITH KAIVAN PARVANI

TRS (The Real Scoop)
Date: March 26, 2022

Has Hunter Drake already found a new flame?

Photographers caught the Canadian singer at Sammies, an eatery in Vancouver's Gastown neighborhood, sharing a cozy meal with PAR-K drummer Kaivan Parvani. PAR-K is opening for Kiss & Tell on their *Come Say Hello* tour; the band is playing their second of three sold-out shows at Vancouver's BC Place tonight.

Drake recently parted ways with long-term boyfriend Aidan Nightingale; reps for both Drake and Parvani were unavailable for comment.

Owen Jogia's Colorful Holi Celebration

Ian Souza's Sweet Birthday Message to Lily Yeoh Sparks Dating Rumors

TEXT MESSAGES RECEIVED BY
HUNTER DRAKE FROM AIDAN NIGHTINGALE

March 27, 2022

Hey
You free?
I miss you
Delivered 11:35 AM

Are you reallly hanging out with that kaivn guy?
I thought you wanted to focus on yourself
Delivered 11:48 AM

You ignornig me???
Delivered 11:56 AM

I'm working
Please don't start against
Again*

I miss you h
I'm not starting anything, i just want to know
I deserve to know

Just leave me alone.

Fuck you

Not anymore

Slut
Delivered 12:11 PM

5

I hate interviews. I never know what to do with my hands.

And I like my voice, but something about being on camera makes me wonder if I sound gay. Which is ridiculous, since I am gay, but how much gay voice is too much?

We all let Ethan do most of the talking. He's funny and quick-witted and the hosts of *Sunday Morning*, Stacey and Nicole, are immediately charmed by him. I smile and nod along and hope I won't have to do any talking until—

"Now, Hunter, you've been through it lately, haven't you?"

I try to give a disarming laugh, because what am I supposed to say to that? I glance toward Janet, who's standing offstage behind one of the cameras, but she shrugs at me.

"Your breakup was so unexpected," Stacey says. She's a skinny white woman with perfect teeth, an alarming amount of eyeliner, and a pencil dress that looks impossible to walk in. "And right before your tour, no less. How have you been coping?"

I hate talking about the breakup. It's no one's business but me and Aidan's.

Everyone acts like they knew what our relationship was like. They didn't see our fights. They didn't see the way Aidan got jealous when I was on tour, the way he texted me every time a tabloid wrote something about me, about him, about us.

They only saw what we shared on social media, what The Label wanted them to see. The cute pictures, the goofy dancing, the love songs. The Label approved all of it.

I shake my head and put on my game face. "I mean, like you said, we're on tour, so that keeps me busy. Plus we're working on our next album, and I've been pretty hands-on with that."

Nicole, who is Chinese-Canadian and also wearing a metric ton of eyeliner and a blue pencil dress, does one of those Sympathetic Interviewer nods.

"So many of your songs are about love. Has the heartbreak made it hard to work at all?"

"I mean," I start, but I don't know how to answer that.

Yes. No. It's not the heartbreak that's hard, it's the attention. It's having people think that who I am on stage is the same as who I am at home. Who I am in bed.

Not literally, thank god. No one's asked about what me and Aidan do—did—in bed. Not to my face.

The Internet is full of creeps.

"It's a team effort," Owen says, grabbing my shoulder. "So when Hunter's feeling down, we step up to help. That's what friends do."

Stacey gives him a TV smile and turns back to me. "Well, it's nice to hear you're keeping your spirits up." She turns to the camera. "When we come back, Hunter's going to lend his keen eye to our Sunday Brunch setup. Invite the girls! You won't want to miss it when *Sunday Morning* returns!"

I look toward Janet again, eyebrows raised, and she nods and starts typing on her phone.

I can't believe I have to do another brunch segment.

Like all gay guys love brunch or are good at place settings or flower arranging or whatever.

The guys head offstage to get their mics taken off, while a PA leads me over to the kitchen set, which seems unnecessary since I could see the kitchen from the couch where we did the interview. TV studios are so much smaller in real life.

Brunch is already laid out on the kitchen island: scrambled eggs, roasted asparagus, a stack of English muffins so perfectly toasted they can't be real, a plate of avocado wedges, little cups of espresso, a carafe of orange juice and a couple bottles of champagne with the labels turned away from the camera. Everything looks perfect and pristine, but there's no steam rising, not even from the espresso. It's all cold or fake or both.

I'm in a light blue button-up, my sleeves rolled Italian-style, and black jeans. It's a new publicity look I picked for this tour, and I really like it.

A different PA hands me a salmon-colored apron to put over everything. I look heinous in salmon: It clashes with my freckles and my hair, which is "burnished copper" according to The Label's marketing but "red" according to normal people. Dad had red hair too, though it had turned more auburn by the time he died.

I think a producer realizes how awful I look, because the PA runs back with a pastel purple apron and ties it on me as we're being counted back in.

"And we are back with Kiss & Tell's Hunter Drake, here to help us plan the perfect Sunday brunch. Hunter, what's your favorite brunch staple?"

I summon up what I hope is a winning smile. "I mean, I'm trash for anything Florentine."

Stacey laughs and rests her hand on my bare forearm. "Well, I'm afraid we don't have any spinach today, but we've got a healthy, protein-rich scramble, sure to give you plenty of energy whether you're getting ready for a day at the park or a night of dancing."

I smile and nod as the ladies walk through the menu, and try not to flinch every time they rest their hands on my shoulders or comment on my hair or how I look in my jeans. "You've got to share your leg day routine," Nicole adds, with a cheesy television glance toward my ass and a wink to the camera.

"Now, no brunch is complete without a good, spicy Caesar, wouldn't you say, Hunter?"

"Well, I wouldn't know. I'm seventeen."

"That's right! Thankfully we've got all the fixings for a mocktail here, perfect for the kids."

They make a virgin Caesar—just Clamato and some hot sauce—and then hand me the cocktail shaker to "see what I've got," commenting on my technique and "strong arms" as I shake the cold metal as hard as I can.

I feel so gross, but I've gotten used to it. Mostly. We've all got our parts to play, and right now mine is the gay boy helping make brunch.

I help the ladies pick out napkins and napkin holders, set the table with mismatched plates and stemware that were all "antiquing finds," and then toast our successful brunch with the virgin Caesar, which tastes awful.

And then it's finally, finally over.

"Hey, thanks for being a good sport," Nicole says once they've gone to commercial again.

"It was perfect," Stacey agrees. "Can't wait to have you back." She gives my arm another squeeze, then takes her mark for her next segment.

I shake myself off and let a PA help me out of my apron and microphone. Janet's waiting by the door, answering emails on her phone judging by the set of her jaw and the furrow between her brows, but she looks up when I approach.

"Good save, Hunter," she says. Janet's about my mom's

age, or maybe a little older, with black hair that's always in a ponytail, brown eyes, and a little mole at the edge of her right eyebrow. She's white but always has a tan, even in the winter, and she's still got a hint of her Plains accent from growing up in Saskatoon. "I told The Label you weren't doing brunch segments anymore, but someone in publicity missed the memo. I'm getting it sorted out now."

"It's fine." I'm used to it by now. It just sucks, being singled out all the time.

"You sure?" Janet asks.

My throat is tight, and I take a couple breaths to try and loosen it up. It's not Janet's fault; she always looks out for us.

"I'm sure."

She gives me a nod. "Come on. The car's outside."

From: Bill Holt (b.holt@thelabel.com)
To: Janet Lundgren (janet@kissandtellmusic.com)
Subject: Re: Brunch again?!
3/27/22 1:32 P.M.

By the way, got updates for you on the FMW shoot. Booked a studio on the Universal lot, 3/30-4/2. How long can the boys shoot and still be fresh for concerts?
Finalizing cast for video now; see attached.

Thanks,
BH

From: Janet Lundgren (janet@kissandtellmusic.com)
To: Bill Holt (b.holt@thelabel.com)
Subject: Re: Brunch again?!
3/27/22 2:15 P.M.

Thanks Bill. I think 10am-4pm is the best we can do. Might be able to push to 9am, but they like to sleep in. Will talk with them and circle back.
Cast looks good.

Thanks,
Janet

6

Sunday night, after our final show at BC Place, we board our bus and hit the road.

We got a new bus for this tour, with comfier beds, a better lounge, and most importantly, a recording studio in the back. When we're parked and plugged in, we can actually record in there, instead of soundproofing a random room with mattresses and blankets.

Once we're through Customs and on I-5, I change out of my show clothes and into a faded Canucks T-shirt and some gray camo leggings. Ian and Owen are in the lounge, playing the new NHL on the PlayStation we've got hooked up to the TV. Ethan wanted an Xbox, but me and the rest of the guys outvoted him because we're not actual monsters.

I grab a spot on the couch, this candy-red pleather thing, and record a short video.

"So, we've just crossed the border into the USA. Did you know I was technically born here? My parents were on a shopping trip when my mom went into labor. Anyway, I hope to see all you Seattle fans at Key Arena tomorrow. Or I guess it's tonight now? Love you all."

I post it and then check my DMs. PAR-K's got their own bus, but Kaivan and I have been talking, sending each other funny memes. Just friendly stuff, despite what the tabloids are saying.

We're just friends, and Sammies wasn't a date.

"Uh, Hunt?" Ashton asks as he sits next to me.

"Uh, Ash?" I smile and bump his shoulder. "Good show tonight."

"Yeah. You're smiling again."

I put my phone down. "Am not."

Ian keeps his eyes on the screen, but he asks, "This doesn't have anything to do with a certain drummer, does it?"

"Hunter Middle Name Drake," Ethan says, stepping into the lounge. "Are you hooking up with the opener?"

"He's a friend," I say. "Unlike you clowns."

Ethan gasps and clutches imaginary pearls as he plops down beside me. "You know we can see your junk in those, right?"

I roll my eyes. I grew up in locker rooms, and then doing quick changes backstage with the guys. We've all seen each other pretty close to naked at one time or another. "You're just jealous your butt is too flat to pull off a look like this."

"Oh yeah? I'd look great in tights!"

"Leggings." I kick my legs in the air and recross them languidly, which makes Ian laugh and miss a goal.

He pauses the game and shakes his chestnut hair out of his eyes. He's got light brown skin, so light he gets mistaken for white sometimes, a sharp nose, gray eyes, and a strong brow that furrows as he studies me. "What was up with that interview anyway?"

"You mean the stuff about the breakup?"

"I mean the brunch segment. It was . . . a lot."

I shrug. "Eh, I'm used to being treated like a handbag."

Owen cocks his head to the side. "Handbag?"

"You know, like an accessory she'd like to collect."

"Oh . . . that's kind of messed up."

His voice is scratchy from the cold he had during rehearsals, and he's got dark circles under his honey eyes, which makes them pop even more against his russet skin. Owen's parents are Indian (Gujarati, he told me, and I'm kind of embarrassed I had to look it up), and he's got this elegant nose, perfectly shaped eyebrows, and beautifully lush black hair. It always smells like coconut and he's constantly pushing it off his face.

"I guess," I say. "I'm kind of used to it. I mean, it is what it is."

"You should talk to Janet, though," Ethan says. "Tell her you don't want to get teabagged."

"Dude! Handbagged!" I swallow a laugh. "She knows. She tries."

Still. None of the other guys get handbagged.

My phone buzzes again. Kaivan.

"You're smiling again," Ashton says, digging his elbow into my ribs.

"Am not! We're just talking."

Owen narrows his eyes and shakes his head. "You owe us all pizza!"

We made a rule last year that anyone who starts dating has to get the group pizza, to make up for if they start acting like an asshole, which all the guys tend to do. Especially Ethan, who can never seem to keep a girlfriend for more than a month.

I was already with Aidan when the rule was made, so I never had to get the pizza.

Besides. "We're just friends."

"Yeah. Sure." Ethan shakes his midnight hair off his forehead and turns back to the TV. "I play winner!"

BUILD A POUTINE ORDER AND WE'LL TELL YOU WHO YOUR KISS & TELL SOULMATE IS

NewzList
March 12, 2022

Pick a potato:
French fry
Pommes frites
Steak fry
Waffle fry

Pick a gravy:
Brown gravy
White gravy
Beef jus
No gravy

Pick a cheese:
Cheese curds
Parmesan
Pepper Jack
No cheese

How about a protein?
Beef short ribs
Fried chicken
Pulled pork
No protein

Any herbs?
Parsley
Cilantro
Rosemary
No thanks

What are you drinking?
Soda
Iced coffee
Lemonade
Water

YOU GOT: Hunter Drake.

You like the finer things in life—nice cheese, rich jus—but you're a purist too, and save the protein for later. You know that all the perfect date really needs is an iced coffee. Load up on poutine and then take a stroll down Davie Street, or see if you can convince Hunter to take you to the skating rink and show off some of his hockey moves.

7

It's nearly lunchtime when I finally wake up. The bus is parked in the loading dock at Climate Pledge Arena. It's quiet, except for the grumbling of my stomach, so I slip out of my bunk, careful not to disturb Ashton, who's still asleep above me.

The lounge has a little kitchenette thing, and I turn on the electric kettle and dig out a Cup Noodles. I know I shouldn't eat them, since the salt always makes me bloated, but they're so good.

Before the water boils, my phone buzzes. Another DM from Kaivan.

You eat already?

I found a place

I'm glad the other guys are still asleep so they can't make fun of me anymore. Besides, it's just lunch with a friend. I change out of my leggings into some jeans, pull on a Canucks hoodie, and find Kaivan waiting for me right outside the bus.

"Hey," he says.

"Hey. Where are we going?"

"It's here in Seattle Center. We can walk, if that's okay?"

"Sure. We need an escort, though." We're not supposed to go anywhere without security other than the venue. And even in the venue, we've usually got escorts.

"I already checked with Nick." Kaivan nods toward a tall, bored-looking white guy standing by the gates.

"Oh. Great."

Kaivan wiggles his eyebrows at me. "Come on."

Nick follows behind us silently, which is awkward, because Nazeer's usually telling dad jokes. Kaivan's hand brushes mine a few times as we walk, and I can't tell if it's on purpose or not, but there's a cool breeze blowing and I end up stuffing my hands in my pockets to keep them warm.

"So where are we going, anyway?"

"You'll see. I came here on vacation a couple years ago."

"Oh yeah?"

Kaivan nods. "My dad locked his keys in the rental car when we went to Pike Place. We were stuck there for two hours."

"No!"

"Yup!" Kaivan's eyes sparkle as he laughs. "My dad was so mad we had to pay for extra parking time."

"Wow."

"Yeah."

Kaivan and I swap stories about Seattle as we walk. Mom used to drive me and my sister Haley down once or twice a year, to go clothes shopping at the bargain stores we didn't have back home. I guess we used to do it with Dad too, but I don't remember that.

Kaivan leads me to this big concrete building. Bold letters spell out ARMORY over the doors, and giant stylized bald eagle sculptures stare imperiously over our heads.

"Wow."

"Yeah, it's pretty 'Murica.' " Kaivan holds the door for me. "It used to be an actual armory, though. Like, for the military. But now it's offices and a really good food court."

Kaivan's voice echoes off the smooth concrete floor. The acoustics in here are truly heinous, which becomes even more apparent as we enter the wide-open food court and see the band playing on a small stage to one side.

It's a cover band, the kind that I imagine formed after a bunch of people in an office somewhere started singing along to the same song at the same time, locked eyes over their cubicle walls, and decided they should form a band.

They're doing an out-of-tune cover of "Poutine," which makes me groan and pull my tuque down lower over my head.

"This seems weirdly appropriate." Kaivan bumps my elbow. "Just wait."

He leads me to one of the little restaurants in the corner.

It's got a huge open kitchen; cast-iron skillets dangle from a rack over a gas range. The tables and counters are made of reclaimed wood, the chairs and stools some kind of recycled metal painted bright red.

I lean in close and mutter to him, "You've got to be shitting me." Because marquee letters above the counter spell out the name of the restaurant: POUTINE.

Kaivan laughs. "What? That's your brand, right?"

Kaivan orders a large poutine with parmesan, which, to be honest, I don't think should count as poutine: It has to have curds, otherwise it's just cheesy fries.

I get myself a small order, with regular cheese curds, plus extra brown gravy because that's the best part.

I turn to see if Nick wants anything, but he's hanging back by the entrance, giving us our space. I get out my credit card, but Kaivan tries to stop me.

"No, come on, it was my idea."

"You paid last time. It's my turn." I remind him.

Our little baskets of poutine come out steaming. Well, mine is a little basket; Kaivan's is huge. My mouth waters.

"I haven't had poutine in so long," I say as we grab seats at the counter.

"Really? I thought it was your favorite."

"Nah, just a good hook for a funny song. It's so many calories."

No one at The Label has ever said it to my face, but they've made it clear in lots of subtle ways that I'm supposed to stay as twinkish as possible. Which sucks, because I've always been too stocky to achieve the true twink look. Years of hockey have given me a big butt and muscular thighs, and though I've slimmed down a bit since my hockey days, I'm still thicker than they want me to be.

"It's so good, though." Kaivan shovels a forkful of fries into his mouth. I dig into mine too. The fries are fresh, so hot they make the tines on my biodegradable fork start to droop.

As we eat, Nick comes up and says, low into my ear, "Looks like you've been spotted." He nods across the food court, where a crowd is starting to form. I pretend I don't see them, because if you make eye contact with someone, it's all over.

"What?" Kaivan glances over. "Oh. Wow."

The crowd is edging closer. Nick's blocking us with his body, but there's only so much he can do. He eyes the crowd and leans down to say, "We'd better go."

I nod and turn to Kaivan. "You good?"

"Yeah. As long as I don't have gravy all over my face."

"Just a bit." I pay him back for Sammies by wiping his mouth for him.

He blushes. "Keep that up, people are going to think we're dating."

"Sorry. It's just tabloids."

"Don't be. There are worse things in life than people thinking I'm dating a cute boy."

Now it's my turn to blush. I clear my throat. "We can take a couple minutes to say hi, right?"

Nick raises an eyebrow but finally nods.

I pull a pair of Sharpies out of my hoodie and hand one to Kaivan. I try to keep a couple on me whenever I can, because there's nothing worse than getting cornered and asked for an autograph only to find that no one nearby actually has a pen.

"Come on. Let's greet your fans."

As soon as I wave toward the crowd, it erupts. People scream, a few cry, phones jut into the air to snap photos. The air crackles with excitement.

"Hi, folks," I say. I pose for selfies, sign posters and autographs, record myself saying "Hello!" over and over.

Kaivan hangs back, until I gesture for him. "You all know Kaivan from PAR-K? They're opening for us!"

And then people are taking pictures of him too, and he gets the sweetest grin as someone asks for his autograph.

"Are you two really dating?!" a fan asks.

"We're just friends," I say.

"Oh my god you totally should though, my friends and I are shipping you!"

I don't know what to say to that. I've always had a hard time with strangers feeling involved in my dating life. Aidan liked the attention, but I always felt kind of gross.

Kaivan's made the mistake of getting drawn into a conversation—you've got to keep moving at these things. I nod at Nick, who clears his throat and uses his presence to press the crowd back a little.

"Sorry, folks," he says in a clear, sharp voice that must've come from time in the military or something. "These guys have sound check."

"Sorry!" I pause and let a few more people grab photos of me. "See you all tonight!"

And then Nick is herding me and Kaivan out a side exit, talking into his Bluetooth earpiece. He's summoned a golf cart for us, and it's humming right outside the double doors. I let him take shotgun while Kaivan and I ride in the back, so we can wave as we ride away.

"That was intense!" Kaivan flops onto the couch of my dressing room.

"I know," I say. "It's cool, though. I mean, I know it's cliché and all that, but we really are lucky to have such great fans. Fans make the band."

"Yeah."

I sit next to him, sink into the cushions, but then I bolt up again. "Shit! We forgot your leftovers."

Kaivan laughs. "It's fine."

I give him my most serious frown. "No, this is unacceptable. I promise I'll find a way to get you more poutine soon."

"Okay, okay." He gives me this look, totally unguarded, and I have to look down at my hands because it's too intense. "Hey. Nice guitar."

He's looking at my Stratocaster sitting on its stand. It's a black Made in America model with a maple fretboard, custom single-coils, and a black pickguard to make it look like David Gilmour's famous Black Strat.

Pink Floyd was Dad's favorite band, even though he wasn't even born yet when they started recording. He was totally obsessed with them. He always said *Dark Side of the Moon* was the most perfect album ever recorded, and David Gilmour's solos are the best ever played.

I mean, it is an excellent album. It always makes me think of Dad driving me to hockey practice in his crappy Honda as he drummed along to "Time" on the steering wheel.

Sometimes I wonder what he would make of me being in a boy band, if he'd be embarrassed by the whole thing. Or by me being gay. He died before I got to come out to him.

I pull the guitar off its stand. "Thanks. Want to?"

"Sure." Our hands brush as I offer it to him.

He tosses the strap over his head, runs his hand along the fretboard, tests the tension in the tremolo arm, plays a few chords. "Feels good. I usually go for Gibsons."

"Yeah. I really like the C neck of a Strat. Plus that single coil sound."

Kaivan picks out a melody and bobs his head along to the beat. He looks like a chicken pecking the ground looking for seeds, and I chuckle a tiny bit.

"What?"

I shake my head. "Nothing. I didn't know you played guitar too."

Kaivan scrunches up his mouth, which highlights the little bow in his full lips.

"Yeah, but Kamran's a lot better. Plus we needed a drummer."

"Lots of bands have two guitarists, though. You could get a session drummer."

"Yeah, but that's always been our deal, right? Me, Kamran, Karim, we all play our own instruments. We're real musicians."

There's something in the way he says it, some line he draws between him and me.

"And me and the guys aren't?"

People say shit like that all the time. Critics who hate boy bands on principle. But it sucks hearing Kaivan say it. It feels like being slammed against the boards.

Kaivan stops playing and looks down at the fretboard.

"I didn't mean it like that."

"Then what did you mean?"

He shifts on the couch so our knees are touching and meets my eye for a second before his gaze drops to my chin. "Just that our whole deal, from when we started, was that we play our own instruments. We're authentic."

I pull my knee away from him. "Me and the guys are authentic too. We write our own songs. I play guitar in every show. Owen plays piano. He's good, too."

The muscles in Kaivan's neck and throat work as he

swallows. "I know. I'm sorry. I didn't mean it like that. Seriously. You guys are awesome. It's just . . ."

"What?"

"I don't know. Sorry." He bumps my knee with his. "Here. Play me something." He raises the guitar to get his head out of the strap, and his shirt rides up just a bit to show his flat, brown stomach and the happy trail disappearing into his waistband.

My throat clamps up again. I take my guitar and play a few bars of "Breathe (In The Air)," which has one of my favorite chord progressions, that switch from D7#9 to D7♭9. As my shoulders relax, I end up leaning toward him. And he's leaning toward me.

Just friends.

But there's something electric about him. Something exciting.

I haven't felt this way about a guy since Aidan.

I swallow. "So . . ." I start to say, but then my door springs open.

We both sit up straighter, and I catch Kaivan in the ribs with my Strat's headstock.

He grunts and rubs his chest as Ashton bursts in.

"Hunt!" He doesn't even react to Kaivan. His eyes are wide and he's breathing hard. "Hunter. Have you seen? Did you hear?"

"What?"

"Where's your mobile?"

I grab it off the side table. I missed a couple messages from Aidan while we were at lunch:

Are yoi sleepin with him????
Why wont you anser me

I roll my eyes and ignore them. I've got a shitload of notifications, too many to make sense of. I start scrolling through them, but Ashton's too impatient. He holds out his own phone.

"Here. Look."

My thumb catches on one of the little cracks in his screen protector. Ashton's the most cursed person I know when it comes to phones.

He's got Twitter pulled up. We're trending. I'm trending.

I tap and find the tweets.

"Oh shit."

KISSED & TOLD: HUNTER DRAKE'S SEXTS POSTED ONLINE

Rainbow News Now—News That Slays
March 28, 2022

Aidan Nightingale, the spurned ex-boyfriend of Kiss & Tell's Hunter Drake, is making headlines after posting screenshots of salacious texts exchanged with the singer. The texts shed new light on what went wrong between the two, revealed the duo's virginal façade to be just that, and answered gay Twitter's most pressing question: whether Drake is a top or a bottom.

In a series of typo-filled tweets, Nightingale claims he posted the screenshots to prove that he wasn't "the bad [guy]" and that Drake's infidelity was to blame for the breakup. Neither Kiss & Tell's management nor Drake himself have commented on the matter.

Interested in being an affiliate?
Click here to find out how.

TWEET FROM @AIDANNIGHTINGALE:

Everyone's thinks I'm the bad hut, that I broke your
heart, they don't know what you did, they dint know
your a dirty bottom slut, they don't know you broke
mine first

MAY 3, 2021

I miss you sm
miss that d 👇👇👇

                    Miss you

did you get the sheets clean

                    Yeah no problem

i'll prep better next time

                    Okay

I'm a little drunj

                    You safe? You have a ride?

wanna ride you

                    Wow slutty much lol
                    Call me when you're sober

JANUARY 15, 2022

                    I can't believe you

What??

                    The pics are everywhere
                    Last night at the Orpheum

He followed me to the washroom
Security got him right after

Just stop lying to me

Nothing happened!!

Yeah well

Maybe if you didn't flirt with everyone

FEBRUARY 15, 2022

Did you talk to TRS?
__Haidan are "stronger than ever,"__
__despite rumors of infidelity"__

I'm tired of people lying about us

They are lies right?

Why do you have to freak out
over every google alert??

Because there's one in every city.

It's humiliating.

Fuck you

I don't have time to wait in line.

I'm not doing this anymore

FEBRUARY 16, 2022

I'm sorry, I was upset.

I didn't mean it.

Hunt?

FUCK YOU

Please?

I love you.

I'M FUCKING DONE AIDAN

HAIDAN: THE TRUE HISTORY

Lion Heart Magazine
May 11, 2021

LH: Okay, let's start at the beginning. How did you two meet?

HD: Well, we . . . you wanna go?

AN: Well, Ashton and I were playing Atom League when this scrawny redhead showed up and he wouldn't talk to anyone, he'd just sit on the bench.

HD: I was so shy.

AN: You really were. How'd you end up being a superstar?

HD: No clue.

AN: But one day he finally got off the bench, and he was a demon! Just incredible. And within a year he was our starting center, and me and Ashton were left and right wings. And we were unstoppable together. We thought we were going to take over the world.

HD: I mean, let's be honest, we kind of hated each other at first.

AN: We did not!

HD: Come on, you know it's true.

AN: I think it was more rivalry than hatred.

HD: Maybe. But then when my dad died, I just kind of shut down. And I don't know if it was pity or what, but Aidan and Ashton kind of adopted me as a third brother. That really meant a lot to me. I mean, things got a little complicated later . . .

LH: When you came out?

HD: Yeah. I was, what? Twelve?

AN: It was the summer before seventh grade.

HD: Yeah, twelve. It took you a little longer to come out.

AN: I took longer to figure things out. But then there was the accident.

LH: You're talking about the accident that ended Hunter's hockey career?

HD: Yeah. It was one of those freak things. I mean, it's hockey, it gets rough sometimes, but the way Ashton and I collided, his blade hit my kneecap just right and . . . well, that was it.

AN: You needed a lot of physical therapy afterward.

HD: Yeah, the recovery was way worse than the reconstruction. There were all these exercises I had to do. But Aidan and Ashton would come over and help me out, make sure I did them, just keep me company. And then one day . . .

AN: One day!

HD: I swear it was like something out of a movie. I mean, Aidan was over by himself, 'cause Ashton had choir rehearsal, and I was feeling really sorry for myself. And Aidan sat with me and held me, and told me everything was going to be okay, and the next thing I knew we were kissing.

AN: I don't know which of us started it.

HD: I blame the painkillers.

AN: You do not!

HD: I know, I know. I was off them by then.

AN: Anyway, things just kind of . . . evolved from there. While he was recovering, Hunter started writing songs . . .

HD: While Aidan was taking over the whole league . . .

AN: And then things blew up when "Poutine" went viral.

HD: You know, it was Aidan who came up with our name. It was a little while before we fessed up to Ashton about things.

AN: Yeah, I know twin telepathy is kind of made up, but he definitely knew something was going on. So someone had to tell him.

HD: The kissing was better than the telling, though.

AN: Aw, thanks. You're not so bad yourself.

HD: Hey!

LH: But Aidan, you kept playing hockey? You never wanted to join in the band?

AN: Not really. That was Ashton's thing. I don't think our parents could've handled it if both of us joined a band. Besides, I can't dance.

HD: That's not true. I've seen his moves.

AN: But for real. I was just glad to see Hunter doing something he loved. And my brother too. He never went back to hockey after the accident.

HD: I think he felt pretty guilty that he got to walk away and I didn't.

AN: Being in the band was good for him. And you too. I like seeing you both happy. Besides, it's pretty sweet having a rock-star boyfriend.

LH: So you never felt jealous?

AN: Not a bit. I don't think that's a healthy thing for a relationship.

HD: Yeah. When there's problems we just talk through them.

LH: Has all the public attention made having a relationship difficult?

HD: I mean . . .

AN: Not really. At the end of the day, we're still best friends, we just kiss a lot now. And nothing's going to change that.

HD: Yeah.

AN: Also, just between us, Hunter's really, really good-looking. I wasn't going to let him get away.

HD: Don't be sappy.

AN: You're the one who writes me love songs.

HD: Yeah, yeah. I do.

8

I'm a supernova.

I'm a black hole.

"Hunter?" Kaivan reaches for my arm, but I jerk away.

He's got a question in his eyes, but I can't look at him. I can't let him look at me.

I think I'm having a panic attack.

Ashton's phone slips out of my numb fingers and falls to the floor, no doubt adding another crack to the screen protector.

"What?" Kaivan asks, but he sounds far away. My ears are ringing.

I can only sort of remember what my accident was like. It's all jumbled flashes: the feel of Ashton's blade against my knee, the crack of my helmet against the boards, the way the world spun and went dark. I had a concussion, and vommed on the way to the hospital.

I've got it again, that urge to vom.

I run to the washroom, lock it behind me. My knee comes down hard on the tiles, but I ignore it and rest my forearms on the rim of the toilet. I retch but nothing comes out. My eyes burn but no tears will come.

"It's going to be okay, Hunt," Ashton says from the other side of the door. "Mom's already calling Dad to find out what happened. We'll get everything taken down."

"No you won't," I groan. "It's the Internet. It's there forever."

I think that's what finally makes me cry. There's no undoing it.

I loved Aidan. And I let him do this to me.

What the fuck is wrong with me?

"Hunter?" Kaivan's voice is low and gentle.

"Go away."

"Talk to me."

"Don't you have sound check?" I ask through a sniffle.

There's a pause. Kaivan and Ashton mutter to each other, but I can't make anything out.

"I'll find you after."

"Don't," I choke out.

"It'll be okay." He taps once on the door, and then his footsteps recede.

"You want some water?" Ashton asks.

"No. I want to wake up and find out this was all a nightmare."

I grab some of the terrible single-ply toilet paper that all arenas seem to use and blow my nose.

"I'm sorry. I don't know what he was thinking. I'm sorry."

"Not your fault. You didn't do it."

Ashton sighs. The door rattles as he leans against it.

I give up on trying to vom and sit back against the door, massaging my throbbing knee. "I can't believe him."

"I know."

I take a shaky breath.

Slut.

Aidan's the only person I've ever had sex with.

And yeah, I liked it a lot, once we figured some stuff out, like how to make sure I was clean.

But it was supposed to be our thing. Personal. A part of our lives we didn't share with our fans.

The Label was pretty clear on that, after Ethan admitted to being sexually active in an interview. There was a whole petition to get him kicked out of the band. Everyone was supposed to think we were all virgins. Wholesome. The kind of guys you could take home to meet your parents.

I've always known exactly who I'm supposed to be: the clean gay. The gay best friend. The guy you get your nails done with. The guy who helps you plan a brunch.

I mean, Aidan and I were dating for two years, people had to guess, right? Maybe that was the point: guessing but never knowing for sure.

That makes me feel sick all over again. Because it's no

one's business but ours. Not our fans and definitely not the Internet's.

I hug myself tighter. The muffled sound of Kaivan tuning his tom-toms filters in over the in-room monitors.

How am I supposed to perform tonight? Everyone in the audience is going to know.

Everyone in the world knows.

Slut.

The door shudders against my back as Ashton slides down the other side to sit on the floor. "Talk to me, Hunt."

"He asked about Kaivan, you know."

"What?"

I rest the back of my head against the door with a thunk.

"Aidan texted me. Wanted to know if I was hooking up with Kaivan. Back home, and again today."

Ashton's conspicuously quiet.

"I wasn't, by the way. We're just friends."

"I know."

"I never cheated on Aidan either."

"I know, Hunt." He lets his own head thunk against the door. "You gonna hide in there forever?"

"Thinking about it."

Ashton's quiet for a second. And then:

"Your phone's buzzing."

"Anyone important?"

Ashton's shadow disappears from under the door for a second.

"It's Aidan."

"Ignore it."

"He says he's sorry."

I choke back a laugh.

"He says he fucked up."

I want to smash something. Rip the toilet off the floor. Go out into my dressing room, grab my Strat, and smash it against the walls like a real rock star.

"Fuck him," I shout through the door. "Fuck you too. Leave me alone."

I don't know why I'm so mad at Ashton, but I am.

I just want to be alone.

Finally I hear his footsteps departing too.

Fuck.

TRENDING: HUNTER DRAKE
TRENDING: #GOODBYEHUNTER
TRENDING: BOTTOMGATE

@jayman01: Hunter has betrayed his fans and he should quit the band before he takes everyone else down. #goodbyehunter

@i_luv_aidan: I just don't get how he could cheat on Aidan. He should apologize publicly!!! #IStandWithAidan

@haidanfan12: You guys there wouldn't even BE K&T without Hunter why are you asking him to leave?! #NoHunterNoBand

@macattacc: My daughters won't stop crying. Shame on Hunter. No one needs to read about that kind of stuff.

@magggs_rt: why is his label even keeping him on after this? don't they have morality clause or something? #goodbyehunter

@h34rtbr34kfever: okay but like do you think Hunter Drake swallows or no?

@leviah59: yaaasss hunter honey bottom pride!!!

@_lady_gege_: I've loved Kiss & Tell since their first single but I can't support them if they condone behavior like @hunterdrake's. He needs to step down! #goodbyehunter

@hdidi04: WTF people, Hunter and Aidan are both 17! Kids make mistakes!

@heckyeah_hunter: So was he hooking up with Kaivan? Is that why they broke up?

@hashtaghashton: Honestly I always shipped him with Ashton anyway.

@samalicious: @hunterdrake @aidannightingale sexts are fine but where are the nudes!

9

The washroom tiles are getting cold, so I unlock the door and throw myself onto the couch. My phone's buzzing with more notifications: tags, mentions, messages. I start reading them but stop pretty quickly because they're just gross. I mean, there are some that are supportive, saying people should let me keep my private life private, but there are plenty more making jokes about it, speculating on how good I am in bed, wondering if it's true I cheated on Aidan, and grossest of all, one person hoping for nudes.

(Aidan and I never sent each other nudes. Back in grade nine sex ed we had to listen to a really terrible lecture about what happens to people who send or receive nudes of minors, even when they're minors themselves, and it basically scarred us for life.)

I'm shivering, but my armpits are sweaty. My face is on fire.

I delete all my social media apps and then throw my phone across the room.

The intercom crackles and then Shaz announces, "Kiss & Tell, fifteen minutes to sound check. Fifteen minutes."

I don't know how I'm supposed to go out there and perform for people who know all about my sex life. Who think I'm a slutty bottom.

I mean, I am a bottom, and there's nothing wrong with it except for the value judgments heteronormative patriarchy attaches to it, but I don't need everyone knowing that.

My throat clamps tight around another sob fighting to get out. My voice is going to be a wreck.

Someone knocks on my door.

"Hunter? It's Janet. You've got ten seconds to get decent before I come in."

"I'm decent," I groan, and she comes inside and sits next to me on the couch.

For as long as I've known Janet—from the moment she emailed us and said she wanted to be our manager—she's always treated us all like adults. Even when we goofed off, made mistakes, she never treated us like we were kids.

But now? Now she's looking at me like I'm a kid.

"You okay, Hunter?"

I shake my head.

"I figured. It's fucked up, and we're going to be sorting things out for a while."

"Sorry."

"No, I'm sorry. I know you like to keep your personal life private. You didn't deserve this."

"How am I supposed to go on tonight?"

"By remembering that there are seventeen thousand fans who are here tonight because they love you. Who might never get a chance like this again. Some of them you invited yourself. I know things suck right now, but you're a professional. And you've shown time and time again how brave you are. Can you be brave tonight?"

I swallow and nod.

"Good. Then put on your big-boy pants and get your game face on."

Maybe Janet was a hockey coach in a past life, because her speech works. I actually do feel a little better.

She pats my good knee and stands.

"Take a couple minutes to collect yourself. I'll tell Shaz you'll be out when you're ready. Okay?"

I take a deep breath and let it out.

"Okay."

Once she's gone, I go back to the washroom and stare at the ceiling until I'm sure I'm not going to cry again, then face myself in the mirror. I'm all puffy and red.

"Keep it together, Hunter," I tell myself. "You can do this."

The show is fine. I hit my marks. I sing my parts. I smile into the cameras. I laugh when I'm supposed to. The spotlights blind me, and I can't see if the audience is staring at me.

But the meet and greet is awful. Everyone is definitely staring at me, acting weird.

A man in his forties asks me if I'm a lights-on or lights-off guy.

A cross-armed girl, accompanied by her equally cross-armed mom, asks if I really cheated on Aidan. Tells me I used to be her favorite but not anymore.

A guy in his twenties tells me about a website that sells enemas in case I'm still having "problems getting clean."

A woman runs her fingers through my hair while I'm signing her poster, and emits this little squeal that makes my jaw clench.

I want to peel my skin off and throw it in the trash.

Eventually, Nazeer steps in and starts insisting there's only time for me to sign autographs, no photos and no conversation. I get him to relax a little for the shelter kids, enough for me to say hi, but I don't get up from behind my table. If someone hugs me, I'm going to start crying again.

I go back to my dressing room when it's finally over, wash my face, pack my Strat. I sling my backpack over my shoulder and turn to find Kaivan in the doorway. He's looking at me with the gentlest smile and the kindest eyes, and I have to look away.

"Hey," he says.

"Hey," I tell the floor.

"You okay?"

I shrug.

"I figured. Listen."

"I get it." I was expecting this. He can't be around me, not with all this news. I'll just drag him down.

I'm a slut.

Kaivan's eyebrows scrunch up. "Get what?"

"Aren't you going to tell me we can't be friends anymore?"

"What? No. That's bullshit. Who would do something like that?"

"Oh." I blush all the way up to my forehead.

"I just . . . I'm sure you have weird feelings about texting or DMing or whatever right now, but I thought maybe I could give you my number? Just in case you wanted to talk? Like, talk-talk?"

"Oh. Okay." I pull out my mobile, but it's dead. "Shit."

"No worries." Kaivan hands me his phone. I put in my number and hand it back. "I'll text you mine."

"Cheers."

He looks at me again, and his eyes are somehow even kinder than before. Warm brown, with dark, gracefully arched eyebrows above. His lips curve into a tiny grin. My skin hums, a soft and constant ground loop.

"Well. See you in Portland?"

"Yeah."

He gives my shoulder a quick squeeze, leans in and kisses me on the cheek. "Call me if you want."

"Thanks."

★　★　★

Once we're on the bus, I get out of my show clothes and pull on another pair of leggings (lightning bolt print), but then I get this really weird feeling, because Ethan was right, you can see my junk in them, plus my butt.

I pull off the leggings and put on my baggiest gym shorts instead.

As soon as I plug my phone in to charge, I get a message from an unknown Ohio number.

Hey it's Kaivan

Hey

I don't know what else to say.

There's a missed call from Mom too. She left a voicemail.

"Hi, Hunter, it's Mom." She sounds overly cheerful, which means she definitely heard the news. "I just wanted to see how you were doing. I heard from Jill earlier about what Aidan did."

There's a pause.

"I'm sorry. It was awful. And you're probably feeling pretty awful right now too. But I just want you to know, whatever you and he did, that was private, and you had every right to expect him to keep it private. And him posting it all was a betrayal of your trust. This isn't your fault. It's his. You didn't do anything wrong."

My heart tightens.

I'm the one who wanted us to have sex in the first place.

I'm the one who started everything.

"Anyway, I love you and I miss you. Call me when you can. Bye."

My eyes start burning again. The guys are all out in the lounge, so I go hide in the studio.

The walls are lined with acoustic foam, the ceiling too, and there's a pair of bare mattresses leaning upright against the back wall that we use to make a little recording booth. In the corner closest to the door is a desk with a Mac workstation and two large displays mounted to the wall.

Even with all the soundproofing, I can still make out the low rumble of the tires on the road. We don't record while we're driving, just play around. I've got another Strat in here, mystic surf green with a rosewood fretboard. It feels calmer than my black Strat, warmer, as I move through some chord changes I've had stuck in my head for the last couple days.

I used to be able to play for fun. Now it's like every time I sit down, if I don't come away with some progress on the new album, what's the point?

The door opens and I mute my strings. Owen steps in, wearing his usual black pajama pants and vintage Transformers T-shirt. "Don't stop. That sounded good."

"I dunno."

"Really." He sits at the keyboard. We both sway a bit as the bus takes a turn. "Come on, let's jam."

We used to do this all the time. Just fuck around playing

whatever we felt like, recording it all in case we accidentally hit on something good. It was fun.

I look down at my guitar but I can't seem to summon up anything, not even a single note. My insides have been scraped away, Zamboni'd and left smooth and frozen.

So Owen starts playing, a simple progression in D minor, kind of melancholy. He meets my eyes and nods, and even though I don't think I can, my fingers do their own thing and I start to play along.

It actually is kind of fun.

From: Bill Holt (b.holt@thelabel.com)
To: Janet Lundgren (janet@kissandtellmusic.com)
Subject: Next steps
3/28/22 11:07 P.M.

Well today has been a shitstorm. Good job wrangling the
boys.

Still learning what the fallout from this will be. H is
hemorrhaging followers right now, not sure where things
will bottom out. Some of the charities H has partnered with
have expressed concerns about image. Matching donations
is good for corporate PR, we'd like to continue if we can work
something out. Will update when I hear more.

Publicity thinks a statement would be good. See below. Have
him post tomorrow morning if possible.

Marketing thinks we need to move quickly to rebrand. New
wardrobe, styling. Think Troye Sivan, floral prints, etc. Going
to recast their music video too; see updated breakdown.
Any word on album number three? Would like to get that in
the pipeline ASAP. I've got a producer in mind if they need help.

More soon,
BH

From: Janet Lundgren (janet@kissandtellmusic.com)
To: Bill Holt (b.holt@thelabel.com)

Subject: Re: Next steps
3/28/22 11:35 P.M.

Thanks Bill. Doing our best out here.

I'll get Hunter working on statements tomorrow. Keep me posted.

Owen's been working on demos for the new album. Some are pretty good. Nothing from Hunter so far, not surprising given what he's been through lately. He'll pull through sooner or later, but go ahead and send that contact.

Best,
Janet
Sent from my iPhone

From: Bill Holt (b.holt@thelabel.com)
To: Janet Lundgren (janet@kissandtellmusic.com)
Subject: Re: Next steps
3/29/22 1:08 A.M.

Gregg's contact attached.

Crazy thought: What if H starts dating Kaivan from PAR-K? Both are gay, have already been seen together, would make a good couple and good story for the press. Talk it over with H, I'll get Ryan to discuss with Kaivan.

-BH

KISS & TELL DOCUMENTARY

Footage transcription
012/01:08:57;00

CHRIS (O/S): It's on the call sheet, right?

BRETT (O/S): That's what mine said.

CHRIS (O/S): You think we should wake him up?

BRETT (O/S): You're the director, man, that's above my paygrade.

ETHAN: Don't worry, I've got a foolproof method. Hunter. Hunter.

HUNTER: Hmm? Mmm.

ETHAN: HUNTER!

HUNTER: (screaming)

ETHAN: BONER ALERT! (laughter) Sorry dude!

HUNTER: Ethan!

ETHAN: This is supposed to be a kids' movie!

CHRIS (O/S): Cut!

10

I am going to kill Ethan.

I mean, it's not his fault I overslept and missed my call for the documentary, but in my defense, I did have a shitty night.

After I get things sorted out with Chris, the director—we're going to reshoot it tomorrow—I brush my teeth and head out to the lounge. Janet's waiting for me.

"Morning," she says.

"Morning." I grab a protein bar out of the cupboard. "Where'd the guys go?"

"Nazeer took them to get doughnuts."

That sounds ominous. Especially since I wasn't invited.

"Is this where we figure out damage control?"

Janet nods. "A statement would be a good start. The

Label's got some suggestions." She hands me a folded sheet of paper. "Sooner is better."

I figured this was coming: time for a Notes App Apology.

"Got it."

"And you've got a stylist appointment this afternoon."

"What for?"

"The Label thinks your look could use some updating."

"What does that mean, updating?"

"They think, given how all this has changed your public image, embracing a more . . . femme look could be good."

"They want me to dress more like a bottom? Is that it?"

"You don't have to. These are all suggestions."

I mean. What else can I do?

"Okay."

"This last one I'm not in favor of, but the choice is yours." Janet purses her lips. "Bill thinks it would be a good idea for you and Kaivan to fake date for a while."

"What?" My whole head tingles. This has to be made up.

"I'll fight them on this if you want. You know that."

"I know."

I close my eyes and rest my head against the window. It's raining, a slow, heavy rain that drums against the bus's roof.

I don't know what to do.

But this whole band was my idea. We wouldn't even be here if I hadn't convinced them to shoot that first video. I can't let them down now. I've got to salvage this somehow.

So I say, "I'll think about it.

"Okay. I'll back you up, no matter what."

"Thanks."

Janet pats my knee and stands.

"Oh, hey," I say before she can leave.

"Hm?"

"You think it's too late to ask Nazeer to grab me a doughnut?"

NOTES APP APOLOGY

Hey friends. By now you've probably heard about
some personal texts of mine that got out yesterday.
I've always tried to keep some parts of my life
private, not because I am ashamed of them but
because they are personal to me and those I
care about. I'm sorry to anyone I've offended or
disappointed or upset.

My ex and I were in a committed, monogamous
relationship for a long time, and everything we did
was safe and consensual and, up until now, private.

I'm going to be quieter on here for a while as I figure
some stuff out. But I hope you'll still support us and our
tour. We're so excited to share our music with you.
Love you all.

h.

11

The doughnuts are ridiculous. Ashton grabbed me one that's orange-soda-flavored and dusted with Pop Rocks, and it's that weird blend of disgusting and amazing that makes the best desserts. I eat it in my dressing room as I post my Notes App Apology. I had to download my social media apps again to post it, and I make the mistake of dipping into my mentions again.

Still a disaster. Plus, my daily batch of dick pics seems larger than usual. The batch, I mean, not the dicks.

I delete everything again, then grab my Strat. Me and Owen landed on a good chord progression last night, but we weren't recording, and no matter what I try I can't find it again. It's gone.

Maybe we really do need help with this album. I hate losing creative control, but we've got to get it out. Most boy bands only have five years of life before they fall apart or implode, and we're more than two years in now.

I run my hands through my hair, massage my scalp.

I don't know what to do.

I end up playing a game on my phone, the kind where you unscramble letters to make as many words as you can. I'm down to only one four-letter word left when Mom calls.

"Hello?"

"Hi Hunter." Mom sounds tired, but even so, her voice is just about the best sound in the world.

"Hi Mom. Sorry, I should've called you back."

"It's okay. Are you doing all right?"

"I'm okay. How about you? How's Haley?"

"You know your sister. Always stressed about some assignment or another."

My sister's kind of a perfectionist, though she'll never admit it, and in fact gets pretty offended if anyone suggests it to her.

"And I'm fine too. Pulled a double yesterday but I've got today off."

"Good."

"How are you really doing, Hunter?"

"I don't know." I hide my face in the crook of my elbow, even though no one can see me. "Angry. Hurt."

"Are you taking care of yourself? Drinking water? Eating right?"

"Yeah."

"Good." Mom goes quiet for a second, and then she says, "I kind of figured you and Aidan were sexually active. You were safe, right?"

A flush sweeps up my chest and neck.

"God, Mom, yes."

"Good. That's all that matters to me: that everything was safe and consensual. Okay?"

"Okay."

"One last thing. I heard from Anthony this morning."

That flush makes its way to my face.

"He asked me to tell you that Aidan says he's sorry."

"That doesn't mean much now."

"I know, honey."

I sigh. My skin is still too warm, except now the heat's moved to the corners of my eyes.

I'm so tired of crying.

"Hunter?"

"Mmhmm?" My throat has squeezed shut.

"It's going to be okay. Maybe not for a while. But it will be. The news cycle will move on. One of your friends will do something just as embarrassing. Isn't Ethan dating someone again?"

"No. I mean, he was dating Kelly K, but they broke up months ago." Kelly K's another of The Label's artists, an Afro-Latina girl from New York who got her start on Broadway. She and Ethan dated for like three months, before they broke up.

"And besides," I say. "It's different for the other guys. None of them are gay. None of them get treated the same as me. There's no shame in straight guys having sex, not like with me, being a—"

I can't bring myself to tell my mother I'm a bottom. I know that's fucked up. I mean, she has to know, if she read everything.

But still.

"Hunter?"

"Yeah?"

"I know things are tough right now. But you're brave and smart and kind. You'll figure things out."

"Thanks, Mom," I say. "Love you—miss you."

"Love you—miss you too. Talk soon."

After the most awkward tutoring session ever—stuck between Jill and Ashton as they both take turns looking at me and avoiding looking at me—I get fitted for my new looks.

It could be worse. Some of the floral shirts are pretty cool. But there's a whole rack of pink hoodies and jackets for me to try, and I look heinous in pink.

"Sorry," Julian, our stylist, says. He's a gay Black man with the most powerful dimples I've ever seen, his hair short and crisply lined. "I know you hate it, but sometimes a little photo documentation is all it takes to get them to stop suggesting it."

"That's fair."

I pose in a couple of the pink pieces as Julian laughs

and takes photos and says "Oh yeah, tomato eleganza."

He even has me try on some pastel shorts that are cuffed mid-thigh. I don't mind showing off my legs, even with the scars on my knee, but these . . .

"Maybe for when we're in Europe," I say.

"You haven't announced it yet, though?"

I shake my head. "We've got a presser when we're in New York."

"Well, let's leave these in the 'maybe' pile at least."

After a couple hours, we finally settle on some new looks that will work.

"Thanks, Julian," I say.

"Of course. That sure was a mess, huh?"

"Yeah."

"Well, we've all been there."

"You had a vengeful ex share your sexts on social media?"

Julian snorts. "No, but I have had more than one vengeful ex. Don't let them get you down."

"I won't. Thanks."

As I trudge back to my dressing room, I get a text from Kaivan.

Where are you?
You doing okay?

Headed toward my dressing room

I'm okay

He's waiting for me at my door, and I try not to smile.

"That a new look?"

I'm in a white button-up shirt with blue flowers (Julian called them gentians, but I've never been a Plant Gay), gray jeans, and a pair of yellow Chuck Taylors, which I actually do kind of like.

"Yeah. The Label wanted it. I guess my old look wasn't 'bottom chic' enough."

Kaivan blinks. "Really? They said that?"

"Not in so many words." Kaivan follows me in and flops on the couch. He's like a rag doll, all loose limbs. He looks so comfortable.

I'm in a straitjacket. A fashionable one, but still. I ease down next to him.

"I mean, if that's the worst that came of it, it's not that bad, right?"

I let out a nervous laugh. "Oh, there's more."

"Like what?"

"Well, I had to do a Notes App Apology."

Kaivan snorts. "I saw that."

"Why are you being so cool about all this, anyway?" Kaivan should be trying to get as far away from me as he can.

"It's not like it's a surprise, you and Aidan having sex. I'm not exactly a virgin myself, you know."

"Really?"

"Yeah. With my last girlfriend. I think I was still trying to convince myself I was straight."

"I'm sorry."

"Don't be. She's still a good friend. And it was good. Just not what I wanted."

"That's good. I mean, that it was good, and that you're friends."

"Yeah."

Somehow he's shifted closer to me, or I've shifted closer to him, but I'm suddenly very aware of the feel of him against me. He's in his usual tank top, showing off those nice shoulders of his, and even through my shirt I can feel the warmth of his skin. It makes me shiver. I scoot away from him.

His brow furrows. "What?"

"There's something else The Label wanted."

"Oh?"

I look at the ceiling, because I can't look at Kaivan. "They want me to . . . god, it feels so silly saying it." I take a breath. "They want me to pretend to date you. They want us to pretend to date. Like . . . fake date."

Kaivan doesn't say anything, and I can't stop myself.

"I guess they think it'll distract from all the Aidan stuff, and people are already speculating, because we were hanging out, and I know it was just as friends, but you know how the Internet is. But Janet's going to get them to back off, because obviously that's not fair to you at all, and I'm sorry for even mentioning it—"

"Does it have to be fake?"

My voice fails me. It's never done that before.

Kaivan blushes.

"What?" I finally manage to squeak out.

"Like . . . does it have to be fake?"

"I don't understand."

Kaivan chuckles. "I like you. And I get the feeling you maybe like me too?"

"I do."

"Yeah?"

"Yeah." I bite my lip to keep from smiling. "But it's just so weird, with The Label and all."

"Just 'cause they want it for a shit reason doesn't make it a bad idea."

"You really want to do this?"

"Yeah. If you want to."

That's just it. I do want to. I want to hold his hand. I want to go eat more poutine and giant sandwiches and curl up and cuddle.

I want to kiss Kaivan.

"I do want to," I admit. "But we have to talk to each other. Okay? I mean, if something's bothering you, you have to tell me." Aidan and I were never good at that part.

"Okay. Yeah. And you'll tell me the same, right?"

"Right." I relax against him and let out a chuckle.

"What?"

"This is like something from a fanfic."

"If this were a fanfic, we'd be making out or something."

"I mean." I swallow. "We could be."

Kaivan looks at me and then away. His smile fades, just a bit. "You know, I've never actually kissed a guy before."

"Never?"

"Never."

Given how perfect Kaivan's lips are, that's basically a crime against humanity. He licks them as I stare.

"Well." My heart starts beating double time. "Would you like to?"

"God, yes."

I reach for his cheek and pull our heads together, angling my nose to the left, but he angles his nose the same way and we bump. I giggle and angle the other way and bring my lips to his.

They're warm and soft and smooth, like he put on Chap-Stick a while ago but it's had time to wear off a little so it's not greasy. He rests a hand on my knee. The other reaches for my hair.

I tug on his lower lip a little, let my tongue dart out to meet it.

That makes him giggle, a nervous one, and I break the kiss. My skin is alive with electricity. "How was that?"

"Awesome," he says. I'm about to ask if he wants to keep going, but his eyes are looking watery.

"Hey," I say.

"Sorry." He sniffs. "It's just, there were days when I

was growing up that I thought I'd never get to do that."

"It's okay. I know what you mean."

"How can you? You've been out forever."

I scoff and rest my forehead against his for a second. He's practically vibrating, and I can't tell if it's nerves or exhilaration.

I take his hands in mine. "I was terrified coming out to my team. I'd spent years basically keeping my eyes closed in the locker room. I didn't want anyone to think I was looking at them. I didn't want to be called an f-word."

To be honest, a couple guys did call me the f-word after I came out, but they got kicked off the team pretty quickly because of the inclusion policy. Also because they sucked and I was really good, and it was a no-brainer who Coach wanted to keep around.

"I get that," he says. "My family was cool. School was okay for the most part. Already knew who all the assholes were."

"Oh?"

"Yeah. Ohio's not exactly the best place to be Iranian-American."

"Really? I thought it was kind of diverse?"

I could swear Kaivan frowns for a second. But maybe I just imagine it.

"I mean, some parts are, but we were in the suburbs. And it's still one degree removed from the South. Like, some parts of Ohio are basically Kentucky."

"Oh. I'm sorry."

He shrugs, but then he laughs. "Sorry, that took a turn."

"It's all good."

I scoot closer to him and wrap my arm around his side. He feels strong and warm.

He licks his lips again.

"Hey," he says.

"Yeah?"

"I'm not sure I got the full experience. You know, with that kiss."

"Oh really?"

"Yeah. Maybe we could do it again?"

I laugh and kiss him again.

SING ME A SONG BY HUNTERGREENEYES

FanWorks Repository
Rating: Explicit
Category: M/M
Fandom: Kiss & Tell (Band)
Relationships: Hunter Drake/Aidan Nightingale
Additional Tags: top!Hunter, bottom!Aidan, hurt/comfort, i don't know hockey but whatever, mutual pining, such angst, first time
Length: 18,000 words (incomplete)
Chapters: 5 of ??

Summary: After Aidan takes a bad hit at hockey championships, Hunter takes a break from tour to come home and take care of his boyfriend. When music fails to cheer Aidan up, Hunter tries more ~direct means~.

Notes: Thanks everyone for all the comments, they mean alot! This fic will update on every other Monday.
Also to everyone asking in the comments: yes, I have seen the tweets, but i'm not rewriting anything. I still think top!Hunter makes more sense, so I guess this is an AU now. ;-)

NEW COUPLE ALERT! HUNTER DRAKE'S REPS CONFIRM NEW ROMANCE

TRS (The Real Scoop)
Date: March 30, 2022

TRS can now confirm that Hunter Drake, the Kiss & Tell singer, is dating Iranian-American drummer Kaivan Parvani of PAR-K, which is opening for Kiss & Tell.

Reps for Kiss & Tell announced the pairing early this morning, and suggested that it was a recent development as Drake and Parvani got to know each other on tour.

Drake recently made headlines when his text messages with ex-boyfriend Aidan Nightingale were posted on Twitter. Drake has since apologized, though the damage may already be done: A number of brands have distanced themselves from Drake, as well as several LGBTQ+ charities.

Parvani came out as gay in a series of social media posts last December, in which he emphasized that he wants to be seen as a musician first, and that "being gay is only one part of who I am."

Starting tomorrow, Kiss & Tell (with PAR-K

opening) will be performing three sold-out shows at Los Angeles's famed Hollywood Bowl.

__Aidan Nightingale Deletes All Social Media Accounts__

__Callum Wethers Denies Dating Rumors__

CASTING BREAKDOWN FOR MUSIC VIDEO SHOOT UPDATED 3/30/22

Kiss & Tell—Come *Say Hello*—"Find Me Waiting"
(3:57)
Director: Tessa Wooten
Casting Director: Natalie Carlisle

Concept: The boys of Kiss & Tell are members of the RCMP, who refuse to party. When they pull over a carful of teens on their way to a campout, sparks fly and they abandon their duties to join the campout.

Cast:
Young Man, driving the car: Ruggedly handsome, a flannel-and-jeans type with a bit of stubble. This is Hunter's love interest.

Young Woman 1, ~~driving the car~~ riding shotgun: A blond girl-next-door type. This is Ashton's love interest.

~~Young Man, riding shotgun: A waifish, shy type. (Ethnic okay.) This is Hunter's love interest.~~

Young Woman 2: A perky, fun-loving type. (Ethnic okay.) This is Ethan's love interest.

Young Woman 3: A short, athletic type. (Ethnic okay.) This is Ian's love interest.

Young Woman 4: A quiet, studious type. Wears glasses. (Ethnic okay.) This is Owen's love interest.

12

I usually like dark days: days when there's no concert, when we can sleep in (at a hotel, even), relax. We used to be able to do tourist stuff—walk around, explore, go shopping—but everything's a lot more coordinated now, with escorts and escape plans. We're not invisible anymore.

Kaivan and I are going to go to the beach this evening, since The Label thought that would be a good "public outing," and Nazeer's been coordinating with a local security company to set things up. I wish we could just catch a cab and go by ourselves like normal guys dating. But I guess it's better than nothing.

Still, I've got to survive this music video shoot first.

It's not the song: I really like "Find Me Waiting," which is another one I wrote with Owen. It's got this moody jazz chord progression, until it switches to triple-time to show off how fast Ian can really sing.

And it's not the crew, which is mostly cool, though more uptight than the ones in Vancouver.

No, it's the whole concept of the video: Sexy Mounties.

We're wearing Red Serges that taper on the sides and stop just above the butt, and I'm once again thankful that I'm not flat-assed because at least I can pull off the black jodhpurs. We've all got our jackets unbuttoned, some more and some less. The costumer has even draped Ashton's to show off his tattoo: a twisting branch of cherry blossoms over his heart, with a few falling petals floating down toward his ribcage.

It's a really awesome tattoo. And Ashton has really nice pecs to display it. (I've never been able to get mine to look like that, no matter how many pushups I do.) Aidan had a nice chest, too.

I haven't heard anything else from him, which I suppose is good, since he can't do any more damage if he shuts up. My anger is cooling into something different, this sharp note of betrayal constantly humming in my gut; but there's an undercurrent of sadness too, because maybe if I'd done things differently, Aidan wouldn't have been so convinced I cheated, wouldn't have felt like the whole world was mad at him, wouldn't have done what he did.

I just don't know.

"One more time, from the top." Our director, Tessa, is hunched over in her director's chair, black hoodie pulled over her auburn hair, staring into a video monitor and drinking from a water bottle larger than her head.

I take a deep breath and find my mark again. I'm doing this bit opposite Garrett, who I'm pretty sure is at least twenty-five. He's got stubble that's practically a beard, he's even whiter than me (and my family is Scottish on both sides), and worst of all, he's six-four, which he's already mentioned twice today.

"Hunter, can you get onto the car any smoother?"

In this part, I'm supposed to hop onto the trunk of the car we've pulled over, toss my hat in the air, and announce that we're going to go party instead of giving them a ticket. It doesn't make any sense, but whatever.

"I'll try," I say, but my jodhpurs make it kind of awkward.

"I can give him a boost," Garrett offers. "I'm six-four."

Three times.

I shake my head. "I got it."

The AD calls for final touches, and my dresser runs out. They button my jacket back up, fix my hair, wipe a smudge off my sunglasses, and run off before I can even thank them. I take my position, leaning my hip against the trunk of the car, holding a ledger and pen, threatening Garrett with a speeding ticket.

"I can give you a boost later," Garrett mutters with a crooked smirk that he must think is sexy but just comes off as desperate.

It's so gross, so ridiculous, I freeze up as playback starts and Tessa calls action.

I'm supposed to toss my ledger away, hop up onto the car, but I'm just staring at Garrett. Who actually says stuff like that?

He grabs my hips and hoists me up onto the car, but I push him away. "Don't touch me, dude. I said I got it."

Tessa calls out "CUT!" A second later, the music stops. "Hunter? Problem?"

Garrett is still looming over me. I push him away and get off the car. "I'm good. Let's go again."

Janet's standing next to Tessa, and leans in to whisper something. Tessa nods and says, "Why don't we take ten?"

"Yeah. Okay. Sure." I run to my dressing room before anyone can stop me.

I hide in the trailer Ashton and I share, clutching a mug of honey-ginger-lemon so hard I feel like I could crush it. My hands are shaky, and I never have shaky hands. I don't even drink caffeine.

Someone knocks on the door. The whole trailer shakes a little. "Yeah?"

The door opens, and I squint against the California sun. Ian pops his head in. "Hey. You okay?"

I shrug. He lets himself in, moves Ashton's backpack off the couch, and sits. He's taken his Serge off but he's still wearing the Stetson, and he cocks it back with his knuckles.

I smirk. "Nice hat."

He chuckles. "Beats the sombrero anyway."

"Oh man, I think I'd blocked that out."

"Are you kidding? Owen still has PTSD I think."

One of our first videos with the label was for "Young and Free," and it had this travel theme, but the costumes were some low-level racist shit. Ian got stuck in a sombrero and other "Brazilian garb," Owen had to do like a full Bollywood number. Ethan was pretty sure his costume was actually Thai and not Vietnamese.

I got put in this rainbow kilt that made no sense whatsoever, but I guess they were worried people would forget I was gay if they didn't cover me in rainbows.

Meanwhile Ashton got to wear a Canucks jersey.

It was heinous, and Janet made them scrap everything and come up with a new concept. And what's worse, everything we shot was on green screen, so we didn't even get to go anywhere.

Ian studies me. "So what happened out there?"

"It was nothing."

"It didn't look like nothing."

I shake my head and stare into my honey-ginger-lemon.

"That guy was just being a creep. I don't know. I'm just being sensitive."

"Did you tell someone?"

"No. I mean, that's not what bothered me. I mean, that bothered me too, but, well. It's hard to explain."

Ian doesn't say anything, just keeps looking at me.

How am I supposed to explain to a straight guy what it

feels like, when people try and force you into a certain definition of what a gay guy is like. Who's a "believable" partner, if you're a bottom? It's the floral shirts all over again.

"I don't know," I say. "Maybe I'm just tired."

Ian sighs and stretches. His long legs bump into the little IKEA coffee table, and his arms smack against the Venetian blinds covering the window behind us. His shirt rides up when he does it, revealing a strip of light brown waist that I avoid looking at.

"Maybe you're feeling forced into a role that's not right for you."

Sometimes Ian does this thing where he says what he thinks and it ends up being alarmingly true. My face starts burning.

"Maybe."

"You should talk to Janet."

"Whatever, it's just a music video. Besides, I've already caused enough trouble."

"Technically Aidan caused it."

"You know what I mean."

There's a knock on the trailer door. A PA says, "Mr. Drake? Five minutes to places."

"Thank you five," Ian and I both call through the door.

I stand and roll out my neck. Ian straightens out his hat and grabs my shoulder. "You know we've got your back, right?"

"I know, Ian. Thanks."

EVERYTHING WE KNOW
ABOUT HUNTER DRAKE'S NEW BOYFRIEND,
KAIVAN PARVANI

NewzList Canada
Date: March 30, 2022

Kiss & Tell's Hunter Drake recently went public on his new relationship with Iranian-American musician Kaivan Parvani of the band PAR-K. For those who aren't familiar with them, here's a helpful primer on Kaivan:

He came out as gay last December.

He's 17 years old, and his birthday is June 7—so he's five days younger than Hunter.

He was born and raised in Columbus, Ohio.

He's a middle child: two older brothers (Karim, 20, and Kamran, 19) and two younger sisters (Parvin, 15, and Persis, 12).

He and Hunter met during rehearsals for Kiss & Tell's *Come Say Hello* tour. They were <u>first spotted together</u> at a sandwich shop in Vancouver.

He used to <u>swim competitively in high school.</u>

<u>He bleached his hair in middle school.</u>

<u>Gay Twitter Reacts to Hunter Drake Being a Bottom</u>

<u>Callum Wethers Under Fire After Being Spotted at Chick-fil-A Drive-Thru</u>

THE BOYS OF PAR-K BRING
MIDDLE EASTERN FLAIR TO POP MUSIC

Gramophone Magazine
November 12, 2021

It's a combination that shouldn't work: three brown-skinned immigrant boys, imbuing their youthful pop with ancient Middle Eastern rhythms and instrumentation and Farsi backing tracks, but PAR-K has done the impossible. Brothers Kamran, Karim, and Kaivan Parvani, the children of Iranian immigrants (the boys also have two sisters), hardly fit the stereotype. Born and raised in Ohio, growing up on a mix of Iranian classics, like Bijan Mortazavi and Googoosh, and American staples like Bruce Springsteen and Michael Jackson, they've forged a synthesis that has listeners eager for more.

After playing gigs in and around the Midwest, PAR-K gained national attention during an audition for *America's Best Band*, where, despite accolades from the judges, they failed to advance to the finals. The Label signed them shortly thereafter, and released PAR-K's eponymous first LP, which reached number fourteen on the Pop Charts and number five on Alternative.

PAR-K made headlines again this spring, when it was announced they would be opening for Canadian boy band Kiss & Tell on their upcoming *Come Say Hello* tour.

We sit down with the Parvani brothers to talk the American Dream, their musical stylings, and their plans for the future.

13

Ashton's on the phone with his mom as we head back to the hotel. I only catch his end of the conversation, but it's enough to suck all the air out of the Escalade.

"Yeah, I know he was drunk, Mom, but I don't think . . . just a beer after the show sometimes, it's fine. You can check the bills if you want . . ." He sighs. "No, I don't think you're playing favorites."

Ashton's lips are pursed, his nostrils flared, as he runs a hand through his hair. It's got this loose curl to it, the kind that I could never achieve except with epic amounts of product and wishful thinking. He's grown it out a bit for the tour, and it looks good on him.

Ashton catches me looking at him. I raise my eyebrows but he just shrugs.

"No, I haven't talked to him, Dad took away his phone . . .

come on, Mom. Yeah . . . yeah. We're on our way to the hotel . . . no, Hunter's busy tonight. Okay, love you. Bye."

He hangs up with a groan and leans back against the headrest. "Don't ask."

"Wasn't gonna."

"You know how Mom and Dad get. They're arguing over whether they've punished Aidan enough for . . . well, you know." He shakes his head and turns to me. "Don't be surprised if Mom tries to get you to take sides. She thinks Dad is going too easy on Aidan."

The damage is already done. What does it matter what the punishment is?

"Sorry." Ashton taps my knee with his fist. "Anyway. What was up with that guy at the shoot?"

"You mean Mister Six-Foot-Four?" Ethan says, leaning up between us. "That guy was a dick."

"Total asshat," I agree. "What was up with you and your partner?"

Ethan's scene partner was a brown-skinned girl with a bright smile and an even brighter laugh. Ethan seemed to be coaxing both out of her with alarming regularity.

"Sam? She was cool. I think she's coming to the show tonight."

"Dude," Owen says, and elbows Ethan. "You did not give her tickets."

"Of course not. I got Janet to do it."

"You are ridiculous," Ian says up front.

"You guys are just jealous."

"Not Hunter," Owen points out. "He's got a date."

I blush, but I smile. "Yeah, I do."

Nazeer's driving us to Santa Monica Pier, which is at the beach, but it's not like it's summer. It's 21°C out but it'll be cooler once the sun sets, plus there's the sea breeze.

After a shower, I put on a pastel-green button-up shirt and a pair of white chinos. They don't feel like me, but apparently they look beachy and femme enough. I text a picture to Julian, who replies with a thumbs-up.

I'm fussing with my hair when Nazeer knocks on my door.

"You ready?" He's in a pair of dad jeans and a Roots sweatshirt with the beaver on the front, and it feels so weird to see him out of a suit that for a second my brain freezes up. "Hunter?"

"Yeah," I say. "I'm ready."

Kaivan's a floor down, and opens the door in just his boxers when I knock.

(I can't believe he wears boxers.)

"Sorry! I didn't know what to wear."

Nazeer stifles a laugh, but I step into Kaivan's room to help.

Kaivan's room is a regular hotel room, not a suite like mine, which makes me feel kind of weird and guilty. His bed is covered with what must be his entire suitcase.

"You look nice," he says, studying me. "What'll match?"

"Thanks." I help him pick out a pair of dark-wash jeans and

a salmon shirt that looks perfect against his warm brown skin.

"You sure?"

"Yeah. It'll be great."

Kaivan disappears into the washroom, which is both a disappointment and a relief, because I did enjoy seeing him in just his boxers. Kaivan's lithe and long, with dimpled shoulders and collarbones I want to trace with my tongue.

I think about hockey drills to make my boner go away. I probably should've jerked off beforehand.

Kaivan finally emerges, dressed and smelling faintly of his woodsy cologne. He runs a hand through his hair, which makes it stick up a bit in front. "Ready."

One of my favorite spots in Vancouver is Jericho Beach. Back when I played hockey, we used to have team picnics there. It's a beautiful stretch of sand on English Bay.

But Santa Monica Beach is pretty awesome too. I've seen it in movies and TV shows and pictures, but it's so alive.

I reach for Kaivan's hand as we walk, and he only hesitates a moment before taking it.

I get it. I mean, I do that mental calculus too, figuring out how safe it is to be out and queer in any new space. But Nazeer's with us, keeping pace a few meters back, and there's a whole security team on crowd control in case we get mobbed.

People wave and smile, pull out their phones to take photos, but it's chill. Nazeer clocks a couple paparazzi, but they're keeping their distance. The whole point is for us to be seen, anyway.

I squeeze Kaivan's hand and enjoy the warmth of it, the feel of the sea breeze in my hair. The Label might've set this up for PR, but the smell of the salt, the little hairs on Kaivan's knuckles, the gentle smile he gives me, those are all real. Those are ours.

I haven't been on a date in forever.

The heavenly aroma of fried dough sings through the air.

"You like funnel cake?" Kaivan asks.

"I've never actually had it."

"You're kidding me."

I shrug.

"Okay, we have to fix this." He pulls me over to a bright yellow stand and orders one for us to share.

The funnel cake is piping hot and covered in powdered sugar, and I burn my fingers as I break off pieces.

Kaivan closes his eyes and gets this euphoric smile as he eats a piece, coating his lips white from the sugar. I grab a napkin and hand it to him, but he just licks his lips ostentatiously.

"Okay," I say. "This is pretty good." It's crispy, but it melts in my mouth.

"Mmm-hmm."

The sun is setting, and we head toward the pier itself. The salt spray dots my lips, and the breeze rustles my hair. I hold Kaivan's hand tighter as we navigate the crowd of tourists vying for the perfect spot for a photo against the sunset. Some turn to gawk at us, and a few snap photos. I blink against the flashes.

Eventually we find our own little spot on the rail, lean against it and stare out over the water.

"It's beautiful," Kaivan says.

He's beautiful, the planes of his face caught in the golden sunlight.

"You ever seen the ocean?"

He shakes his head. "First time. But we used to go to Lake Erie in the summer."

I rest my head against his shoulder, and he rests his head against mine.

"This is nice," I whisper, so quiet I'm not sure he can even hear me over the surf, but he plants a soft kiss into my hair and nods so that his chin rubs against my head. His stubble combs through my hair and sends a shiver down my spine.

Farther down the pier, there's a shriek.

I snap up, looking for Nazeer, but we haven't been recognized. Instead, toward the end of the dock, there's a woman on her knees, holding out a tiny box to another woman, who's covering her face.

"Aww." The second woman nods, and they embrace and kiss as everyone on the pier starts clapping. I pull my hand out of Kaivan's and we both join in.

"Hey," he says. "Let's photobomb it."

We sidestep a bit so we can be in the background as they

photograph their engagement. Kaivan's laughing and grinning, but I take his neck and pull his face to meet mine. I kiss him, and he tastes of funnel cake and salt as he kisses me back.

And then I forget about the newly engaged couple, because Kaivan wraps his hands around my waist, tracing my hipbones with his thumbs, and I slip my hands into the butt pockets of his jeans.

This is probably the most romantic moment in my life. I tell myself to remember every detail.

This is the kind of moment people write songs about.

But there's no lyrics in my mind, no chords, not even a single note. Just Kaivan, and the way his jaw dances against mine.

"Ahem." Nazeer's standing right behind us. "We're on a schedule, guys."

I sigh. Our whole date's been planned out down to the minute.

Kaivan laughs against my mouth, which feels so funny it makes me laugh too.

"All right," I say, and we break apart, but the couple has noticed us—noticed me—so Kaivan and I agree to take a couple of pictures with them, instead of behind them.

"Be gay, do crimes!" Kaivan shouts as Nazeer snaps the photos, which makes us all crack up.

We congratulate them again before making our way back up the pier toward the Ferris wheel.

"I can't believe we're doing this," Kaivan mutters.

"Is it okay? Do heights bother you?"

"No, it just feels so cliché."

"I'm pretty sure Ferris wheels are gay culture." I point at the enormous wheel looming above us, its sides glowing with colored lights. "It's even got rainbows."

Kaivan snorts, but his eyes sparkle and he gives me the softest smile that makes me want to kiss him again.

He lets me grab a seat in the car first, then cozies up beside me. I link our fingers as we start rising.

"Okay," Kaivan says as we ascend. "I admit the view is pretty awesome." The sun is half an orange, sinking below the horizon. It reminds me of home.

I tell Kaivan about Jericho Beach, about the way the sun looks as it sets over English Bay and how there always ends up being either a barge or a cruise ship in the way. I tell him about all my favorite spots, parks and coffee shops and cool little stores.

Kaivan tells me about Columbus, about Ohio, about his friends back home, about being on his school swim team.

"I used to be pretty good, but I quit."

"Why?"

"Everyone said swimming was gay."

"Oh."

"Yeah. If I'd realized I actually was gay, I might've stayed."

"Really? I think I knew when I was, like, eight. I kept lingering at the underwear aisles."

Kaivan snorts. "You were a thirsty kid, huh?"

I blush. He says it jokingly, but all I can hear is Aidan calling me a slut.

He pauses. "What?"

"Nothing."

"It's not nothing," he says. "You said we had to be honest with each other, remember?"

"Well, that was poor planning on my part," I mutter.

Kaivan laughs. "You can tell me."

"Just, after all the stuff with Aidan, and people thinking I'm . . . I don't know. I mean, I was a kid. I was curious."

Kaivan nods. "I didn't mean to make you feel bad. Hey, I like the underwear aisle too."

I groan and pull my hand out of his to cover my face, because I'm blushing even harder.

"You're missing everything," Kaivan says.

I rest my head against his shoulder as we watch the beach spread out below us. It actually is really pretty. Not as pretty as home, but LA's not so bad. The car pauses at the top, and for a second, I forget that I'm Hunter Drake the singer. I'm just plain Hunter, on a date with a boy I like, and the feeling is so perfect I want to cry.

I wish it could last forever.

As we descended, the noise of the crowd starts to reach us, screams and shrieks. The security detail has thrown up a couple barricades.

I sigh.

"What?" Kaivan asks.

"I mean, I kind of hoped we could just have a chill date."

"Isn't that the point of all this, though? To be seen?"

"I know, I know."

Kaivan holds up a pair of Sharpies. "And hey, I came prepared this time."

"Nice."

The crowd closes in almost immediately once we're back on solid ground, Nazeer doing his best to make a little bit of a buffer, but there's a lot of people and only one of him.

Kaivan pulls his hand out of mine to uncap his Sharpie. I do the same.

Right away, people are shoving phones in my face, or passing me posters to sign. I smile and say hi, tell people it's nice to meet them, ask if they're coming to any of the shows. The crowd is just as friendly (and frantic) as always. Maybe more.

Maybe The Label was right about all this. Because they don't seem grossed out by me or angry or disappointed. They all want a piece of Hunter Drake.

My neck tingles, a flutter of piano keys against my skin. So many people, and they all still want me.

Someone grabs my ass. I jump, messing up my signature, and try to salvage it into something recognizable, but someone else grabs my ear before Nazeer puts himself between us. Kaivan's pulled away from me, and I move to stay with him, shoulder to shoulder, because there's so many of them and they're all looking at me, crying out for me. Wanting wanting wanting.

A hand runs through my hair, pulls hard enough to pluck out a few strands, and someone screams in triumph.

"Ow!"

"Okay, that's enough." Nazeer takes my shoulder, says something into his earpiece, and starts carving a path through the crowd. It shifts to follow us, and I worry we're never going to escape. I love greeting our fans, connecting with them, talking to them, but this is too much.

What a shitty way for a date to end.

We reach the security chokepoint and break free into the parking lot. Nazeer keeps his hand on me until we make it back to the Escalade. Kaivan's breathing hard, a wild light in his eyes, and he laughs as we buckle up.

My own chest is tight.

"That was crazy." He beams at me, but I can't smile back. "Hunter?"

"I'm okay." I should be used to all this. I don't know why it bothered me so much. "That was a lot."

"Yeah." He takes my hand again. "But it was a good date, huh?"

I mean, some of it was pretty good. The parts where it was just us.

"I still owe you a good-night kiss," I tell him.

"Oh yeah? I'll make sure to collect."

"Keep it PG, you two," Nazeer says from the driver's seat, and we both laugh as he merges into traffic and heads back to the hotel.

THE BOYS OF PAR-K BRING
MIDDLE EASTERN FLAIR TO POP MUSIC

Gramophone Magazine
November 12, 2021

Continued from page 37 . . .

GM: You mentioned growing up on Iranian music, but American music has influenced your sound as well. Do you have any particular inspirations?

Kaivan: You know, the greats. Springsteen, Dylan. And some English stuff too, like U2.

Kamran: Isn't Bono Irish?

Kaivan: Whatever. You know. Real music. It's kind of frustrating, really, that we always get lumped in with, like, boy bands, poppy stuff like that, because I think our music has a lot more depth than that. What's that Canadian one that's getting all the attention now?

GM: Kiss & Tell?

Kaivan: Yeah. It's not like it takes a lot of talent to sing about girls and heartbreak and prom and maple syrup.

Kamran: And boys. The redhead is gay.

Kaivan: Really?

Kamran: Yeah.

Kaivan: Oh. Still, it's all manufactured, you know? It's like they came from a checklist.

Karim: I don't know, it's still pretty cool to see a boy band where the people of color outnumber the white boys.

Kaivan: Yeah, but look at them. None of them are that dark-skinned, so it's colorism at work. And their names? Ethan, Ian, Owen? It's assimilation porn. It's a safe version of multi-culturalism. Just like all their songs: safe and vapid.

Kamran: I don't know, I kind of like their stuff.

Karim: I think what Kaivan's getting at is, we're out here actually trying to say something with our music.

Kamran: Yeah. We're more than just pretty faces and large noses.

From: Cassie Thomas (c.thomas@thelabel.com)
To: Bill Holt (b.holt@thelabel.com), Janet Lundgren (janet@
kissandtellmusic.com)
Subject: Beach date
3/31/22 9:17 A.M.

Great numbers coming out of last night's date. See 1st
spreadsheet for the breakdown from various outlets. LGBT
outlets are most heavily favored, as you can see, but a few
more family-friendly places picked up the story as well.
Hopefully we can see more market penetration there as
Hunter's image recovers.

The photobomb of the lesbian engagement has done good
numbers as well, see 2nd spreadsheet.

This is a good start, but the team would like to see some more
intention going into wardrobe choices. Does Kaivan have
anything sportier? Hunter's look is fine, but could go further.
Make sure they come across as a well-matched couple.

Focus group also shows that no tongue is better for kissing
photos; let's see if we can pull them back a bit on this
element.

-Cassie

From: Bill Holt (b.holt@thelabel.com)
To: Janet Lundgren (janet@kissandtellmusic.com),

Cassie Thomas (c.thomas@thelabel.com)
Cc: Ryan Silva (ryansilvamanager@gmail.com)
Subject: Re: Beach date
3/31/22 10:02 A.M.

Thanks, Cassie. Numbers look good. Janet, see what you can do with Hunter. Looping in Ryan as well to coordinate with Kaivan.

Sales should have new data for us soon to see if this is moving the needle.

From: Janet Lundgren (janet@kissandtellmusic.com)
To: Bill Holt (b.holt@thelabel.com), Cassie Thomas (c.thomas@thelabel.com), Ryan Silva (ryansilvamanager@gmail.com)
Subject: Re: Beach date
3/31/22 12:05 P.M.

I'll talk it over with Hunter and see what we can work out. Keep in mind, Hunter's on board but there's a limit to what he'll do, as I mentioned in our brainstorming session. Authenticity is important to him.

Best,
Janet
Sent from my iPhone

14

"You are so basic," Ethan says around a mouthful of pizza as I tell the guys about my date.

"Oh, like your dates are so fancy," Owen says, and digs his elbow into Ethan's side. "How many girls have you taken to Playland?"

"Hey, roller coasters are romantic." Ethan swallows and then looks from Owen to me. "You should write a song about how love is a roller coaster or something!"

Owen grabs another slice. "Maybe you should."

"Maybe I will."

It would be nice if Ethan did. Or if I could. Every night I stare at my notebook, trying to come up with lyrics, but I'm empty.

"Otherwise me and Hunter have to do all the work."

Owen grins at me, but I avoid his eyes. Right now it's just him doing all the work.

I grab another slice of pizza, the smallest one I can find, since I'm feeling kind of bloated. One of the hardest things about being on the road is eating healthy, because no city ever has "vegetables" as their can't-miss local specialty.

Kaivan said LA is famous for Iranian food, and he wants us to go to Westwood. The Label didn't think that was "high-profile" enough as a date, but Kaivan's trying to convince Nick to take us.

"Five minutes to sound check," Shaz announces over the intercom.

I scarf down the rest of my slice, chug a bottle of water, and then one of the local crew escorts us to stage.

Ian whistles as we emerge onto the stage of the Hollywood Bowl. The sun is shining, the sky is a bright gray that hurts my eyes.

Rows of seats and boxes spread out before us, hemmed in by trees and hills.

We've been in lots of cool venues before, and certainly bigger ones, but this might be the most historic.

"Wow," Ashton says at my side.

"Yeah."

He grabs my shoulder, gives it a squeeze, and I meet his goofy smile with one of my own.

"We're at the fucking Hollywood Bowl."

"We're at the fucking Hollywood Bowl!"

"Language," Jill calls from offstage, where she's taking photos of us with her iPhone. Ashton's mom is a full-body photo taker: She leans her whole torso when she's trying to find the right angle, and tilts her head way back before she snaps a picture.

"Sorry, Jill," I call out. She hates it when we swear.

I learned the f-word from my first hockey coach when I was eight years old.

We take our marks, run through the first verse and chorus of "Heartbreak Fever," and then I hang back to check all my guitar settings, because I've never played outdoors like this before.

"Don't pick up any air traffic," Ethan says as Patricia fiddles with my wireless pack.

Patricia laughs, but I don't get it.

"Huh?"

Ethan stares at me.

"Dude. Spinal Tap? The army base scene?"

"What's Spinal Tap?"

Patricia clips the belt pack to me and stands, her arms crossed. Her jaw slides from side to side and her lips bunch up, which means she's playing with her tongue piercing inside her mouth.

Ethan steps closer, his fingers steepled beneath his chin.

"You mean to tell me that you, Hunter Middle Name Drake, are in a band, on tour, and you have never seen *This Is Spinal Tap*?"

"I guess not," I say.

"We're watching it!" Ethan announces. "Next movie night. We have to fix this. This is a hate crime!"

Ian laughs at him, but Ashton comes over and says, "Don't worry. I haven't seen it either."

Patricia gives us both the most withering look I've ever experienced. "Babies. I'm working with babies."

"You're only twenty-five!" I say.

"Babies!" she shouts, and spins on her heel.

"Hey, Hunt, you got a minute?" Ashton asks.

"Yeah, gimme a second, though, I need Patricia to check something."

She's at my guitar rack, checking everything, and I pull out my acoustic: a Gibson Hummingbird older than me. I found it at this hole-in-the-wall vintage guitar shop on Alma Street.

"Can you check the frets? It's never been away from Vancouver before," I explain. "I'm not sure it likes the desert."

Patricia's runs her left hand up and down the neck.

"They do feel a little off. Leave it to me."

"Thanks." I look for Ashton, but he's squatting at the edge of the stage, talking to his mom. Kaivan and his brothers are in the house too, taking pictures and laughing. Kaivan gives me a little wave, and I smile and wave back.

"You've got it bad," Patricia says with a snicker.

"Come on, I've seen you when your partner comes to a show."

Patricia sticks her tongue out at me, and I do it right back, and then we both crack up.

"Now let me get to work, you pest."

"Cheers. I'm gonna go see if Kaivan wants to make out in my dressing room."

"Gross! Babies! You're both babies!"

LET THE MOONLIGHT IN
BY HASHTAGHASHTON

FanWorks Repository

Rating: PG-13

Category: M/M

Fandom: Kiss & Tell (Band), PAR-K (Band)

Relationships: Hunter Drake/Kaivan Parvani

Additional Tags: One-shot, Canon Compliant, fade-to-black, implied therapeutic blowjob, acrophobia not homophobia

Length: 1300 words (complete)

Chapters: 1 of 1

Summary: When the passenger car of the Santa Monica Ferris wheel breaks down, Hunter and Kaivan are stuck at the very top, all alone, and Kaivan is afraid of heights. Hunter knows one way to get his boyfriend to keep calm until they're rescued.

Notes: I know, I know! A non-Hashton fic! SCANDAL! But this idea popped into my head and I ended up writing the whole thing in like an hour lol.

Thanks as always to my beta The_Mandy_Lorian_.

Also, what are we calling this ship anyway? Haivan is too close to Haidan, but Kunter is not great when you say it out loud lmao!!

HUNTER DRAKE AND KAIVAN PARVANI ATE IRANIAN FOOD IN LA AND THE PICTURES ARE EVERYTHING

NewzList Canada
Date: April 2, 2022

Editor's note: An earlier version of this story misspelled Kaivan Parvani's name. We apologize for the error.

It's only been a few days since Hunter Drake and Kaivan Parvani went public with their relationship, but the new couple has already made a splash, strolling along the beach, sampling funnel cake at the Santa Monica Pier, and photobombing another couple's engagement pictures. Now they've been spotted at an Iranian eatery in Los Angeles.

This was apparently Hunter's first experience with Iranian cuisine; the singer documented the entire meal in a series of photos and videos, including an improvised song about kabobs that, while never quite rising to the artistry of Kiss & Tell's viral hit "Poutine," managed to leave Kaivan in stitches.

Kiss & Tell is playing the last of three sold-out shows at the historic Hollywood Bowl tonight.

Ashton Nightingale Talks About the Meaning Behind His Tattoo

24 Times Masha Patriarki Clapped Back So Hard, Their Victims Had Whiplash

15

"Okay, Hunter, get ready," Ethan says as he fiddles with the big TV in the lounge. "Tonight we're going to rock you tonight."

"Uh, what?"

But Ethan ignores me, so I find a comfy spot on the couch and stretch out my aching knee. It usually handles concerts okay, but adding in choreo for the music video has worn me out. At least we're finally finished, and I'll never have to deal with Six-Foot-Four Garrett again.

What a dickbag.

"Here, Hunt." Ashton hands me an ice pack and flops down next to me. He's in a gray tank top and black shorts, his damp hair held back by a headband. We're all in our pajamas, except for Paul, another of the camera guys, who's stationed in the corner, recording B-roll for the documentary.

It feels weirdly meta, to be watching a fake documentary about a rock band, while making our own real one.

The bus sways gently as we all settle. Ethan smacks his spacebar and starts the movie.

A bearded man in a trucker hat pops on-screen and starts talking, but I can't hear him.

"Is this a silent movie?" I tease, but Ethan grumbles and fiddles with his settings until the audio starts coming out of the TV.

Owen tosses bags of Sour Patch Kids at me and Ashton, Ian reaches behind him to turn down the lights, and Ethan takes a spot on the floor, wrapped in a blanket. "Okay. Everybody quiet!"

We stay up way too late, because after the movie, we end up watching random YouTube videos for another hour. At some point, I'm not sure when, I fall asleep on Ashton's shoulder, until he finally pokes me awake.

"Time to turn into a pumpkin," he says. "Come on, Hunt."

I shake out my limbs until the pins and needles go away. The ice pack on my knee has turned to lukewarm water, so I tuck it in the little freezer as we head back to the bunks.

Paul the camera guy is dozing on one of the seats, and someone (almost certainly Ethan) has filled the hood of his jacket with Sour Patch Kids wrappers.

I follow Ashton back into the bunk area and let him use the bus's tiny washroom first. When it's my turn, I go in to brush my teeth and pee. That's basically the only things any of us do on the bus, as there's an unspoken no-shitting-except-for-emergencies rule, and there's a blanket no-jerking-off-on-the-bus-in-general rule too, more for cleanliness than prudishness, I think.

Ashton pulls his shirt off and is about to climb up to his bunk, but then he turns to me.

"Hey, Hunt?"

"Yeah?"

"This thing with Kaivan . . . you want it, right?"

"What? Yeah."

"Okay. I just know The Label's been weird about things, since Aidan and . . . yeah."

"I mean, they're definitely in favor of it, but Kaivan and I both like each other. It was our decision."

"Okay." He twists his lips back and forth. "I just worry about you. You barely had time to be yourself before you started dating again."

I clap him on his shoulder, but then let go right away, because it reminds me too much of Aidan's shoulders, and how I used to give him shoulder rubs. I wonder if Kaivan likes his shoulders rubbed. He has really nice ones.

I shake my head. "It's okay. This isn't a rebound and it's not fake. And I'm being myself with Kaivan. Really. I like him a lot."

"Okay."

Ashton climbs into his bunk. I roll into mine below him

and pull the curtain shut. I turn on the little light and pull out my notebook, trying to capture something: the brilliance of hanging out with your friends and watching a funny movie, or the warmth of sharing a meal with the guy you like, or even just the exhilaration of performing.

But there's this anxiety clawing at me too, because if I put it down into a song, it's going to get out. People are going to know.

I'm so tired of everyone thinking they know everything about me.

I scratch out all the shit lyrics I wrote, turn off my light, and roll over.

A PAGE OF HANDWRITTEN LYRICS FROM
HUNTER'S NOTEBOOK

F#m???

I thought that I was
Broken but then you
Spoke and made me feel
Alive
Alive
Alive

These feelings put in
Motion all I wanted was a
Token of affection and
Your love
Your love
Your love

THANKS I HATE IT

COME SAY HELLO: *THE REVIEW*

Gramophone Magazine
February 2, 2022

Canadian boy band Kiss & Tell topped the charts last year with their eponymous debut album, a joyful, tongue-in-cheek explosion of youthful exuberance. Their follow-up, written almost entirely by band members Hunter Drake and Owen Jogia (Ian Souza supplied lyrics for one song, the fast-paced "Click"), is less solid: While the vocals remain golden, the songs are less so, lacking the electric gay energy we've come to expect from Drake. *Kiss & Tell* was a celebration of queer life (and immigrant life, courtesy of Jogia), but this new album seems almost subdued. Even "Your Room," presumably about Drake's longtime boyfriend Aidan Nightingale, could be mistaken for any number of heterosexual ballads.

VERDICT: A decent effort, but listeners hoping for deeper explorations of more diverse experiences will be disappointed.

16

We're in Las Vegas when I wake up. The bus is parked behind T-Mobile Arena, nestled between a couple of semis. I asked once, and Janet said each of our shows takes twenty semis' worth of gear. And there's three sets of twenty semis, because while we're performing one show they're tearing down the previous one and setting up the next.

I don't know how the crew does it. We're ten days in and I'm already tired.

I roll out of my bunk and head to the lounge to grab some water. Paul's still there, but he's awake this time, and the little red light on his camera is on.

I immediately clench up my stomach, because I took my shirt off during the night and I don't want to look puffy.

Thank god I waited for my morning wood to go down before getting out of bed.

Thank god I'm in shorts instead of my leggings.

We're supposed to act natural for stuff like this, but it's kind of unnerving to be filmed. My chest and stomach are turning red and itchy, a full-body blush, and I scratch at my belly and chug my water bottle until Paul says, "Thanks, that was good."

I relax and turn to face him. "Cool. Sorry about all the candy wrappers. I think it was Ethan."

Paul scoffs. "I've dealt with worse. You guys are a hoot."

I assume that's a good thing, since Paul doesn't seem too angry.

"Cheers."

I finish my water and then head back to brush my teeth, because my mouth tastes like the inside of my skates. Something about the air on the bus, I think.

I pee too, do my morning skincare at the tiny sink, and find Owen waiting for me when I get out, his hair a total mess. Owen's always tossing and turning when he sleeps on the bus.

"Oh, sorry." I slip by him. "All yours."

"No, I'm good," he says as I tuck my stuff into my backpack. "I thought maybe we could spend a little time in the studio?"

I glance at my notebook, full of scratched-out shitty ideas. I don't know how Owen keeps churning songs out, when I'm a dried-up well.

"I had a couple things I wanted to get your opinion on?"

I follow Owen back. "Bobby plugged us in, right?" I ask as Owen starts turning on the equipment.

Bobby's our bus driver. He's a good guy, but one time last year he didn't plug us in when we got to a venue and we didn't realize it, and ended up draining the battery playing video games all day.

"Already checked." Owen sits in his chair, a worn black pleather office chair he brought from home. He says he can't work in strange chairs.

I wheel over one of the other chairs and plug in my headphones while Owen opens up his latest session.

"Here. This is what I've been working on." He taps the spacebar and his demo plays.

It's mostly him on piano, with simple drum and bass tracks laid down underneath. Most of Owen's stuff tends to be in major keys, but this one is in C minor, which gives it this reflective vibe that I really like. It's fresh and unique. Perfect for our third album.

"Dude," I say when it finishes. "I love it."

It's so good. And I'm so pissed at myself that I didn't come up with it.

"Thanks. It's still pretty rough." Owen's one of those guys that doesn't handle praise very well.

"No way. It's perfect. You have a name for it?"

"Figured once you write some lyrics we can decide."

"Deal."

"Okay, here's the next one."

164

Owen opens another demo and hits play. This one is way more synthesized, faster and edgier, and just as good as the first one. He plays another after that, and then a fourth.

This lump of guilt solidifies in my stomach. He's done so much, and I've done nothing.

"Okay," Owen says. "How about you? Any luck?"

I shake my head and look down to hide my blush. "No. Sorry."

Normally I let Owen see all my stuff, even the shitty ideas, because sometimes between the two of us we can transform them into something good. That's where "My Prize," from our first album, came from: I had some half-assed lyrics, Owen had a half-assed bass hook in his head, and somehow when we put them together, magic happened.

"Come on," he says gently. "You know I don't judge."

"It's just . . ." I swallow away the lump in my throat. "I mean, everything is hard. Everything feels more personal than usual."

Owen nods. "That's when you write your best stuff, though."

"I guess." I mean, he's not wrong. My best songs have come from when I was writing from the heart. But my heart's burned and blackened from all its time in the spotlight. "I just feel so raw lately. Exposed."

"I get that." He scratches his nose. "But it's just me, dude. Come on."

He's right. It's just him.

I open up my notebook to find my spot when the studio door opens and Janet leans in, phone clutched in her left hand.

"Oh, you're working." The surprise in her voice stings. "Good."

"Yeah, just going over some new demos and stuff," Owen says.

"Cool. Make sure to send copies to Gregg too."

Owen nods, but I ask, "Gregg?"

"He's a producer Bill put me in contact with. He's going to help pull the new album together."

"He's . . . what?" I've got an angry blush coming on.

Janet glances down at her phone and starts typing something into it. "Since you've been having some trouble, Bill thought some fresh ideas would help. Don't worry, he's not taking over."

That just makes me worry more.

"Anyway, you're all set for this afternoon, right? Settled on wardrobe and everything?"

"Yeah. I mean, we're going skating, so nothing fancy."

"Great. All right, keep up the good work. Bill said it's really helping to move the needle."

And then she's gone.

When I turn to face Owen, he won't meet my eyes.

"You knew about this Gregg guy?"

He nods and fiddles with the computer's touchpad to wake it up from its screen saver.

"Janet asked me about it a couple days ago."

"And you said yes?"

"Yeah. You were dealing with the Aidan stuff and . . . yeah."

"Well." I swallow and try to keep my voice as even as I can, given Owen's just elbowed me in the throat. "Well. Make sure to send the demos over, I guess." I unplug my headphones and go.

I've got to get ready for another date.

THE NEW CLOSET: HUNTER DRAKE AND THE PERFORMANCE OF HETERO-RESPECTABILITY

Pride Today
by Gavin Malone
April 2, 2022

Unless you live under a rock, you probably know Hunter Drake: the fresh-faced redhead who makes up one-fifth of Canadian boy band Kiss & Tell. From the moment their first song dropped on YouTube—a catchy, humorous ode to the ultimate Canadian comfort food, poutine—he's made his name as one of the most famous out gay teens in our pop culture landscape.

Gay men (and boys) have always existed in tension with boy bands: Their carefully curated images, intended to appeal to teen and tween girls, so often appeal to queer boys as well. But up to now, there's been an air of unavailability that made them all the more alluring. These singers are simultaneously symbols to aspire to, and representations of the forbidden straight men we've all, inevitably, crushed on at some point.

Not so with Hunter Drake: His queerness makes him at once more approachable and less. Because beneath that openness lies cynicism.

As Kiss & Tell's star rose, so too did Drake's, tied inextricably with his very public romance with former hockey teammate Aidan Nightingale. They were the picture-perfect gay couple: two attractive, white, healthy young men, known for hand-holding, chaste kisses, and photogenic dates. In short, they did everything society tells young gay men to do: Be safe, be cute, perform your queerness for the masses in a digestible, harmless way.

Drake certainly leaned into that, using his relationship to sell albums, and more insidiously, to sell an image of himself—of queer life—that appealed to all the people who think the fight for queer rights ended with marriage equality.

Now, at last, the curtain is drawn back. In a series of angry (and grammatically inept) tweets, Nightingale aired his grievances against Drake following their breakup, exposing a relationship that was full of jealousy, infidelity, and painfully awkward sex. (We've all been there, haven't we?)

Now we know Drake was never who he pretended to be for his fans, for the media, for the public.

And yet he was willing to embrace that image for money and fame. To hide parts of himself to be socially acceptable.

The new closet might be more spacious, but it's still a closet, one Drake has been painfully, forcibly outed from. And while we can have sympathy for the circumstances, we still need to ask ourselves:

Is his really the example we should be following?

Gavin Malone is a queer theorist, pop culture analyst, part-time nerd, and full-time cat dad. Follow him online @gavmalone.

17

The Label managed to book us private time at a rink close to T-Mobile Arena, and they sent Rick and Paul to film our date, along with Chris to direct us.

I mean, I get why we're doing all this, but part of me wishes we could just skate and talk and have some fun and not need "direction."

"Have you been skating before?" I ask as we lace up.

"It's been a long time. We used to go to this rink when I was really little, until Kamran decided he hated it. I don't remember much."

"It's okay, we'll take it slow."

I finish lacing, but Kaivan's still on his first skate.

"Need a hand?"

"Maybe."

I get on the ground, resting on my heels in front of Kaivan, and take his boot between my knees. "You want them nice and tight." I take his laces and give them a big tug, then start lacing up his skates properly.

"I wasn't expecting you to get on your knees this early in our relationship," Kaivan says, and I freeze for a second, because Paul's camera is right over my shoulder and suddenly I can see how the whole scene looks. Hunter Drake, on his slutty knees again.

A blush starts creeping up my neck.

"I'm not sure I'm ready for marriage," Kaivan says with a laugh, and I breathe again, grateful he's making it a joke about marriage instead of blowjobs.

I finish lacing him up and lean back.

"Feel okay?"

"I don't know."

I stick my fingers between his shin and the tongue of his boot. "Seems good." I lace up his other skate. "Come on."

I step onto the ice and turn to watch Kaivan. He holds on to the wall and starts to walk, his legs shaking like a newborn deer taking its first steps.

"Bend your knees," I say, sinking deeper into my stance. "So your shins press against the tongues of your skates."

He does, but he also sticks his butt out, which is hilarious and cute.

I bite my lip to stop my smile.

"What?"

"Nothing." I back away from him. "Come on. Easy."

Eventually I'm able to coax Kaivan away from the wall, and after a couple laps he begins to relax and enjoy it. I spin around and face him again, speeding up so he has to chase me a little bit.

"How do you go that fast?" he says. "And backwards."

I laugh. "Years of practice."

I slow down again as we pass a penalty box. "Here. Take a break."

He sits on the bench and starts shaking out his legs, wiggling his ankles, while I stay on the ice, doing rocking horses to stay warm.

Chris makes his way over. He's bundled up in a dark gray peacoat and fuzzy scarf. His ears are pink but he didn't bring a hat, I guess because he's too worried about his hair, which is silver and styled almost as heavily as Ashton's.

"Hunter?"

"Yeah?" I pull up to the boards.

"This is all good and stuff, but can you skate a little . . . uh . . ."

I blink at him.

"It's just, you're coming across really aggressive."

"Hockey's an aggressive sport." Besides, this was nothing.

"What if we do a bit where you fall and Kaivan can catch you?"

"Dude. I've been skating since I could walk."

Chris clears his throat. "Yeah, but we're building a narrative here. Our audience is going to have certain expectations."

"Our fans know I can skate."

"Well, can you at least be a little more . . . loose?"

Chris has been pretty cool up to this point. A little uptight and sometimes oblivious, but this . . .

"Are you saying you want me to skate more gay?"

"What? No!" he says, in a way that clearly means yes. "Just chill out some, you know? You're on a date. It's fun. Here, I'll let you get back to it."

He shuffles away.

Kaivan stands, a big grin on his face. He kisses me on the cheek, and then whispers in my ear, "What a shithead."

I laugh and hold his hand as he gets back on the ice.

I don't know how to skate gayer, but I do at least skate slower, keeping pace with Kaivan as we talk and laugh.

"My glutes are on fire," he says. "No wonder you . . ." He trails off and avoids my eyes, looking down at the ice.

"Don't look down," I say, and he looks back up at me but he's blushing.

"No wonder I what?"

He clears his throat. "No wonder you have such a nice butt."

"Thanks." I dart in and kiss him, real quick. I've never kissed a guy on the ice before, not even Aidan. I like it.

Kaivan laughs and leans in to try and kiss me, but he straightens his knees and starts to topple over. I catch him and let us gently fall to the ice, so he winds up on top of me.

"Oops," he says. "That wasn't so smooth."

"It's okay." I lean up and kiss him again, a little longer. He kisses me back, sucks on my bottom lip, brings his hand up to stroke my chin.

I giggle. "Hey, we'd better keep it PG," I whisper. "Can't skate with a boner."

"Well, they always say that sex sells," Kaivan says, but I get a chill that has nothing to do with the rink. Straight sex sells. Gay sex means you need a "rebrand."

"That was great," Chris says from the nearest box. "Can you do that bit again?"

I sigh and rest my head against the ice.

Kaivan chuckles. His breath whispers against my neck. "Sure."

After a couple hours, Kaivan's beat, and my knee is hitting that limit where I know if I push it anymore, I'll regret it.

I lead Kaivan back to the box and sigh as my feet leave the ice.

"What?" he asks.

"Nothing. I just miss hockey is all."

"How come you quit, anyway?"

I'm surprised—almost offended—Kaivan doesn't know the story.

But then I get this weird excitement, that I get to tell him myself, that he didn't just read about it on the Internet like so many countless strangers. So I sit next to him and pull up the right leg of my sweats to show him the scar across my knee.

"Dude." He reaches out to trace the pale line connecting my quads to my shin. "What happened?"

"Total knee replacement," I say.

"No, I mean, my grandma had the same surgery. But what happened?"

"It was kind of a freak accident. Ashton was going for a goal, but the other team's D-man got the puck away from him. I went after him, so did Ashton. I got the puck back, but then we . . . kind of collided."

"I thought that happened a lot in hockey."

"It does. But it wasn't a check, I didn't see it coming, and neither did he, and I ended up against the boards with his blade in my patella."

Kaivan shudders.

"After that things were pretty much over for me. And Ashton quit with us."

Sometimes I wonder what would've happened if Aidan had quit too. If he had joined the band, or at least joined us on tour.

Maybe things would've been different.

Then again, maybe things would've been even worse.

Kaivan wraps his warm hand around my knee and squeezes it. It feels nice, right where his thumb presses against the soft spot, but weird too, because I can feel pressure in my scar but not actual touch.

"I'm sorry," he says.

"Don't be." There are days when I still miss it. When I wish the accident hadn't happened.

But my life is pretty good.

I lean my head against Kaivan's shoulder. I don't know if Rick's still filming us and I don't care, because this is real, whether it's filmed or not.

This is real.

ASK THE EXPERT: HOW DO I TALK TO MY KIDS ABOUT HUNTER DRAKE?

ParentingSense.com
April 3, 2022

Dear Ask the Expert,

My kids (14 and 12) love Kiss & Tell. They follow all the boys closely, know all the trivia, can sing every song. Hunter, the gay one, is their favorite. Up until now it's been fine: Compared to my kids' TV habits, Hunter and his boyfriend were practically wholesome. But recently there were some revelations about Hunter, including stuff about his sex life. Not just that he was having sex before marriage, but also some more explicit mentions of specific sexual activities.

I'm not really comfortable with my kids obsessing over him to the degree they do. My wife and I definitely weren't expecting to have to explain anal sex to our children at this age.

I used to think Hunter was a good role model, but now I'm at a loss. I don't want my kids thinking his behavior is acceptable, but they still love him and his music. What should I do?

Sincerely,

Fumbling Father

Dear Fumbling Father,

Keeping an eye on our kids' media consumption is never easy, especially when that media makes a hard right into more adult territory. Kudos for having the hard conversations with them. (For other parents struggling with having "the talk," check out our guide for age-appropriate ideas.)

My own daughters were heartbroken by the Hunter Drake news: both that he'd been cheating on Aidan, and that he was engaging in behaviors they found "gross."

Ultimately, it's our jobs as parents to help steer our children toward healthier idols. In general, I don't recommend forbidding anything; rather, have safer alternatives ready to offer. Have you heard of Callum Wethers? He's an up-and-coming gay country artist with great songs, a bright smile, and a much cleaner public persona. My daughters love him.

Best of luck,

Ask the Expert

18

After a change of clothes—me into a light blue sweater with billowy sleeves and a V-neck that I can fit my whole torso through, Kaivan into dark jeans and a leather jacket of all things—we head to this cookie place The Label found.

It's a tiny cookie shop in a little plaza, not inside one of the ginormous hotel-casino monstrosities, and it's got a line out the door. Nazeer parks in a valet spot. He rolls down the window and passes over a few bills, then hands me some sunblock, since I burn super quick and super red.

"You want some?" I ask Kaivan. He's jiggling his knee as he stares out the window.

"Huh? Oh. I'm good."

"You nervous?"

He shakes his head. "You ready?"

I wish it was just us, getting cookies together. Not doing a whole big production. But Janet said this was moving the needle. Helping the band.

So I screw on my smile and nod.

The scent of cinnamon and vanilla fills the plaza, mixed with gasoline and exhaust fumes. Nazeer stays at my back as we get a spot in line.

The shop has got speakers mounted underneath its awning, playing Top-40 type stuff, but as we get closer I hear a familiar guitar riff, one that starts our encore every night.

"Oh, no," I groan.

It's not like we just met
We've been friends for a while
But there's something I never told ya

It's a secret I kept
How it burned me to lie
But it was just so hard to own up

Kaivan's laughing, mouthing the words to the song.

I mean, I'm still proud of "Poutine," but we recorded it when my voice was still changing, so I sound all scratchy. Also, my writing has gotten better since then. Me and Owen always say we want each album to be better than the one that came before.

Oh—

If I could only share it
This feeling that's inside
It's bubbling to the surface
It's getting hard to hide

Oh whoa, our love would hardly be routine
We go together as perfect as poutine
Like French fries covered in gravy and bits of cheese
Just give us a chance, I'm begging you on my knees

"Where'd you come up with this anyway?"

I shrug. "I was on painkillers. And I really wanted poutine one day. And it just . . . came to me."

"But like, where did it really come from?"

"Uh, that's it?"

Kaivan blinks. "Oh, really? I thought that was just a line. I figured The Label wrote it or something."

I shake my head. "No, we signed with them after. I told you, we write all our own songs. We did it for both albums. Produced them too."

"Really? Cool."

I'm blushing again, and I've got a timpani behind my

sternum. Will I still be able to say that, once fucking Gregg has his grimy hands in our third album?

"Why do you sound so surprised, anyway?"

Kaivan shakes his head. "Nothing, sorry. It's just—"

But he's cut off by a scream. Nazeer's head whips around, and I follow his gaze. A group of girls has spotted us. Their phones are already out.

Every fucking time.

"Here we go," says Nazeer. He pulls his phone out of his breast pocket and starts talking. "We've got some local guys to help with crowd control."

"Should we wait for them?"

But Kaivan's already stepped out of line, toward the coalescing crowd. "Come on! Let's go say hi!"

He pulls a Sharpie out of his pocket. I follow more slowly, keeping closer to Nazeer.

I don't know why I'm so anxious. This is the job. I like greeting our fans. We wouldn't be here without them.

But right now, there's a mass of humanity wanting, wanting, wanting, when all I really wanted was to get cookies with my date.

Someone pulls up their sleeve and asks me to autograph their shoulder, but I have a strict no-body-parts policy, so I end up signing their T-shirt instead. I hate signing T-shirts, they always turn my Sharpies nubby.

Hands brush my shoulder, tug on my sleeves, and someone pulls the tuque right off my head.

"Hey!" I say, but then wince at the screaming that follows. Nazeer steps closer.

"Come on," he says. "This is getting too intense."

I nod, try to wrap my hand around Kaivan's arm, but he's drifted out of reach as he poses for selfies.

"Kaivan!" I shout, but he doesn't hear, so I step away from Nazeer to get Kaivan's attention. "Kaivan!"

"What?"

"We need to go." Someone grabs my arm and yanks it hard, twisting me to the side. My knee's already tired from skating, and it hates twisting like that, so I stumble and fall. My palms sting against the concrete.

Nazeer gets me back on my feet, and Kaivan takes my hand as we push through the crowd, Nazeer's power elbows carving us a path to the car. I spot a couple other local security guys, pushing the crowd back, as they shriek and cry and shout my name, Kaivan's name, sing and chant.

I can't breathe.

This was supposed to be fun.

Kaivan keeps waving at people, so I rest my hand on his back, just to make sure he stays close and doesn't get pulled away. I feel a pinch at my ass, look over my shoulder, but I can't tell who did it.

Nazeer gets us both in the car, says something to the valets, who start clearing a path for us to leave.

I take a deep breath and lean back.

"Hunter? You okay?" Nazeer asks.

"I'm fine."

"You're shaking." Kaivan rests his hand on mine, but I pull away. "Hunter?"

My heart is banging against my ribs. I've got this deep thrumming in my ears, a bass drum inside my skull.

"Sorry. I'm fine." I take his hand and sigh. "We didn't even get cookies."

When we get back, Kaivan and I hole up in my dressing room. His feet and calves are cramping, so I offer to give him a foot massage, which is something Aidan and I never did.

It's not as sexy as I thought it would be. In fact, it's not sexy at all. Kaivan's feet smell like rental skates, and he keeps grunting as I hit the most tender spots.

My heart's still racing from getting mobbed, so I keep quiet and let Kaivan talk.

It's nice, letting him tell me about his brothers, his sisters, his mom and dad. Eventually, he asks me about mine.

"It's just me and Mom and Haley," I tell him. "But she's at UBC now."

"What about your dad?"

"He died when I was little."

Kaivan's face falls. "Oh. Sorry."

"It's okay. It was a while ago. Seven years this past January."

"What happened?"

"Car accident."

"I'm really sorry, Hunter."

"It's okay." I use my thumb to make circles around this spot in Kaivan's arch that feels like a marble, and he hisses. "Too much?"

He shakes his head. "It's fine. Feels good."

I press again, and this time he winces and yelps.

"Okay, it hurts."

I chuckle. "Sorry." I lean across his legs to kiss him.

"It's cool." He pulls his foot out of my hands and scoots closer, returning the kiss, sliding his tongue against my Invisaligns, which is a super weird feeling. His hands find my hip crease and his thumbs dig in gently.

On our last tour, one of our stops was in this old concert hall in Toronto, a 3,000-seater with a huge pipe organ in it, and they let Owen try playing it. He was heinous at it—pipe organs are so complicated—but it was loud, so loud I felt the sound waves vibrating every molecule in me.

That's what happens when Kaivan touches me, squeezes my waist, nibbles on my lower lip. When I run my hands through his hair and pull his tongue back into my mouth and suck it gently. He lets out this sound, somewhere between a gasp and a groan, and I'd do anything to hear it again. But instead he breaks the kiss and leans back to breathe.

I wish I could capture this moment, replay it in slow motion over and over, write a song to explain this feeling.

(God knows I need to be writing.)

"That was good," he says with a sigh.

"Yeah?"

"Yeah."

My face is heating up, because I've got a boner and it's probably super obvious. I shift around a bit, but that doesn't fix it, so finally I just reach down and adjust myself.

Kaivan chuckles. He was checking me out.

He reaches down and adjusts himself too, gives me a shy grin when our eyes meet.

It's kind of scary how much I'm into him. With Aidan, it was a slow crescendo of feelings, but this is a sudden swell of horns and strings and percussion, filling my chest until I can't breathe.

"I really like you," I say, because otherwise I'm going to explode.

"I really like you too."

From: Cassie Thomas (c.thomas@thelabel.com)
To: Bill Holt (b.holt@thelabel.com), Janet Lundgren
(janet@kissandtellmusic.com), Ryan Silva
(ryansilvamanager@gmail.com)
Subject: Latest metrics
4/6/22 4:12 P.M.

Just an update on how metrics are looking. Hunter and
Kaivan's dates have been getting good press, and social
media engagement has been up 20%.

Go-karting was the most successful; a few of the photos have
become memes and gone viral. Escape room was the least
successful; engagement was lackluster. (See attached for stats
on these, plus their hike.)

Let's keep honing wardrobe choices.

-Cassie

From: Bill Holt (b.holt@thelabel.com)
To: Janet Lundgren (janet@kissandtellmusic.com), Cassie
Thomas (c.thomas@thelabel.com)
Cc: Ryan Silva (ryansilvamanager@gmail.com)
Subject: Re: Latest metrics
4/6/22 4:38 P.M.

Attaching latest sales data here as well. PAR-K has seen a

surge since they started dating; K&T has leveled out after their dip and is climbing again. Good job, team. This is the outcome we were hoping for.

-BH

From: Ryan Silva (ryansilvamanager@gmail.com)
To: Bill Holt (b.holt@thelabel.com)
Subject: Re: Latest metrics
4/6/22 4:57 P.M.

Awesome news Bill, numbers look excellent. What do you think about moving up there single release for memories? Take advantage of good pr?

Thanks,
Ryan

From: Janet Lundgren (janet@kissandtellmusic.com)
To: Bill Holt (b.holt@thelabel.com), Cassie Thomas (c.thomas@thelabel.com), Ryan Silva (ryansilvamanager@gmail.com)
Subject: Re: Latest metrics
4/6/22 11:35 P.M.

Great news. I'd love it if we could cut back a bit on the number of dates they're being scheduled for; want to keep

Hunter fresh for his concerts, and still working on third album. Plus the doc crew being split means less coverage for the other boys.

Best,
Janet
Sent from my iPhone

QUEER COMMUNITY?
WHAT QUEER COMMUNITY?

Mode.com
by Gabby Schenck
April 7, 2022

Unless you're part ostrich you've probably seen queer culture's latest power couple, Hunter Drake and Kaivan Parvani, making headlines. They're nearly impossible to avoid, as various social media algorithms keep shoving photographs of them down our collective throats.

Hunter Drake has been a queer darling since he first rose to fame: He was out and proud even before Kiss & Tell's star began to rise, and has embraced his gay identity in his songwriting, his philanthropy, his activism, and his entire platform. We know him.

Not that Hunter has been perfect, as his frequent tabloid appearances show, but he's been steadfast in his support of his community. He embraced us as we embraced him, scandal and all.

Which makes it all the more strange to see him dating musician Kaivan Parvani, of Iranian-American band PAR-K. PAR-K is fairly new to the scene—their first album released just last year—but they gave every indication, in marketing, music videos, and lyrics, that they were entirely heterosexual. Kaivan embraced the image of an attractive, straight young man, before coming out late last year in a series of posts in which he emphasized his desire to be seen first and foremost as a musician.

That desire seems to have been tossed aside, as Kaivan has now taken to flaunting his relationship with Hunter at every possible opportunity, going on dates at <u>a Phoenix Go-Kart Track</u>, <u>a themed escape room in Denver</u>, and <u>splashing around in the Great Salt Lake</u>.

Kaivan hardly seems like Hunter's type, and the whole relationship smells of a cynical grab for publicity.

More cynical still, despite his newfound fame and platform, Parvani seems totally disinterested in uplifting his community; happy to reject it when it suited his musical goals, and to embrace it when it promised monetary reward, he has yet to make the sort of public efforts that Hunter does.

Kaivan has a unique opportunity to use his fame to advance the cause of queer liberation. So why isn't he?

19

It turns out Albuquerque is actually kind of a cool town. The Label finds me and Kaivan a cute spot for brunch in Old Town, which is basically the historic district. We pose for photos with the café owner and sign a few autographs, but thankfully nothing too intense.

After, me and the guys pack into the studio to listen to another of Owen's demos. It's starting to smell a little bit, the smell of too many boys in tight quarters, the smell of the road. It reminds me of locker rooms after a tough game, of sweaty skates and stinky pads and a hard-fought victory.

I kind of like it, even though it's a little gross.

"Here. I just got this back from Gregg." Owen sits at the computer and hits play.

I recognize the chord changes from Owen's demo instantly, but now there's a voice singing too. It's kind of scratchy, way

193

lower than any of our voices, so it's straining to hit some of the high notes.

I can barely hear it
When you scream and you shout
My name, my fame, my blame,
Still you just sit and pout
All I ask is one last kiss,
But you say there's a drought

Ooh, baby, we're done
Ooh, baby, I'm over and out.

Oh, I've tried to make you listen
You don't care, you just flout
All these things I don't want
You've been talking about
So I'm packing up my gear
No, I don't have a doubt

Ooh, baby, we're through
Ooh, baby, I'm over and out.

It's edgy, almost sarcastic-sounding. And worse, it's actually kind of good. I can see what it could be when it's finished. It could be great.

This angry drumming starts up inside me, banging around

in my stomach before moving up into my throat. Fucking Gregg.

When it's done, Owen's beaming. "So what do you think?"

Ethan grabs Owen's shoulder and shakes him. "It's awesome."

Ian nods. "It's got potential."

Ashton just looks at me, and one by one the other guys do too.

"Hunter?" Owen asks.

"It's okay," I manage to get out, but Owen looks like I've punched him.

"You don't like it?"

"I didn't say that, it's just . . . I mean, it doesn't sound like you. Like us."

Owen glances at Ashton, who just shrugs, and then back to me. "What do you mean, it doesn't sound like us?"

"Just, it sounds like it's had a stranger working on it is all I'm saying."

"Well, Gregg helped with the lyrics. But once we're done with it, it'll be all us."

"I guess," I say. "I mean, it'll always have Gregg's name on it, won't it?"

"Why are you being so weird about it?"

"I'm not being weird!"

"Listen," Ian says gently. "We know you've been under a lot of pressure lately, with the Kaivan stuff and the tour and all."

"Yeah," Ethan says.

"What's that supposed to mean? The Kaivan stuff?"

Ashton clears his throat. "Hunt. It's cool, but you've been pretty distracted lately. Spending way more time with him than us."

"Yeah, because I'm supposed to, because The Label asked me to, because people won't support us if they think I'm a slutty bottom. I'm doing this for all of you." I can't believe the way the guys are acting. Like I'm being selfish. "You're supposed to be my friends. I'm doing this for you guys."

"We are your friends," Ashton says.

But Ethan says, "You're doing this because Aidan fucked up and we're all paying the price."

"Dude," Ashton says. "Not cool."

"You know, you guys don't know what it's like to have every part of your life examined. To have to be on all the time, to always be performing yourself and never get to just be. So sorry if I'm a little slow. I'm doing my best, okay?"

The guys are quiet. Ashton looks at his feet. Owen turns back to the computer. Ethan folds his arms over his chest.

Finally, Ian says, "We know you are. We just want to help, okay? We want to take some of that pressure off."

I wipe at my eyes again. I don't know what's wrong with me. We've fought before, about instrumentation and arrangements and who sings which parts, and it's never made me cry before.

"Whatever. It's fine."

"Listen." Owen turns back to face me. "If you don't like it, we can do something different. With the song."

"I like it. It's fine," I say. Because it is. It'll be good, once we've had time to make it good. I know it will.

I'm just so tired.

"It's fine."

"It's not even that it wasn't good," I explain to Kaivan. We're in his bus, on his couch, playing *Overcooked*. It's this game where you're cartoon chefs trying to prep and deliver meals while your kitchen catches on fire or gets struck by lightning or whatever. My little alligator with a bow tie is chopping salmon and throwing it across a river filled with piranhas.

It's addictive.

"I mean, it was catchy. It was fun. I just . . ."

Kaivan's all elbows as his unicorn washes dishes. He's one of those guys that plays video games with his whole body. I like that about him, though, the feel of being pressed up against him as he plays.

"Just what?"

"I don't know. We got into a fight, I guess, and the guys were saying some stuff, and it just really made me think."

"Oh?" He bumps his shoulders against me but doesn't take his eyes off the screen. "About what?"

"Just, I was thinking about the other guys, and how like,

they just get to be themselves. They don't have to 'dress like a gay guy' or whatever. They don't have to perform their identity for our fans, the way I do. And it's kind of exhausting."

Kaivan goes quiet, rushing to plate a sushi roll and get it to the service counter in time. His lips twist side to side, like he's chewing on something but doesn't want to say it.

"Did I say something wrong?"

"No. You're entitled to your feelings."

"But?"

"But . . ." He pauses the game. "That's a really weird thing to say, you know? We're all doing it. You don't think me and my brothers are out there performing our identities? I've never done a single interview where I didn't get asked about being Iranian. And like, Ethan and Ian and Owen, you said yourself they got put in racist costumes for one of your videos?"

"Yeah," I say, but my voice isn't working right.

Kaivan's face is a storm cloud. "It's just, you're not the only one having to perform, you know?"

"Sorry. You're right. I didn't think about it like that."

I mean, it's not like any of the guys ever talk about that stuff with me.

I guess I don't talk about my stuff with them either, though.

Kaivan's face softens. "It's okay. I'm not mad."

"You should be. I'm being a dick."

"Just a little." Kaivan laughs, presses against me again.

"Listen, it's okay to feel bad about it, you know? Just, you're not the only one going through it. That's all."

"You're right. Sorry. Thank you."

Kaivan kisses me on the nose. "It's all right. Now come on. We've got to get this sushi delivered."

KAIVAN PARVANI IS NOT HERE FOR YOUR STEREOTYPES

Pride Today
by Xavier Wang
December 8, 2021

Kaivan Parvani, 17, is the drummer for the groundbreaking Iranian-American pop group PAR-K, formed with his brothers Kamran, 19, and Karim, 20. The group's debut LP climbed the pop and alternative charts when it dropped this summer, but Kaivan found a different sort of attention when he announced via Instagram that he's gay.

"High school was a nightmare," Kaivan explained over the phone. "Like, being Iranian was bad enough, in a school that was ninety percent white. It felt like every news cycle, my brothers and I had to deal with some sort of racist jerk or another. It was mostly just talk, but bullying is still bullying, you know?"

After PAR-K's top ten performance on *America's Best Band*, Kaivan's parents allowed him to quit public school and work on getting a GED while focusing on his music. Both of his brothers had already graduated at that point.

"Yeah, it was kind of a relief. So much of high school was just about surviving. Especially as I started to realize I maybe liked guys. There was this one kid in middle school, everyone always said he was gay, because of the way he dressed, the way he talked, the music he listened to, lots of boy bands and stuff. People were just merciless to him. And he was white! I knew I couldn't just be out and gay, not when I was already brown."

When asked about being queer in a cultural heritage that has at times even denied the existence of homosexual men, Kaivan is quick to point out that Iranian-Americans are not a monolith.

"My parents were the first people I told. Well, second, I guess, but only because my brothers already kind of guessed. They've been so supportive. I think people get this idea of Iranians that they, that we, all hate gay people or something. But just look around, there's plenty of homophobia right at home too."

Ultimately, Kaivan hopes to break down stereotypes and bridge East and West, gay and straight, through his music.

"I don't want people to only know me as Iranian, or as gay. I'm a whole person. I want to make music that brings people together. Good music, you know? Stuff that'll stand the test of time. Not this manufactured crap, like all these boy bands where you can't even tell which one is singing. It's plug and play. Me and my brothers, we want people to be able to tell us apart. At the end of the day, I just want to be myself, without everyone else's expectations holding me back. That's what I want."

Xavier Wang is a journalist, specializing in stories of diaspora, third culture experiences, and queer studies. They live in New York City with eight house-plants and the world's most thoughtful partner. You can find their articles in Pride Today, The New Yorker, *and elsewhere.*

HUNTER DRAKE'S SCHEDULE—
ALBUQUERQUE, NM/AUSTIN, TX
April 7–8, 2022

NB: Hunter will arrive in Austin early for a photo shoot and interview with Q *Magazine.* Separate car service/escort has been arranged. All times CDT unless noted.

2300MDT Approx. end of meet and greet, depart for ABQ Albuquerque International Sunport

2345MDT Flight to AUS Austin-Bergstrom International Airport

0220 (April 8) Arrival at AUS Austin-Bergstrom International Airport

0300 Arrival at Four Seasons Austin

0930 Car service will pick up Hunter at the SERVICE ENTRANCE

1000 Arrival at photo studio

1230 Lunch provided at studio

1500 Car service takes Hunter DIRECTLY TO VENUE

1730 Sound check

20

My wake-up call comes way too soon. I mean, it's not objectively that early, but I lost an hour changing time zones, and then I stayed up too late talking to Kaivan because he was still awake when I texted to let him know I landed, so I didn't even get to bed until nearly 4:00.

I've got a local escort today, this military-looking white guy who just goes by "Hodges." He's kind of scary, to be honest. Nothing like Nazeer who, despite his imposing frame, carries himself more like our Group Dad than anything.

I meet Malone at the hotel's service entrance, where his black sedan is idling, and he drives me to this tall, art deco building by the river, the kind that looks like it should be full of bankers or architects or law firms. On the twelfth floor, there's an advertising agency with a whole photo studio inside. The walls are white, the lights are soft, and everyone seems to be wearing scarves even though it's not that cold inside.

Hodges drops me off with my stylist, this tall, thin guy with blocky glasses, platinum-blond hair, and a gray scarf.

"How are we, honey?" he asks as he pulls back the curtain on a dressing booth.

"Okay I guess. How about you?"

"Living the dream. I'm Aaron by the way, he/him."

"Hunter. He/him."

"I know who you are, mister." He hands me a pair of faded black jeans so soft, I have to check the seams to make sure they're really denim. "Nervous?"

"A little."

"Why? I bet you have photo shoots all the time."

"Yeah, but this time it actually means something, you know?"

Aaron smiles. "Well, don't worry. We'll take care of you. It's all family here."

I let my shoulders relax and breathe a little deeper. There's nothing quite like being in an all-queer space.

I've missed that feeling.

"Your publicist says you're going for a new look?"

"I guess."

"Hm. You guess?"

"I don't know, they think I don't dress enough like a bottom."

"What do bottoms dress like?"

I gesture at my clothes. "Sweats and a tuque, I guess."

Aaron cackles. "Well, we'll try something just a tad more stylish for your shoot." He hands me this white shirt with an asymmetrical neck and a cool, ripply texture to the fabric, then a pair of sleek black leather boots. "Try these on. You need anything? You've got on underwear, right?"

I nod.

"What kind?"

"Boxer briefs."

"Thank god. Callum showed up in the baggiest boxers I have ever seen. It was like a circus tent in there. I thought a clown car might come flying out of the changing room."

I blush, thinking of Kaivan's well-fitted boxers. "No circus tents for me."

"Good. Mind if I check the style?"

The way he says it is professional, not creepy, so I pull out the waist of my sweats to show him my black boxer briefs with gold threading in the waistband.

"Cute," he says, and I flush with approval. "But I think we'd better get you into something seamless."

My boxer briefs do have a seam right down the middle.

Aaron steps out and comes back a few seconds later with several pairs of briefs so soft they're water in my hands.

He pulls the curtain closed and I get dressed. I pick a pair of teal briefs and study myself in the mirror. I don't usually wear briefs, but these have a nice shape to them, and they support me well.

I slip my jeans on. They're kind of tight, especially the thighs and butt, but the length seems fine. I zip the boots up, pull the shirt on, and step back out.

"How's this?"

"Hmm." Aaron has me step up to a three-way mirror and starts fussing with the way the shirt falls across my shoulders. "How do the jeans feel?" He slips his fingers into the waistband and yanks on them. "Tight?"

"More in the thighs."

"Can you squat?"

I try, and the jeans fight me for a second before they let out this mournful ripping sound.

"Shit! Sorry."

Aaron laughs. "I've dealt with worse."

"It's my hockey butt."

"Let me try something else."

Aaron returns with dark blue jeans that fit perfectly, and he swaps the white shirt out for a plain black V-neck cashmere sweater.

"You look great," he says when I step up to the mirror again.

I study my reflection. I haven't worn something like this since the whole "rebrand," but I like it. It's comfortable and practical and stylish. Not loud or sparkly or bottom-chic. It's just me.

"There's that smile," Aaron says.

"Thanks. I love it."

I wish I could dress like this all the time. Just tell The Label to go fuck itself and wear what I want.

"Perf. Come on, let's get you to hair and makeup."

The hair stylist (Jai, they/them), who has the most luscious long brown hair, gives me a wash and the slightest of trims before styling me in the tallest angled pompadour I've ever pulled off.

I didn't even know my hair could stand up like that.

Jai looks over my shoulder in the mirror. "Good?"

"It's amazing."

They swivel the chair around and pulls out an eyeliner pencil. "Finishing touches."

"Do we have to?" I kind of hate getting eyeliner. It's not the sharp object near my eyes, though that's not great. It's just, I don't like people touching my eyelids.

"We don't have to," Jai says. "But it'll make the green really pop. It's up to you."

I grit my teeth and nod.

Jai is quick and gentle, but I still dig my hands into my armrests as they work. Once they're done, they stand aside so I can see myself.

"What do you think?"

They're right: Eyeliner does make my eyes pop. Usually they're kind of a forest green, but with the contrast they look more jade.

"Fierce."

"Yeah it is." Jai pulls the plastic bib off me. "You're all set."

"Thanks, Jai."

The shoot is for Q *Magazine's* "Icons" issue, an annual piece celebrating twenty-five queer luminaries making a difference. It's a huge honor, but to be honest, I feel like a faker, being included with activists and lawmakers who are all way older than me.

In fact, I'm the second-youngest person this year. Callum Wethers is sixteen.

Callum's a country artist who made headlines last year for coming out at fifteen and "shattering country music stereotypes," as if Melissa Etheridge and Lil Nas X and a bunch of others didn't already do that. He's a white boy with blond hair, cornflower-blue eyes, and the jaw of a thirty-year-old farmer: basically every stereotype of an all-American country musician rolled into one. Except for the liking boys part.

He's wearing a white button-up shirt, light blue jeans, and a pair of pink low-top Chuck Taylors.

"Hunter Drake!" he says when he sees me. He has a wide, open smile (his teeth are so white and so straight they might have been manufactured), and he goes for a hug before I can stop him. "I finally get to meet you."

"Yeah. Nice to meet you."

"I can't believe we're doing this together. It's like, you inspired me, and now I get to inspire more people. It's amazing."

"It is pretty cool, eh?"

He smiles at me like I'm a camera. "Yeah! Like, I really wanna show how diverse country music can be. And show all the people out there that gay people are just like straight people. Like, I can sing about a boy and it's fine. Love is love, right?"

"Yeah." He sounds like he's doing an interview, all canned answers. "Sure."

He keeps smiling at me, but his eyes look more nervous than anything. I can't tell if he's excited to meet me or over-whelmed by all this or if he's just not used to being treated like an actual human being anymore.

So I ask, "How's it been, with all the attention and stuff? Lots of pressure, I imagine."

"Huh? Oh, it's been okay. I mean, I get some haters and all that, you know, the 'Adam and Eve, not Adam and Steve' stuff. But really, it's been great, getting to live my truth. You know how it is."

"That's good."

"Yeah. Plus it's not like I'm dating anyone or sleeping around. I'm really just focusing on my music right now."

I can't tell if he's trying to be a dickbag or if he just doesn't think before he speaks, but thankfully Lou (she/they), one of the photographer's assistants, comes to grab Callum for his shoot.

"Let's talk more after, okay?" he says over his shoulder.

"Sure."

I would rather eat one of the ring lights.

I go to the wall and start to lean against it, but then I remember I've been dressed and styled, so I stand up straighter.

"You look like you need a Valium, honey."

"Sorry?" I turn and find Masha Patriarki, Nonbinary Drag Monarch, in all their glory, looking right at me.

They've got this enormous red wig (ketchup red, not copper red like mine) and a tight dress that must've been spun from rainbows and glitter, because it changes color wherever the light hits it. Their makeup is incredible: dark brown skin glowing, eyebrows perfectly arched, cheeks and nose contoured to a knife's edge, lips painted dark but flecked with glitter to shine like the night sky.

They even smell good, something with rose and honey.

When I don't respond, their eyes soften. "You okay?"

I clear my throat. "Yeah. Yeah, I'm just . . . kind of starstruck."

Masha's eyes crinkle up as they laugh. "Well, I don't blame you. It's not every day you get to meet royalty."

I blush. "I'm Hunter, by the way."

"Oh, I know who you are."

They know who I am.

"I loved your TED Talk."

Masha gave this amazing talk about how important queer activism is (or Drag-tivism, as they put it) to address inequities in housing and health care and employment. And then they ended it with a fantastic drag number about the legacy of queer protest, from Stonewall to today.

I mean, Masha's a queer icon. They're the real deal.

I'm just a pretender.

"Thanks. I like your music."

"Really?"

"Yeah, it bops. But I like you supporting youth shelters more."

I blush so hard I'm probably redder than Masha's hair. "I was just . . . trying to do what you talked about. Using my platform for good."

"Look at you." They swat my chest lightly. "What else are you up to?"

"I'm not sure yet," I admit, and feel even more like a phony, because I could be doing more. I should be doing more.

I mean, in addition to their public speaking, Masha's got a foundation set up to support Black and brown queer youth, and a separate advocacy group that lobbies for nondiscrimination laws.

"Well, you're still young. You've got time to figure it out."

"I guess. I just don't know. Maybe I messed everything up."

Masha arches an eyebrow so high it disappears into their wig.

"Messed up how?"

"Uh, I don't know if you heard about all the stuff my ex posted online."

They bat their eyelashes at me. "Oh I heard, honey."

"Yeah. Some of the shelters and charities and stuff have kind of distanced themselves from me."

Masha purses their lips. "Most of those shelters depend on funding from corporations looking for tax breaks. Corporations full of straight people. Straight people hate being reminded that queer people have sex. And you did just that."

"I just feel like I let them down."

"You didn't," they say. "I've lost plenty of sponsors before, and I'm sure I'll lose more. The important thing is to do what you believe in."

"I'm going to try."

"Good." They study my face. "Your eyes look fierce."

I smile for real.

"You ever think about doing drag?"

"Maybe someday, when all this is over," I say. "I've even got the perfect name: Little Red Hiding Wood."

Masha cackles. "I love it! What do you mean, when all this is over? Why wait?"

"The Label always said that drag wouldn't be a good look for me."

"Oh really? Why is that?"

"I don't know," I say. Except I'm pretty sure I do know. "I think they have a certain idea of what a gay guy looks like, what I'm supposed to do in the band. Before all the stuff with Aidan it was *be masc, be sporty, be a guy*, and now it's all *be femme, be gentle, wear this floral shirt*. They don't want me to be complicated."

Masha blinks at me. "What they think is their business. What you do is yours."

213

They're right, of course. I know they're right. But I don't know what to do about it.

"Masha?" Lou calls out. "We're ready for you."

Masha nods at Lou and then turns back to me with a theatrical wink. "Keep your chin up, Little Red Hiding Wood."

Q Magazine

QM: You made quite a splash, coming out when you did. Why risk it? Especially in country music, which has historically been quite conservative.

CW: I don't know, I just felt like I had to be me. People always think, 'Oh, country kids, they're all the same, driving big trucks and wearing cowboy boots, and all their songs are the same, about girlfriends leaving and dogs dying.' But there's lots of people that live in the country. One of my best friends is Black. And the QSA kids at my school were in 4H too.

But, I guess the real reason is, I want country music to be something everyone can enjoy. And me being out can maybe help people realize that we're not so different. We want the same things, and heartbreak feels the same if you're gay or straight.

QM: Speaking of heartbreak, you've been pretty quiet on the dating front. Are you seeing anyone?

CW: I don't really have time for all that right now. I'm really just focusing on my music. Like, I'm gay, but I don't want to be known for my dating life. I want people to know me because of my music, because I made a song that helps them get through their day, that makes them smile. That's what matters to me.

QM: If you'd asked me last year who I expected would make The Icons Issue, a sixteen-year-old country singer would have been far from the top of my list, and yet here you are. Who are your icons? Who inspires you?

CW: To me, my parents are always going to be icons, because they raised me to hold my head high and be who I am. And I'd never be here without musicians like Taylor Swift and Kacey Musgraves. You know. The greats.

QM: Dolly Parton?

CW: Oh yeah, for sure. Dolly's great.

QM: What's next for you?

CW: Well, I'm going on tour this summer, and I'm hard at work on my next album. Plus my parents are helping set up this thing that'll help mentor young musicians in rural areas, but we're still figuring all that out. And you'll probably laugh, because it sounds like such a stereotype, but I got a pickup for my birthday and I'm still trying to fix it up.

QM: Sounds like you've got a lot on your plate.

CW: For sure, for sure. But I wouldn't have it any other way. You only live once, right?

Callum Wethers's first album, *Callum,* is available for streaming now on all major platforms.

Photography by Margie Holden. Styling by Aaron Waters. Hair and makeup by Jai Culber.

Q Magazine

QM: One of our other icons this year is Callum Wethers. How does it feel, knowing you're inspiring young musicians to come out and live their lives openly?

HD: I don't know. There's been lots of queer musicians before me. Freddie Mercury. Elton John. Troye Sivan. Janelle Monáe. I don't feel like much of an inspiration. I mean, there's been other guys in boy bands that came out too.

But I'm glad Callum's getting to live authentically. That's really cool.

QM: All the boy band members that came out did so later in their careers, though, not at the start. That couldn't have been easy for you. Were you worried about any sort of backlash?

HD: I guess, but it wasn't like I could go back in the closet. I was already out when I was playing hockey, and then when we did our video for "Poutine," it was just for fun, so I didn't think I needed to pretend to be straight or anything. Like, who cared if some random guy in a YouTube video was gay? So then when we got big, it was kind of too late.

But the guys have always had my back. And our manager, Janet.

The Label has been pretty cool too.

QM: You mentioned the guys, your bandmates. Is it hard being in a band with four straight boys?

HD: Yeah, but not in the way people imagine. It's not like I'm pining after any of them. Not that they're not good-looking, because they are. But what I mean is, back home I had more queer friends, I had the QSA at school, I had spaces like this where everyone's queer. I don't know, I just feel lighter in queer spaces. Does that make sense?

QM: It does.

HD: Good. I think this interview is the most queer people I've gotten to talk to in a long time. Well, if you don't count the receptions and stuff.

QM: You're talking about the VIP receptions after your shows?

HD: Yeah, I got it set up so we give out fifty tickets to local queer youth every show. It feels weird to say that: "queer youth." Like I'm not one of them. But anyway, that goes so fast, it's not like it's community. It's just a moment. An awesome moment, but then it's over.

QM: It sounds like you're selling yourself short. You've made it fairly public how much you're donating to shelters across the nation.

HD: And Canada too.

QM: And Canada too. That's not nothing.

HD: It sounds kind of glib, but it's just money, right? I mean, Masha Patriarki is out there leading protests, giving talks, pushing for real change. Sometimes I feel like a phony, to be honest.

QM: Give yourself some credit, at least. This is The Icons Issue.

HD: Thanks. I try.

QM: You've been pretty public about your relationships too. Don't you think there's something powerful about representing queer love to the general public?

HD: I don't know. It's hard being in a relationship, and even harder when you're having to navigate the public eye. It takes a lot of work, a lot of communication, and that's not always easy with a spotlight on you. It's been pretty tough at times.

QM: You're referring to your breakup with Aidan Nightingale?

HD: Yeah, but even when we were dating. We stopped being people and became this idea instead. And that really messed with my head. Aidan's too, I think, but you'd have to ask him.

QM: Aidan insinuated you were less than faithful to him in your relationship, but you've never talked about that publicly.

HD: How am I supposed to? I mean, there's kind of a power differential, isn't there? With me being in the band and all? If I say he's wrong, everyone will go after him, and he was already getting treated worse than me anyway.

I mean, our fans are great, don't get me wrong, but there's lots of randos on the Internet who like starting shit.

QM: That's fair.

HD: Listen, can we cut that last part out though?

QM: If you're sure. I think people might be interested to hear your take on it, though.

HD: I know they would, but it doesn't feel right, talking about him when he's not here.

QM: That's fair.

QM: What's next for Hunter Drake?

HD: Well, we're working on our third album right now. And we're shooting a documentary of our tour, which has been fun but kind of hectic, having cameras around all the time.

Plus I'm trying to figure out how to do more good, on a larger scale. Maybe a foundation or something. I haven't figured it out yet, though. I want to make a difference. Not just for people who come to the shows, but for queer people everywhere.

QM: You've got a lot on your plate!

HD: Yeah. I guess. But I've got this platform, and I've got to use it, right?

Hunter Drake can be heard on Kiss & Tell's debut album, *Kiss & Tell*, and their follow-up, *Come Say Hello*.

Photography by Margie Holden. Styling by Aaron Waters. Hair and makeup by Jai Culber.

Q Magazine

QM: This is your third year running as one of our Queer Icons. What would you call that? A hat trick? A triple?

MP: A turkey, like in bowling. Lord knows I've got the feathers for it.

QM: A lot's changed in three years, though. That first year, you had gone viral for your TED Talk. Now you're a best-selling author, an award-winning humanitarian, a cultural icon.

MP: Don't forget the sore loser of a congressional run.

QM: That too. How does it feel, to look back and see how far you've come?

MP: Tiresome. I've been doing this for ten years. I've gone from being ignored to being vilified to being everyone's Magical Negro. People expect me to sashay in, fix their white problems, and shantay away again. They'll read my books, put my sayings on T-shirts, but they won't do the work of smashing our white supremacist hetero patriarchy. And it's built into the name, honey!

QM: And yet it's still hard to think of people doing more work for queer liberation right now than you.

MP: Someone has to.

QM: What does that work look like? Say we're together like this again next year. What kind of future would you like to see?

MP: I wish I knew. We're still dreaming what queer futures look like. Especially for Black people, Indigenous people, people of color, fat people, disabled people.

I'll tell you what doesn't work: conforming. Giving in to the expectations that the white supremacist hetero patriarchy puts on our behavior, on our expression of ourselves, our identities, our love. The future won't be built by us becoming them. It'll be built off of them slowly, painfully, learning that we're human too.

QM: Wow. That's powerful, and I fear you're probably right. But that's a rather bleak outlook. Is there anything giving you hope right now?

MP: I run on hope, sweetie. Hope, white wine, and a healthy bit of spite.

You know what gives me hope? How many young people I see at book signings, at shows, at talks, who get inspired to go do the work. I mean, look at your list this year, five of them are under twenty-five! Two of them are actual children!

It's easy to focus on how messy and imperfect people are, but the next generation is already making their voices heard. Pushing for change, demanding inclusion, advocating for radical, transformative justice. And that's just the loud ones. There are the quiet ones too, who are making powerful statements of their own just by living, just by existing, just by surviving in this system that wants to tear them down. Still they rise.

That's what gives me hope.

Masha Patriarki is a dragtivist, community organizer, *New York Times* bestselling author, TED Fellow, and *NAACP Image Award* winner.

Photography by Margie Holden. Styling, hair, and makeup by Masha Patriarki. Additional styling by Aaron Waters. Additional hair and makeup by Jai Culber.

21

"How'd it go?" Kaivan asks. We're in my dressing room, cuddling on the couch, my head nestled into the crook of Kaivan's shoulder. He keeps running his hands through my hair.

I stifle a yawn. "It was okay."

"Just okay?"

"I don't know. Got me thinking about some stuff. Oh! But I got to meet Masha Patriarki."

"Really? What were they like?"

"Awesome. So smart and cool and just . . . I don't know. I wish I could be like them."

"I like you just the way you are." Kaivan plants a kiss on my forehead. I snuggle closer to him.

"I met Callum Wethers too. You know that country music artist who came out a while back?"

"Uh-huh."

"He's an actual monster, though. Like, the whitest white gay I have ever seen. And before you ask, yes, I've looked in a mirror."

Kaivan snorts. "Did he smell like hay and fresh-mown grass and sunshine?"

"Nah, he smelled like Axe. But anyway, he was all like, I just want to be known for my music, not for being gay." I do my best Texas accent. *I'm Callum Wethers, I'm just like everyone else except I suck dick. Except I don't suck dick because I don't want the bad press.*

Kaivan shakes his head. "I mean, he's not wrong, is he? Look what happened to you. Maybe he doesn't know any other way to survive."

I blush, because he's right, but still. "We shouldn't have to survive by appeasing straight people, though."

Kaivan chuckles.

"What?"

"You sure about that mirror? You don't think I survive by appeasing white people sometimes?"

"Sorry. I deserved that." I sit up straighter. "And I get what you're saying. But, I mean, we can't control what other people think about us."

"Maybe not, but we can give them their choice of targets. Callum's narrowing it down, that's all."

"I guess." I chew my lip. "Are you worried about it?"

"About what?"

"About dating me. About people only knowing you for that." I try to say it casually, but my tongue feels like I've licked a cymbal. "That always bothered Aidan. Feeling eclipsed. And he got shittier and shittier the worse it got."

Kaivan cocks his head to the side. I study the line of his neck muscles, the way they stretch. He's in his black tank top for the show, the one that shows off his collarbone, which is one of my favorite things ever. (Especially kissing it. Or licking it. Or nibbling on it.)

"I'm not Aidan. I don't feel eclipsed."

"But what about all this stuff The Label has us doing?"

"Hey, if they want to keep paying for our dates, that's fine with me. Let them." Kaivan starts playing with my hair again. My whole nervous system lights up, meridians vibrating in artificial harmonics.

"Aren't you worried that they're going to turn us into people we're not, just so they can sell more albums?"

Kaivan sighs. "That's the name of the game, boy."

"What? Riding the gravy train?"

He laughs gently. "See, I know Pink Floyd too."

"I knew there was something about you." I relax against him. His hand in my hair is so soothing, I could almost fall asleep.

"But I get what you mean. And I do want to be known for my music too. For what I create, just as much as who I love."

He said love.

I'm not freaking out. But he definitely said love.

"I wish we could just be real."

"Me too." Kaivan rests his chin against my head. "Mmm. Your hair smells nice."

"Really?"

"Yeah. It reminds me of something."

"My conditioner's got almond oil."

"Ah. It smells like my mom's baking."

"Mmm." I close my eyes and inhale Kaivan's scent. "You smell nice, too."

He chuckles, and his chest vibrates against me. I'm think I'm getting one of those weird sleepy-boners, which is probably obvious in my sweats, but I can't move. I let our breaths sync up, find his free hand, and twine our fingers together.

I don't want to give this up. I don't want to have to choose between being with someone and being a musician. It's not fair.

Kaivan shouldn't have to choose either.

He said love.

"Hm." Kaivan murmurs into my hair. "Do you hear a saxophone?"

"Mm." I don't hear anything except his heart. I relax completely against him, an unwound guitar string, every bit of me loose.

But then it happens.

The dressing room speaker blares to life, playing the porn-sounding saxophone line from "Careless Whisper" at full volume.

I startle fully awake again, push away from Kaivan so fast I fall off the couch.

"What the fuck," he asks.

I run to the door and yank it open. Ethan's running down the hall, cackling, clutching one of the crew's walkie-talkies.

"Ethan!" I shout at his retreating form.

He glances back, and he laughs louder. "BONER ALERT!" he squawks into the walkie-talkie as he rounds the corner, laughing the whole time.

"Not cool!" I shout, but it echoes in the empty hall. "Ethan!"

But he's gone.

I adjust myself so my boner's trapped against my waistband and go back inside.

In the dressing room, the music has switched to Marvin Gaye's "Let's Get It On," and I can't decide if that's better or worse. Kaivan laughs so hard he hiccups, and that makes me start laughing too. I shake my head, close the door, and turn the volume on the speaker all the way down.

"Those assholes," I say, but I don't really mean it. I've been in on some pranks before, like the infamous Mustard Incident, so I had this coming.

Kaivan's still laughing, but I catch his eyes lingering on my sweats. "Boner alert, huh?"

"Leave me alone," I say, tugging my shirt down. "It was a sleepy-boner."

"Ah." He pulls me down onto the couch. "Were you sleepy?"

"Yeah. I'm awake now, though."

"Oh yeah?"

"Yeah."

"Good, 'cause I've got to get to sound check, and I was worried you were going to drool on my shirt."

"Rude!"

He laughs as he plants a kiss on my cheek and gets up.

"See you after?"

"Yeah."

From: Bill Holt (b.holt@thelabel.com)

To: Ryan Silva (ryansilvamanager@gmail.com)

Subject: Re: "Memories" release change

4/8/22 3:15 P.M.

See attached marketing plan. We're confident this will make best use of new press around Kaivan. FYI Sales is happy with the new identity-driven focus, think it will see good numbers. Lots of in-house excitement for this.

-BH

From: Ryan Silva (ryansilvamanager@gmail.com)

To: Bill Holt (b.holt@thelabel.com)

Subject: Re: "Memories" release change

4/8/22 4:15 P.M.

Marketing plan looks good, will get the guys to sign off. Glad everyone is excited! Thsnks bill.

Ryan

22

"Wow, Austin," Ashton says into his mic. "This has got to be one of the most spectacular shows we've ever had. Wouldn't you agree, guys?"

The crowd screams. Ashton always says some variation of this, no matter what city we're in, but it's actually true tonight. The crowd is electric. There's nothing else like it.

"Did you say 'Austin' or 'Ashton'?" Owen quips as he settles at the piano.

"Are you making fun of my Canadian accent, eh?"

That gets a laugh.

"Anyway, this next song isn't one of ours, but it is one of Hunter's favorites. Isn't that right, Hunter?"

I nod. I'm at my pedal board, holding my Hummingbird, playing a few chords to check my tone. "Yeah," I say. "My dad used to play this in the car on the way to hockey practice, do you remember?"

"I remember he couldn't sing in key, but that never stopped him."

"Or you for that matter," Ethan adds, which gets another swell of laughter.

"Gentlemen," Ian says, stepping between Ashton and Ethan to break up the fake fight.

This is part of our bit every night too. It feels kind of cheesy, but it's worth it to play Dad's favorite song every night.

"Anyway, this is a song by a band called Pink Floyd. It's called 'Wish You Were Here.'"

The crowd screams again, which is probably just regular excitement and not because they recognize "Wish You Were Here." It came out before Dad was even born.

But it really is one of the best songs ever written. And I don't just sing it for Dad, though I do wish he was here. It's about more than that. It's about longing and loss and connection.

If I could write just one song that's half as enduring, I think I could be happy with that.

Maybe someday.

We're still buzzing, skipping down the halls to our dressing rooms after the show. I can't stop smiling. None of us can. Some shows are just like that. Euphoric.

Owen catches up with me and throws his arm over my neck. "Good show."

"The best," I agree.

"Hey. I'm sorry about yesterday, with the song and all. I didn't realize it mattered so much to you, that it's all us."

I mean, it does matter to me, but not as much as our friendship. Not as much as the band.

"No. Listen." I shake my head. "I was out of line. And it's a good song, really."

"Yeah?"

I nod, even though my ears burn, because it really is a good song, I just wish we didn't need fucking Gregg.

"Well, I still need your help with it. Maybe we can work on it tomorrow?"

"Yeah."

"Thanks, Hunter."

He stops at his dressing room, and I keep going to mine.

"Hey, Hunt?" Ashton asks right before I close the door. "You got a minute?"

"Yeah, lemme get ready for the meet and greet real quick."

"Oh."

"It'll just take a sec."

I pull off my show shirt, wipe off as much sweat as I can with the scratchy white dressing room towels, then pull on a new one. It's another floral shirt, with purple orchids on it. I check myself in the mirror and stop.

I don't look like me anymore. I look like a cardboard cutout version of Hunter Drake. A dress-up doll version. And I hate it. I hate that this is who I've become. A fake.

I want to be real. I want to be the kind of guy who does

what feels right instead of what other people want. I think about what Masha said.

What The Label thinks is their business.

What I do is my business.

So I dig through my clothes and find a light blue collarless button-up at the back of the rack. Julian picked it out for me last year for an interview, and I liked it so much I asked if I could keep it.

I pull it on, roll up the sleeves, and fix my hair as best I can.

"Okay, ready," I say when I emerge, but Ashton's talking on the phone. He sees me and holds up a finger, but then he sighs and turns away.

"No, Dad, I don't think—yeah. Uh-huh."

I wait a second, to see if Ashton's going to get off, but he's still talking and I've really got to get to the meet and greet, so I wave and head off without him.

It's a great meet and greet too: The energy from the show is still crackling in the fluorescent lights and ugly ocean-print carpet of the reception suite. I asked once why so many reception suites had such heinous carpeting, and Janet said it's because carpets with busy patterns don't show wine or vomit stains on them, which, gross.

Speaking of Janet, she gives me a raised eyebrow, since I'm not in my "new look," but I smile and shrug at her. After a second, she smirks and shakes her head.

Brett hangs out behind me, capturing footage as I sign

autographs, pose for photos, give a couple hugs, listen to stories, offer advice as best I can.

A girl tells me she thinks she might be bisexual, but doesn't know if she wants to come out, so I tell her that the main thing is to make sure she's safe and has a good support network around her, and she can figure things out (and even change her mind if she wants) later.

A nonbinary adult tells me that our music helped em rediscover eir own love of singing, and ey joined a queer chorus in Austin to meet other people like em.

A dad tells me that me being both gay and a hockey player made it easier for his lacrosse-playing son to accept being queer.

I wish every story was good. I wish every night could feel like this.

"Hi!" I give my best smile as a mom and two kids make it to the front of the line. "What're your names?"

"Alexis," the taller one says, and the shorter one says, "Carly."

"C-a-r-l-y?" I confirm as I sign their poster.

Carly nods.

"We brought you a gift too," the mom says.

"Oh, you didn't have to!" It's always sweet when fans bring gifts, but it's impossible to manage stuff like that on tour, so a lot of it ends up thrown away or damaged even if we try to keep it.

"No, please. We all picked it out for you." She opens her purse and pulls out a rainbow feather boa. I'm painfully aware of Rick's camera on us, so I freeze my smile as the mom lets her kids hand it over.

"Wow." Don't be a dickbag, Hunter. Don't be a dickbag. "Thank you."

The mom holds up her phone. I wrap the strangling feathers around my neck and pose for a quick photo.

"It's perfect!" she says. I just keep smiling, and give them a wave once they head off, but I've got a hockey puck lodged in my throat.

I mean, this isn't the first feather boa I've been gifted, and it won't be the last, but it's worse having the whole humiliating thing caught on camera.

"Hold up," Nazeer says to the next person in line. I don't even know where he came from. It's like he knew. "Why don't you take five." He hands me my water bottle and nods toward the side door.

"Thanks."

The side door opens into a wide, curving hall with polished concrete floors and metal guard rails on the walls. I unwind the feather boa from my neck and let it fall to the floor.

I shouldn't let it get to me. I can't let one well-intentioned microaggression ruin a whole night for me.

I close my eyes, take a deep breath, roll out my neck, sip my water. But I still can't quite find that euphoria from before.

It's hovering out of reach, a high note just beyond my register.

A door bangs open farther down the hall. Footsteps echo off the concrete, along with the sound of wheels. They must be loading out the show already.

I straighten up, shake myself out. The show must go on, and so must the after-show. There are still people waiting for me, people who deserve a smile.

I turn back to the door, but catch Jill coming around the curve of the hall.

"Oh. Hey, Jill."

And then I see the person walking behind her, dragging a black roller bag, a beat-up Ravens duffel bag slung over his right shoulder.

Aidan Nightingale clears his throat.

"Oh. Uh. Hey, Hunter."

TRAVEL ITINERARY

• APRIL 8, 2022 •

ONE-WAY FIRST CLASS TICKET FROM
YVR TO **AUS** FOR <u>AIDAN NIGHTINGALE</u>

DEPARTING YVR
8:05AM

LAYOVER IN DEN

ARRIVING AUS
10:20PM

23

accidentally crush my water bottle, sloshing water up and over my hands and arm.

I don't say anything to Aidan. I don't look at him. Just turn on my heel, put on my biggest, fakest smile, and go back to the meet and greet.

Smile. Sign. Repeat. Nazeer can tell something's up, and he keeps the line moving at a quick clip, though he slows down when the shelter kids come through.

They're happy to see me and I'm happy to see them, though two in the back ignore me as they argue loudly about their favorite animé. A few of them give me gifts too: poems, drawings, an overlarge T-shirt from the shelter's booth at last year's Pride that's big enough for me to swim in. They're sweet and funny and brave and generous. I feel like a shitbag because I know all these gifts are going to end up in the trash with the rainbow feather boa.

Still, I don't let them—or the cameras—see it. I laugh and joke until their chaperone starts gently urging them toward the door, thanking me one last time.

"Cheers," I tell them. "It's my privilege."

Once they're gone, and the room is empty, I lean forward and run my hands through my hair, massaging my scalp. I wish Kaivan was here. I wish it was him touching me, soothing me.

I don't want to deal with Aidan. I want Kaivan.

"That bad, huh?" Nazeer asks.

"Aidan's here," I groan into the table.

"Oh. Hm." He steps away, to wrangle the guys maybe, or find out what the fuck is going on. I don't want to talk to anyone. I keep my head down as I hurry back to my dressing room to get my shit.

I throw my clothes into my bag, pack my Strat, but I get that urge to smash it again. I don't, but I want to.

Kaivan knocks on my door—he always knocks the same way, one sharp rap.

"Yeah," I say.

"Hey. Good show." He wraps his arms around me from behind, kisses my cheek, but I stiffen against him. "What?"

I pull away and turn to face him. He gently holds my elbows. "Aidan's here."

"He . . . really?"

I nod. "Showed up during the meet and greet."

"What, he just came to the show?"

243

"No, he was in the service hall with his mom and some luggage. I don't know."

Kaivan's expression turns stormy. "No one told you?"

"I don't . . ." Fuck. "Ashton wanted to talk to me after the show, but then he was on the phone. With his dad."

Hot betrayal sings through my veins. I think my eye twitches.

"That's messed up. Are you going to be okay?"

"I'll be fine. I'm just pissed off." A laugh bubbles out of me, even though nothing's funny. "Sorry."

"Don't be." He pulls me close again.

"It's totally over between us. Me and Aidan. Just so you know."

"I figured," he says into my hair.

"And I never cheated on him either. I don't know if I ever told you that. But I didn't."

"I wasn't worried about that. I trust you."

"Why are you so nice to me?" I don't know why I ask it. I just feel so small and worthless. I hate this.

"It's your hockey butt."

I snort and rest my forehead against his chest. "Wow."

"It'll be okay, Hunter."

"I know." I sigh and straighten up. "I know."

Ashton's waiting for me outside the bus. I avoid his eyes as I stow my luggage underneath, but he blocks the little stairs to get on.

"Hunter, listen . . ."

Anger bubbles up inside me, but I keep my voice low.

"Did you know he was coming?"

Ashton looks at his feet. "I tried to tell you, but . . ."

"But what?"

"It was all so last minute. And everything was weird yesterday. And then today, you were busy, and I tried but Dad called and you know how he is."

I want to shout at him, but I don't, because he's always getting caught in the middle: between his mom and dad, between me and Aidan.

I take a deep breath and try to even out the timbre of my voice.

"What's he doing here?"

Ashton pushes his hair off his face. "Dad sent him to be with Mom for a while. They were fighting all the time, and . . . Hunt, he got kicked off the team."

"He what?"

"I guess he showed up to practice drunk."

I can't imagine that Aidan. I don't want to.

I don't know if I'm ready to deal with him being in pain. Not when I'm still pissed off at him.

"Aidan's a mess, Hunt. And he's my brother. What would you do if it was Haley?"

My anger cools just a bit, because he's right. I'd do anything for my sister. Not that Haley ever needs anything. She's so independent she wouldn't even let

Mom set up her bed when she moved into her dorm.

"I get it," I finally grumble. "I get it. But a little warning would've been nice."

"I didn't know he was coming inside tonight. I really was going to tell you."

"Fine."

Ashton's shoulders unclench.

"Where's he sleeping?"

"Here. I'll switch with Ian and bunk with him at the back."

Ian won the rock-paper-scissors tourney at the start of the tour for the lone solo bunk, though it was also the one closest to the toilet.

"That okay with you?"

"It's fine," I mutter. "As long as he wears clean socks." Ian always sleeps with one leg dangling out of his bunk. Last tour Ethan got a foot in the face when he got up to pee in the middle of the night.

Ashton nods and follows me onto the bus. Aidan's in the lounge, sitting on the couch with his phone in his hands.

I want to smack it out of his grasp as soon as I see it. But he's just playing a game.

"Hey," he says, and stands up. "I didn't mean to surprise you like that."

"It's fine," I say. It's not fine. But I'm tired.

"Hunter, I—" he starts, but I cut him off.

"Listen, Aidan. I'm sorry that shit's hard for you right now."

To my own surprise, I really am sorry, even if I'm pissed too. "But I think it's better if we don't talk. Okay?"

Aidan presses his lips together. He and Ashton used to be hard to tell apart. I mean, I always could, but most strangers couldn't. Now, though, the difference is stark. I mean, he's bleached his hair (a classic gay cry for help); plus he's got circles under his eyes, and scraggly patches of facial hair on his chin and upper lip.

Aidan never could grow a beard, no matter how hard he tried.

But the worst part is how small he looks. Not shorter—he's a quarter inch taller than Ashton, which used to be a constant source of good-natured ribbing—but just small. Like there's less of him here.

And the part of me that used to love him wants to cry a little bit, because he doesn't really look like the Aidan that was my Aidan anymore.

From up front, Bobby calls out, "Wheels up!" and the bus lurches into motion.

"I'm going to bed."

From: Janet Lundgren (janet@kissandtellmusic.com)
To: Bill Holt (b.holt@thelabel.com)
Subject: Re: Plus one
4/8/22 10:08 P.M.

Aidan's arriving tonight. Jill was adamant that it was either this or she pulls Ashton out of the tour, which is obviously a nonstarter. Can't say I blame her, but it's still a shitshow in the making. Ashton is covering all costs for him.

Ashton also said he would take care of telling Hunter, thank god, but gird your loins just in case you need to bail someone out of jail later.

Best,
Janet
Sent from my iPhone

From: Bill Holt (b.holt@thelabel.com)
To: Janet Lundgren (janet@kissandtellmusic.com)
Subject: Re: Plus one
4/8/22 10:43 P.M.

Agreed it's a shitshow, but not much to be done. Probably best to have H and K do something extra cute for next date to show their relationship strong.

Footage transcription

047/03:29:15;00

ETHAN: So it's a little after one in the morning, and we are on our way to Dallas. We've got two dark days and then a show on Tuesday. We usually like to unwind a little after a show before we go to bed. You build up all this energy at a concert, kind of feeding off the crowd, but once it's done, it's like, you've got to cool off for a while. Usually we watch a movie or play video games or something.

ASHTON: No, no, mix first, then steam.

IAN: Got it.

AIDAN: Not the fish, fish stays fresh.

OWEN: I need more chopped meat.

ETHAN: As you can see, Hunter's gotten us all hooked on a new game. I call next round!

AIDAN: Doing dishes!

IAN: Where's the fire extinguisher again?

ETHAN: I'll probably be replacing Ian because he's terrible at it.

IAN: Hey!

ETHAN (British accent): Ah, and here we have a young gay man in his natural habitat: sitting awkwardly in an armchair, hunched over his notebook. Note the beady eyes, the flush cheeks, the cheerful freckles that belie the darkness inside.

HUNTER: This is an attack.

ETHAN (regular voice): What're you working on?

HUNTER: Nothing. Just some ideas I had.

(phone beeps)

ETHAN (British accent): Quiet! He's just heard the siren sound of a mating call. This specimen has been known to act surly when separated from his mate.

HUNTER: Shut up.

ETHAN (British accent): This species has been known to woo prospective partners with love songs.

HUNTER: Shut up! (gets up from couch and heads to bunks)

ETHAN: Aw, come on, I'm just kidding.

(shaky camera, footage questionable)

HUNTER: Ethan, Aidan's right out there, so can you, like, cool it? This is already weird enough.

ETHAN: My bad, dude. I was just teasing.

HUNTER: Whatever. It's fine.

Dm/Gm/Dm/Bb

Close a door to the world
But don't tell me you left it cracked
I always feel the eyes
Watching me
Waiting for me to fail
At these awful lyrics

What do I have to do
To make it so you
Will be happy with me
What do I have to say
To make it okay
For us to something something??

I don't know what's wrong with me
It's got to be something
Some reason I keep trying

Everything feels familiar
Nothing feels right
Falling into the same old patterns
Shit what rhymes with patterns?
SATURNS???

I DON'T KNOW

24

Our hotel in Dallas is pretty nice. After calling Mom and catching her up on the whole Aidan drama, I grab some room service and then head to the gym.

It's pretty empty: a few uptight-looking business people on the treadmills, a couple doing yoga, and an old guy with a towel around his neck wandering back and forth between the weight machines.

Ethan's there too, on one of the rowers, sweat trickling down his hairline. His form is impeccable. He was on the rowing team, back when we were in school.

No one looks at either of us as I take an elliptical machine next to him. That's probably the best thing about staying at fancy hotels: It's all boring adults who don't know or care who we are.

Ethan nods at me as I pop in my earbuds and pull up my

workout playlist. It's mostly rock, a little hip-hop, just stuff with good bass lines and steady beats.

I might've added a few of PAR-K's songs too, because they're fun and high-energy and I love Kaivan's drumming. It keeps me going as I use the elliptical, which I find tedious because I hate feeling like I'm not going anywhere. But I have to use them, because they're the easiest on my knee.

"What're you grinning about?" Ethan asks.

"Nothing."

"You've got it so bad."

"Leave me alone."

Ethan and I hit the free weights after. We're not supposed to do any heavy weight lifting, just light stuff, since The Label wants us toned but not bulky. Like, skinny enough to still be twinkish, but defined enough to look good if we wear tank tops.

Ethan does look good too: He's got those little veins running down his biceps. I've never been able to cultivate them.

"Sorry if I made it weird last night," Ethan says as I sit on the bench for shoulder presses. "I wasn't thinking."

"Not your fault," I say between reps. "Everything is weird."

Ethan takes the bench next to me. "I feel that. None of us have to share a bus with our exes."

"We'd need a whole extra bus for yours," I say, which makes Ethan chuckle. He's got more exes than all of us combined, though he never got the kind of scrutiny that me and Aidan dealt with.

"They were mostly flings," he admits. "Kelly was the last one that was real."

"Oh."

"Yeah." He sits up and glances back toward the doors to the gym, but we're all alone in the weight room. "She was my first."

"First . . . like, sex?"

"Yeah. I really liked her."

"Really?" I always figured he was already having sex when we were still in school, with all the girlfriends he had.

"Really." He gets this sad smile on his face. "Sometimes I wonder if things would've been different, if we weren't in the public eye. If we'd gotten to just be."

"What do you mean?"

"Dude . . . we both got constantly dragged. Really racist shit. And like, the insults were bad enough, but there was all the insidious stuff too, stuff that sounds fine but wasn't. Know what I mean?"

A blush creeps up my neck and cheeks, because if I'm being honest, I had no idea. I thought everyone just loved Ethan and Kelly.

"Me and Aidan got that too. Especially after we broke up. Aidan got a lot of grief."

"Dude, after the breakup was rough too. And way worse for Kelly. Still is. We text sometimes." He grunts as he lifts. "People scrutinizing every relationship she has. Every outfit she wears. It's vile, the stuff people say. You know some asshole started a website that's just a countdown until she turns eighteen?"

"Gross!" I've dealt with my share of creepers, but not a website.

"Yeah. She always said it was rough being a Black girl on the Internet but I didn't really get it until I saw some of the messages she got."

I don't know what to say to that. I get homophobic comments pretty much daily, but I know that's different.

"Sorry," I finally say.

He shrugs. "You're not the one doing it."

"Yeah, but like, does it still happen? To you, I mean? Comments and stuff?"

Ethan rests his weights on his chest and turns to look at me, his eyebrows scrunched up. "Dude. It's been nonstop since we started."

"Oh. Really?"

He sits up, pulls his phone out of his pocket, scrolls for a second, and passes it over to me.

"Shit," I mutter. It's filled with messages of people calling him racist names for being Vietnamese, insults about Vietnamese food. I'm pretty sure some of them aren't even insults for the right culture, but I don't want to find out.

"Dude." My neck is burning. "I'm sorry. I didn't realize. I'm sorry."

"It's whatever," he says, shrugging. "It's not like it's all bad. Most is good. But yeah. There's plenty of assholes."

"Yeah, but still." I wonder if it's really this bad for Ian and Owen too. If Kaivan gets shit like that.

Ethan picks up his weights again. "I'm used to it. I kind of knew what it would be like, going into all this."

"I didn't," I say. "I mean, I knew what it would be like, I just didn't think it would be this . . ."

Ethan studies me, dark eyes thoughtful. "Intense?"

"Yeah."

"I feel that." He leans back and gets ready to lift again. "Come on. You'll never get swole with all this talking."

"Hey, you're the one with chicken legs!"

"Better chicken legs than noodle arms!"

"Wow. Rude!" But I pick up my weights and keep lifting. "But. Well. Thanks, Ethan."

He huffs a breath and grins at me.

"No problem."

From: Ryan Silva (ryansilvamanager@gmail.com)
To: Bill Holt (b.holt@thelabel.com)
Subject: Re: "Memories" drop 4/15
4/11/22 12:15 P.M.

The boys are super excited for friday, specially kaivan. Can we reschedule his interview for am of 4/14? He has a date with hunter in pm. Otherwise promo timeline looks good.

Ryan

From: Bill Holt (b.holt@thelabel.com)
To: Ryan Silva (ryansilvamanager@gmail.com)
Cc: Cassie Thomas (c.thomas@thelabel.com)
Subject: Re: "Memories" drop 4/15
4/11/22 2:09 P.M.

We're excited here too. Good momentum for the boys. Copying Cassie in to make arrangements for interview.

-BH

From: Cassie Thomas (c.thomas@thelabel.com)
To: Bill Holt (b.holt@thelabel.com)
Subject: Re: "Memories" drop 4/15
4/11/22 3:14 P.M.

I'll get on that. Also, any idea why Hunter's messing with his styling? It's not bad but it's not cohesive for his brand. We should try to keep all elements focused in the run-up to Friday.

-Cassie

25

It rains Monday afternoon, a heavy fall that lashes the windows of Ashton's suite. Thunder rumbles in the distance, and I take a moment to just listen to it. We never get thunderstorms like this back home. I love the way it blankets the world. I could watch it forever.

The guys are all crowded on the couch, playing even more *Overcooked*. Last night, they unlocked a level where you can roast turkeys and potatoes with flame throwers.

Getting them addicted may have been a mistake.

"Potatoes! Potatoes!" Ashton shouts as his chef, a husky with chunky glasses, shoots a burst of flame at a conveyor belt filled with turkeys.

"Hey," Aidan says, voice soft and meek.

Aidan Nightingale has never been meek in his entire life.

"Oh. Hey." I glance at Aidan and then away, stare at downtown Dallas instead, because Aidan is still a hollowed-out shell of himself, and I can't stand it. I can't stand how sorry I am for him, when I should be furious.

I mean, I am angry. And hurt. And sad.

But I have all this—a tour, friends, Kaivan—and Aidan has nothing. How can I hate him when he's so pathetic?

"You got a second?"

The way he says it, you'd think he was asking for my kidney or something.

"Okay."

"Um." Aidan rubs his hands together. His fingernails are trashed, chewed to jagged nubs. I don't remember him doing that before. He used to have really nice hands.

And he still does. They're just a bit beaten up. I want to take them in mine, an old instinct that won't die, but I shove it away. We are not holding hands.

"Listen," he says.

I'm listening.

"I never got the chance to tell you to your face. Hunter. I'm sorry. For everything. I wanted you to hear me say it."

Cymbals crash in my chest. I want to check him against the windows. I want to cry.

I want to be mean to Aidan. I want to make him hurt the way he hurt me.

I want him to stop hurting. I want us both to stop.

I don't know what I want.

"What exactly falls under 'everything'?"

He brings his thumb up and chews on his nail. "Just . . . everything. The texts. The fights. Thinking you cheated on me."

"I didn't."

"I know. I know." He sighs. "And I'm not expecting you to forgive me or anything. Just, I'm sorry."

I look him in the eyes. They have this ring of darker blue around the edges. I used to love staring into them.

"Why'd you do it?" I whisper.

Aidan blinks and breaks my gaze, stares at the rain instead.

"I was drunk. And lonely. And I knew I'd fucked up, but I wanted it to be someone else's fault. Your fault. Anyone's."

"That's really fucked up, Aidan."

"I know." He looks up at me again, just a quick glance. "I don't know what else to say except I'm sorry."

I don't know what else to say either.

"Okay. Well. Thanks, I guess."

He nods. He looks so pathetic, hair flat and lifeless, shoulders rounded, hands trashed.

I want to tell him everything is okay, that I forgive him. I want him to stop being this weird, small version of Aidan and be like he used to be. Maybe then I wouldn't feel so guilty for being angry.

"Listen."

But before I can say anything, Owen shouts out, "Kaivan!"

I look back, and sure enough, Kaivan's at the door. Owen steps back to let him in.

I fight smiling as hard as I can, because the guys will never stop teasing me if I let them see how happy Kaivan makes me. But I'm failing, because Ethan takes one look at my blushing face and starts cackling.

I cross the room and take Kaivan's hand. "Hey," I say.

He glances back toward Aidan, who's watching us, but then turns to me and smiles. He kisses me on the nose, which gets another laugh out of Ethan.

"I didn't know Ashton had a whole suite." Kaivan studies the room: floor-to-ceiling windows, a lounge with a whole sectional and TV, a little kitchenette thing, sliding frosted glass doors that lead to the bedroom.

"Oh. Yeah. We usually get them."

"You've got one too?"

I nod. It's basically identical to Ashton's.

"Wow."

"Sorry," I mutter.

"It's cool." His gaze follows Aidan as he disappears into the bedroom he and Ashton are sharing. "What were you talking to him about?"

"He was trying to apologize."

"Wow."

"Yeah." I sigh. "I just . . . it's weird, seeing him again. And seeing how much he's changed. He looks so much . . . less."

"Yeah, but he did that to himself. You don't have to forgive him just because he's all sad now."

"I know." I take Kaivan's hands in mine. They're strong

and warm and definitely not trashed. His nails are smooth and shaped. "So. What brought you up? Came to show the guys how the game is really played?"

I nod toward the TV, where the whole kitchen has been engulfed in flames. Ethan and Ashton are shouting at each other, while Ian just shakes his head.

Kaivan snorts. "Nah. Just missed you is all."

I blush, drop his hands and wrap my arms around his waist instead. "I missed you too."

"You owe us more pizza if you make out in front of us!" Owen shouts from the couch.

I hide my face against Kaivan's chest. "Come on. Come play with us. At least for a little while."

"Okay."

The rain took all the humidity with it, so the air is crisp and slightly cool as we walk the docks at the Mandalay Canals. Who knew Dallas had canals in it?

"Technically, it's Irving," Kaivan says.

"I thought it was pronounced Ir-vine?"

He smirks. "That's in California."

"Oh."

He sticks his hand in my back jeans pocket and pulls me closer to him, plants a kiss on my cheek.

"What was that for?"

"Just you being funny."

I roll my eyes as we approach the gondola.

"This feels so extra." I study the boat: It looks like something out of Venice, complete with a tan-skinned gondolier in a straw boater, striped shirt, and red handkerchief. The gondola itself is black and low to the water, with an open top, just big enough for the two of us to sit facing each other. Some of the other gondolas—like the one the camera crew and Nick are getting into—are bigger, with covered tops and room for maybe six.

I bet this would be really romantic without the whole production.

I mean, it's still sappy and romantic, and I can't stop grinning.

Kaivan gets aboard first and holds out his hand for me.

"Cheers," I say as we settle in.

"I'm Sebastian," the gondolier says.

"Hunter," I say. "That's Kaivan."

He laughs. "I know who you are." He's got just a hint of a Mexican accent, a faint roll to his r's.

"Well, thanks for putting up with us."

"Are you kidding? This is the coolest thing that's ever happened to me."

He pushes us out with his oar, and I grab the sides of the gondola as we sway side to side.

"Have you been on a boat before?" Kaivan asks.

I shake my head. "It's weird."

He just laughs at me with his tongue between his teeth. He reaches for the sleeve of my shirt. "Hey. Is this new?"

"Oh. Yeah. Julian ordered them for me, and Nazeer picked them up." I'm in a soft green sweater and black jeans. Julian helped me find a couple other pieces too, ones that looked fun and more *me*.

"You're not going to get in trouble?"

I shrug. "I don't know. Maybe. But I'm tired of being so performative, you know? I was thinking about what you said, and some stuff that Masha said, and just, like, what I want to be doing, you know?"

Kaivan purses his lips.

"You look great, by the way." And he does: He's in a salmon-colored button-up that highlights the warmth of his brown skin, and light blue jeans that show off his calves. I want to wrap my hands around them.

"Thanks, baby." He leans in and kisses me, but I lean back. "What?"

"I think we need to have, like, a committee meeting on pet names."

"You sing *baby* in half your songs!"

"That's because it's gender-neutral and easy to rhyme!"

"Hm." He glances toward the camera boat, shifts closer to me. "So what would you suggest to the committee?"

"I don't know. I think Kaivan is pretty perfect just the way it is."

He blushes at that. "Come on."

"No, really. I like your name. It's beautiful. My name's just, like, a noun."

Kaivan snorts, but then he takes my hand and draws me closer, kisses me again, and I don't pull away this time.

Kaivan and I have kissed a lot at this point, but he surprises me with this kiss: It's aggressive, almost forceful.

"Ow," I mutter as he butts his chin into mine, and my teeth clack.

"Sorry," he says. I rub my jaw for a second, but then he pulls me close again. I put my hand against his chest.

"Hey," I laugh. "Give me a second." I don't understand why he's being so aggressive. He wasn't like this when we were squeezed onto the couch with the guys, exchanging quick pecks between levels.

Kaivan leans back, but keeps his fingers twined with mine. I take a breath and watch the buildings glide by us. Most of them are made of stone or brick, painted in bright colors to look vaguely European. Ivy hangs down from cobbled arches. The sunset paints everything golden.

For a second, I can imagine we really are in Italy. Just the two of us. Me and my boyfriend. I wish I could capture this moment, this feeling of a life that's almost normal.

When our first video started blowing up, Mom sat me down and told me that if we decided to follow through, start a real band, that I might never get to live a normal life. At the time I was fine with that.

Even before Kiss & Tell, I thought I was going to be in the NHL. I guess I never thought I was made for a normal life.

Now, all I want to do is make this gondola ride last forever.

Hold Kaivan's hand, and watch the way the light plays with the amber streaks in his brown eyes. Just for a few perfect minutes.

But then the camera boat passes us. Brett's got his camera on his shoulder, focused on us, while next to him, Rick has got his own camera focused on the crowd gathering on the sidewalks, taking pictures of us.

Kaivan pulls me in for another kiss, gentler this time, but still kind of weird. Usually when we kiss, it's a chord progression, a steady rhythm of tension and release.

But this time it's a guitar solo: not a soaring one like David Gilmour, but a forceful one, like a Norwegian death metal band. His tongue is all over mine. His fingers run through my hair. Usually I like it when he does that, but this time it feels . . . weird. Dissonant.

I break the kiss again. From the sidewalk, some of the gawkers are cheering and clapping, and Kaivan blushes and gives them a wave.

"Dude," I say, scooting back a bit. The gondola rocks. "Sorry," I say to Sebastian.

"No problem," he says. "It's harder to tip than you think."

I nod, turn back to Kaivan. "What's going on?"

"What do you mean?"

"You're acting weird."

"Weird how?"

"Like . . . I don't know. You don't usually do this much PDA."

"Do you not like it?"

"I mean, it's fine I guess, but . . ."

"But what?"

"But I just feel like maybe there's something going on."

"Nothing's going on," Kaivan says, but he purses his lips.

"Remember we said we were gonna be real with each other?"

He deflates a bit. "Yeah. You're right." He chews his lip for a second. "It was just weird, seeing you with Aidan."

"Oh." A stone drops into my stomach. "Kaivan, me and him are done. I promise."

"I know. It's just . . . I don't know . . ."

"Are you jealous?"

"A little. You have all this history with him, and I—"

I take Kaivan's hands. "But I have a future with you."

That makes him blush. He smiles at me, and I lean in and give him a real kiss.

But then he ruins it by saying, "Thanks, baby."

I groan and cover my blushing face. "Don't. I hate it."

"You love it," he says, but that just makes me blush harder.

There's that word again.

Kaivan scoots closer to me and pulls me in for a hug. This feels normal again. The way Kaivan likes to hold me, the way I like to be held. He plants a kiss in my hair, and I relax against him.

"You're right," I say into his chest. "I do."

ASHTON AND AIDAN NIGHTINGALE GET MOBBED BY FANS OVER A "TASTY QUESY"

NewzList Canada
Date: April 11, 2022

Ashton Nightingale and his brother Aidan surprised guests at Dallas taqueria TASTY TACO when they showed up for the restaurant's famous Tasty Quesy, a spinach and cheese dip the eatery touts as "the reason God invented tortilla chips."

After sampling the Tasty Quesy, the brothers sipped Jarritos and enjoyed tacos (both puffy and authentic) before taking time to sign autographs and take photos with their fans, including Tasty Taco owner Mike Ponack. "My daughter is obsessed with Kiss & Tell," he said of the surprise guests. "I couldn't believe it when one of our servers told me who it was. You think with rock stars and the like, they'll be rude or demanding, but these boys came in and ordered like everyone else, said please and thank you, didn't make a fuss or anything. I guess it's true what they say about Canadians being more polite. Ashton even signed an autograph for my daughter! I'm pretty sure I won Dad of the Year."

Aidan Nightingale has been out of the public

eye since splitting with Hunter Drake—and leaking their intimate messages in a since-deleted post. So far there's no word on why he's suddenly traveling with the band, or whether this means he and Hunter (who, when last we checked, was dating PAR-K drummer Kaivan Parvani) have reconciled.

Kiss & Tell play at Dallas's American Airlines Center tomorrow night as part of their *Come Say Hello* tour.

Ashton Nightingale Answers Fan Questions While Wrangling Kittens

Hunter Drake and Kaivan Parvani Spotted on Romantic Gondola Ride—in Texas!

26

"**S**orry it's a mess." It looks like five suitcases have exploded all over the floor of Kaivan's hotel room.

"It's cool." I shiver, even though Kaivan's room isn't cold.

My skin's still humming with nervous energy, an amp on the cusp of overdrive. After our gondola ride, we spent nearly an hour taking photos, signing autographs. I posed for photos pretty sporadically, because if you pose for everyone, you can get trapped, but Kaivan said yes to every request.

I don't blame him, with a new song coming out Friday. Fans make the band. Me and the guys have been really lucky on that front, and I want that for Kaivan too.

But it was a shitty way to end our date. I think Kaivan thought so too, since he invited me up to his room.

"I'm getting my laundry done before we hit the road tomorrow," he says, gathering up armfuls of clothing and shoving them into the closet. A pair of lime-green trunks with black accents spills out of his arms, and I catch them for him. They're silky and cool to the touch, from one of those gay lifestyle brands that's always sending me DMs trying to partner for "paid content."

I mean, they are nice. I wonder what Kaivan looks like in them.

I wonder what he's wearing right now.

I swallow.

"Ah," Kaivan says, a blush creeping up his cheeks. He takes the underwear and tosses it on top of the pile. "Sorry. I'm trying something new."

"Don't be. They're really cute."

Kaivan pulls off his button-up and adds it to the pile, then tries to slide the closet door shut. It catches on a sock, but he finally manages.

Now it's my turn to blush, since Kaivan's shirtless.

"What?" he asks, grinning. "You've seen me before."

"I know." But I blush harder. Kaivan's jeans are hanging low on his hips, showing the red waistband of his underwear. Also not boxers.

"I'll put something on." He turns back toward the closet, but I grab his hand.

"It's cool."

He bites his lip for a second.

A clap of thunder startles us both. Kaivan squeezes my hand harder.

274

"Shit!" I go to the window, pull back the sheers. It's dark out, but rain has started dotting the glass, obscuring the lights of the city. "Glad we missed this."

"Yeah." Kaivan steps up behind me.

I shiver again. His skin radiates warmth against my back.

He hugs me from behind. "You cold?"

I shake my head. "Nah, I'm good."

I like the way it feels, his chest rising and falling against me as he breathes. Cozy, steady, safe.

"I love thunderstorms," he murmurs. "They remind me of home."

"Yeah?"

"Yeah."

I start to sway a bit, and Kaivan syncs with me. I hum a little, just nonsense, and Kaivan chuckles.

I turn my head and kiss him. His lips are warm, and so is his mouth when he parts his lips and lets my tongue in. I've got a flutter behind my sternum.

I draw little circles around Kaivan's tongue with mine, twist around so I'm facing him, but I accidentally step on his foot, and he staggers back, still holding me. He breaks the kiss and laughs.

"Smooth."

"Excuse me, I was getting a crick in my neck!"

He laughs harder, jumps onto the bed with his arms splayed, bounces twice before he settles and reaches for my hand again. I let him pull me onto his bed. It's been turned down, and there's a chocolate on the pillow—or there was, until it got bounced off when Kaivan jumped onto the bed.

"Better?" he asks as I settle on top of him.

"Yeah." I kiss him again, lips, jaw, ear, that little tender spot right behind. I rest my hand against his chest, feel the texture as he breaks into goose bumps. His breath hitches when I brush my thumb across the nub of his nipple, which surprises me, because I always figured that was something pornos made up. My own nipples don't really do anything, but sure enough, when I touch Kaivan's other one, he does that same sharp inhale.

"Feel good?" I ask.

"Yeah."

I like making Kaivan feel good. I like the little hiccup noises he's making. I start kissing his chest, then plant my mouth over his right nipple and suck on it. He's got a little ring of hairs there. I pull one out of my mouth and keep kissing, then do the left one.

"Hunter." He runs his hand through my hair, sending a glissando of desire up my spine.

I kiss lower, down the valley of his stomach, to his waist.

He's hard in his jeans. I wonder how he compares to Aidan. I wonder if he'd let me go down on him.

Aidan always said I gave amazing head. (Not that he had any basis for comparison.)

Aidan said I was a slut too.

That glissando turns into a wave of ice. My throat clamps

shut, which is less than ideal if you're thinking of giving someone a blowjob.

So I kiss the divot of his belly button, and then all the way up his chest, teasing each nipple before I end up back at his jawline.

He lets out this sweet laugh, uses a gentle hand to make me stop.

"Hunter?"

"Yeah?"

"What . . ." His pupils are dilated. His nostrils flare. "What was that?"

"What was what?"

"I thought maybe . . . I mean, I kind of wanted you to keep going."

I wanted to keep going too. I don't know what's wrong with me.

"Hey." He sits up, his thigh brushing my own boner where it's trapped against my hip.

I shake my head. "I just got in my own head."

"About what?"

"Just . . . I need to take it slow is all." My throat's still not working right. I swallow again. "Aidan's the only person I've ever been with. And he told the whole world about it. And that hurt, a lot. And I don't know if I'm ready to be vulnerable like that again. Yet."

"Oh, Hunter." He rests his hand against my face. "I'm sorry. That's messed up."

"I know."

"And now you're stuck with him again. Fucker."

"Yeah. It's messed up."

Kaivan sits all the way up, and I get off his lap. Without his body heat against me I shiver again.

I adjust myself so I don't snap my dick in half as I start to get off the bed. "Maybe I should go."

"You don't have to," he says. "We can just cuddle."

"You sure?"

"Yeah. It's a big bed. Maybe not as big as the suite ones, but . . ."

I don't know why he's so worried about the bed. "It's perfect."

I lie back down, and Kaivan pulls me close until our sides are pressed together, and I rest my head on his shoulder.

His hand traces little circles over my arm, my shoulder, rests in my hair.

"This okay, or you wanna spoon?"

"Maybe when we don't have boners anymore."

He snorts, kisses my temple. "Okay."

I close my eyes and let my breath sync up with Kaivan's, our hearts beating a steady counterpoint.

I love the way he makes me feel.

There's that word again.

But I do.

WHERE ARE THE SEX-POSITIVE BOY BANDS?

Mode.com
by Evan Molle
April 10, 2022

We see it every generation: Attractive young men and women taking the stage, clad in tight jeans and black shirts, giving voice to our collective desire. Gyrating hips and exposed skin promise sex, drugs, and rock and roll.

Music and sexuality have always intertwined. From the Rolling Stones' notorious *Sticky Fingers* album artwork to David Bowie's sexually fluid career, from Grace Slick wanting "Somebody to Love" to Britney Spears asking "If U Seek Amy," popular music has always offered a framework for contextualizing human desire.

But no musical archetype has so carefully and callously embraced the notion of virginal naïveté as the modern boy band. They exist in eternal paradox: available and yet forbidden, boyishly innocent but with mischief in their eyes. Innuendo is king, but respectability is queen, and so the boy band machine keeps cranking out plastic people with all the sex positivity of a Ken doll.

That is, until Hunter Drake, of Canadian sensation

Kiss & Tell, made headlines recently for a series of texts leaked by his ex-boyfriend. The texts pull back the veil on Drake's seemingly chaste relationship, revealing that not only had he been sexually active for over a year—he was a proud bottom. (Drake has never commented on tabloid reports that he was involved in sexual activity outside the relationship.)

It was a watershed moment, one that could have opened honest conversations about sex positivity, safe practices, consent, and even bottom-shaming. But aside from a vague apology posted across his social media, Drake has otherwise refused to comment on the matter, even as he embarked on a new relationship with Kaivan Parvani, another seemingly virginal boy bander, their chaste dates splashed across social media.

It's a shame, or perhaps a betrayal: Instead of using his unique platform to educate his millions of fans, Drake continues to hide behind shame and taboo. He could be using his own experiences to highlight the urgent need for sex positivity; instead, he perpetuates the veneer of propriety and larval sexuality that the boy band industry has always embraced.

Young people deserve better.

27

Kaivan's not in bed when I wake up, and I miss the weight of his arm holding me, the warmth of his body against mine as we cuddled. And we did just cuddle, as much as part of me wanted to do more. As much as he seems to want more.

I do want to have sex with Kaivan. I don't know why I'm so hesitant. I always loved it when Aidan and I did it. Even if it was bad or awkward or messy, it made me feel close to him. It made me feel beautiful. It made me feel wanted.

And it made me feel vulnerable. I'm just not ready to be that vulnerable again.

"Morning," Kaivan says from the washroom, where he's doing his hair. "Sorry. I didn't mean to wake you. We've got a photo shoot in an hour."

"Nah, it's cool." I stretch, arch my back, and roll out of bed. My shirt and jeans are rumpled, my hair looks like I've been in a hurricane. Kaivan grins at me as I wrap him in a hug from behind and meet his eyes in the mirror. "Thank you. For everything."

"I didn't do anything."

"You listened. And . . . just because I need to take things slow now, it doesn't mean it's going to be like that forever. Okay?"

Kaivan wiggles his eyebrows. "Sounds good, baby."

"Ugh." I push away from him. "You're impossible." I step back in and kiss him on the cheek. "Have a good day, okay? Have fun at the shoot."

"I will."

I'm just getting dressed after my shower when Ashton knocks on my door, his skate bag over his shoulder.

Thank god I came back to my room. I'm not sure I'm ready for anyone to know I spent the night with Kaivan.

"Hey, Hunt," he says. "We found a rink. Want to come with?"

"Who's we?"

He flattens his lips for a second before he admits, "Me and Aidan."

On the one hand, ice time always sounds good. I'd go every day if I could, and if my knee would hold up.

On the other hand, I'm not keen on being stuck on the ice with Aidan. Or in a car for that matter.

Ashton steps all the way inside and closes the door behind him.

"I don't think that's a good idea," I finally say.

"Come on, Hunt. We never get to hang out anymore."

"We just hung out yesterday!"

"But that was all the guys, not just you and me. You're my best friend. I miss you."

"I miss you too," I say, and collapse on the couch. It's bright blue and angular and probably the most uncomfortable piece of furniture I've ever sat on. Ashton sits next to me, rests his elbows on his knees. "I know I've been busy lately, but I really like Kaivan. Like, a lot."

"I get that, Hunt. And I get that The Label is putting pressure on you too. But would it hurt to take some time and hang out with me?"

"Not just you, though."

"He's my brother, Hunt."

"I know. But what am I supposed to do? He hurt me. I don't know how to tell you how much what he did hurt. How shitty it was."

"But you never even tried."

"You said it. He's your brother. How could I?"

"He's my brother, but you're my best friend." He runs a hand through his hair. It's messy, but he still manages to make it look good. "You gotta trust me to tell you when it's too much, okay, Hunt? I can be Aidan's brother and be your friend too. And I can do them both separately, if that's what it takes. But I hate seeing you both hurting."

I run a hand through my own wet hair. I hate that Aidan's

miserable. I hate seeing Ashton torn in two. I hate that I feel guilty.

"Fine," I say. "I'll try. But if it's a disaster, this is it. Don't ask me again. Okay?"

Ashton's smile hits me like a spotlight. "Really?"

"Yeah. Wait. The doc crew's not coming, right?"

I'm definitely not *skating more gay* in front of Ashton and Aidan.

"Just us. Unless you want to invite Kaivan too?"

"He's busy with promo. Their new single is dropping Friday."

"Ah." Ashton stands, offers a hand to pull me up, then gives me half a hug. "This means a lot to me, Hunt. Thanks."

Aidan's waiting with Nazeer at the elevators when I join them, dressed in sweats with my tuque pulled low and my skate bag over my shoulder.

Aidan doesn't have a bag. He's staring out the window by the elevator, biting his nails again.

I clear my throat. "No skates?"

"Left them at home."

Aidan without his skate bag strikes me as deeply wrong.

Nazeer takes us down one of the service elevators to the hotel's loading dock. We've been in lots of hotel loading docks, and there's this heinous smell that haunts every single one: a combination of trash and cleaning chemicals and rancid food that clings to the back of my tongue, even when I breathe through my nose.

I take shotgun, while Aidan and Ashton pile in behind us. It's a quiet, awkward ride, so finally, Nazeer turns on the radio—and it's playing one of our songs. "Your Room," which I wrote about Aidan, back when things were still good.

I look at you now
I see how you've changed
Through all the years

See how you've grown
See how you've shared
Your heart with me

I've never said it before
Been afraid to hope
For the moment you
Meet my eyes and ask me up

To your room
Your room
We can shut the whole world out
And let the sunlight in

To your room

Your room
We can be ourselves
Set down our fears
In your room

I can't believe it's this fucking song. I close my eyes and try to stop my face from turning red. Because the boy is different, but I'm still that same Hunter, unwound because the boy I like invited me up to his room, held me and kissed me and made me feel so loved.

I just hope things turn out better this time. They have to.

I grab the knob and change channels. "Okay?" I ask Nazeer.

He just shrugs and keeps his eyes on the road.

I glance back. Ashton's bobbing his head and drumming his fingers on his knees, and Aidan's staring out the window, but he catches me looking and meets my eyes for a second.

He has this weird, sad smile.

"It wasn't all bad, was it?" he asks, his voice low. "It was good. Sometimes. Wasn't it?"

I want to punch him.

I want to hug him.

I don't know what I want.

"No," I finally say. "It wasn't all bad."

It turns out Nazeer called ahead and booked private ice time for us, because no one else is at the rink except for two people at the front desk, and there's a CLOSED FOR PRIVATE PRACTICE sign on the doors.

Aidan heads to the rental counter, manned by a friendly-looking bald man with glasses. I hang back with Ashton.

"I can't believe he didn't bring his own skates," I say, scrunching up my nose.

"I can't believe he agreed to come today. It was like pulling teeth, convincing him. But I needed this." Ashton elbows me. "I think maybe you did too."

"We'll see."

For someone who had to be dragged along, Aidan comes to life once his blades hit the ice. He takes off, no warm-up, and Ashton gives chase, both of them going faster than I can manage anymore. I take it slower, warming up my knee, watching them shout and try to show each other up. I laugh as Aidan pretends to lose control and slams into the wall, splaying his arms out like a bug that struck a windshield.

He's right: It wasn't all bad.

Some of it was actually really good.

Eventually, Ashton and Aidan slow down and start skating next to me. Or rather, Ashton skates next to me, and Aidan skates a little behind.

Ashton's cheeks are flushed, his eyes sparkling with joy. Sometimes I think he misses this even more than I do. And he was good at it. I wish he never gave it up.

But then, if he didn't, we wouldn't get to be in a band together.

"Whew," Ashton says. "I've gotta pee. Be right back."

He takes off toward the gate, leaving me and Aidan alone.

It's quiet for a moment, only the sounds of our blades on the ice, and then:

"Well, that was subtle."

I laugh. "He never was good at that."

I drop back a bit so I can actually see Aidan as we skate, but I keep my distance. The air in the rink is brisk but somehow close, a blanket pressed over my face.

My skin prickles.

"I'm glad Ashton made me come," Aidan says. "I haven't been on the ice in a while. I guess you probably heard about me? And the team?"

"Yeah."

"Not my finest moment."

"I can think of worse." I say it before I can stop myself.

"Yeah." Aidan's cheeks are flushed. He stops abruptly, and instinct makes me stop too. "I know you're tired of hearing it, but I really am sorry, Hunter. For sharing the texts. And for the stuff I said. I don't think you're a slut. I mean, I liked it too."

"Then why did you say it?"

Aidan purses his lips and blows out a breath. "Aside from being drunk, you mean?"

I nod.

"I think . . . everyone was mad at me. Everyone was saying

288

I broke your heart. That I did something wrong. I just didn't want to be the only wrong one."

"But if everyone was giving you grief, why not just ghost? People would've moved on."

"Because that was all I had left. You don't get what it's like. You and Ashton, you both got super famous, but I was just . . . all I had going for me was being your boyfriend. Once that was gone, it was like . . . you both left me behind."

Aidan always had more going for him than that. I loved who he was: passionate, competitive, a killer hockey player, thoughtful and so tender when I was recovering from my surgery. I loved the real Aidan, the one the public didn't get to see.

I wish I could've made him see it.

"So then why didn't you join us?" I stuff my hands in my pockets. "If you felt that way. Why didn't you want to be in the band?"

"I'm not talented like you guys. All I know how to do is play hockey."

"You could've come along anyway. If you really wanted to."

"And spend weeks, months, watching fans scream at you and Ashton while I, what? Hid backstage with Mom while she compared me to Ashton every other breath?"

He's got a point: Jill's always favored Ashton for some reason.

"Anyway." He swizzles away from me and then right back.

I wish he'd told me all this back when we were dating. Back

when it could've made a difference. Instead of punishing me for . . . what? Being successful?

"Just. God. I know I keep saying it, but. I'm sorry. Truly. I hope you can believe me, even if you don't forgive me."

I've known Aidan Nightingale for more than half my life. (I did the math on that. We passed the halfway mark last fall.)

And it would be so easy to hate him, if he wasn't wound into every memory I have, the good ones and the bad ones. If he hadn't flanked me, Ashton on my other side, as I cried at Dad's funeral. Hadn't celebrated birthdays with me. Hadn't shared inside jokes. Wins and losses.

Hadn't been my first everything.

"I believe you, Aidan," I say. Because I do. "I don't know if I'm ready to forgive you, though."

He takes a deep breath and nods. "That's fair." He gives me a sad smile, right as Ashton hits the ice again.

"Race you, Aidan!" he calls out.

"You're on!"

"MEMORIES": PAR-K'S NEW SINGLE IS A BOLD DEPARTURE

Gramophone Magazine
April 13, 2022

PAR-K—the Ohio-based Iranian-American band—is back, this time with a catchy single. After an attention-grabbing debut LP last year, "Memories" demonstrates an exciting evolution of their exotic, Middle East–infused sound.

Making use of syncopated drumbeats, a Persian-inspired chord progression, and wistful lyrics drawing from poets like Rumi and Hafez, the song might feel like a departure from PAR-K's usual saffron-flavored bubblegum pop; but the vocals, delivered deftly enough by the three Parvani brothers, with drummer (and songwriter) Kaivan taking the lead, manage to keep it firmly in PAR-K's tweenage wheelhouse.

VERDICT: A delightful and unexpected single, delivering poppy fun with diverse elements.

THE BATTLE FOR HUNTER'S HEART

Rainbow News Now—News That Slays
April 15, 2022

Is Hunter Drake giving Aidan Nightingale another chance?

The former couple were spotted leaving private ice time at a Dallas rink on Tuesday, and laughing over smoked meat platters at a Kansas City barbecue joint on Thursday.

The pair previously split in February; in late March, Aidan leaked a number of embarrassing private messages from the time he and Hunter were dating. The two had not been seen together until Aidan began traveling with Kiss & Tell during their tour.

Meanwhile, Hunter has been linked to Kaivan Parvani for at least the last three weeks. The pair have been seen on a number of public outings, including most recently at a butterfly garden in Houston and a romantic gondola ride in the Dallas area, but the couple hasn't been spotted together publicly since Monday.

Did Hunter split with Kaivan? Is reconciliation on the horizon?

So far, both Kiss & Tell and PAR-K's management have refused to comment.

Interested in being an affiliate?
Click here to find out how.

28

Happy single drop!!

Kaivan doesn't answer, but I don't blame him. Release days are always hectic.

It's hard to buy gifts on the road, unless you've got a dark day, but the musicians' dressing room always has way more alcohol than they can actually consume.

I don't know if Kaivan drinks, but without any better options, I snag one of the little half bottles of champagne that the musicians won't miss, and make a little card out of a page ripped from my notebook.

It looks childish. I'm not good at drawing, or even just nice handwriting, but hopefully the bubbles will make up for it.

I knock on the PAR-K bus, and Kamran answers. He's taller than his brothers, and even though he's only nineteen, he's managed to grow a mustache.

"Hey. Looking for Kaivan?"

"Yeah."

Kamran scratches his bare chest, which has a patch of hair in the same spot as Kaivan's. I guess none of the Parvani brothers have to manscape the way me and the guys do.

"He had another interview this morning. Probably in his dressing room now."

"Cheers. And congrats on the single."

"Thanks, man."

I find may way through the backstage halls of the Xcel Energy Center, peek in on the stage. Our lighting crew is testing all the lights one by one, swiveling them around and pointing them all over the arena, which still has a bunch of signage for the Minnesota Wild all over.

For a second, I imagine what it would've been like to come here and play them. Or even play for them, though I always hoped that if I got drafted, it would be for a Canadian team.

But I'm still here. And it's fucking amazing.

I find Kaivan's dressing room, give his door a couple sharp knocks.

"Happy release day!" I say as soon as he opens it.

"Thank you." He smiles, but he's got dark circles under his eyes. "Sorry I didn't answer earlier."

"No worries." He stands back to let me in. "I got you something. And by *got*, I mean liberated from the musicians' dressing room."

I hand over the half bottle of booze, along with the little card. It's got two kissing stick figures on it, one of them with my best attempt at a stick-hockey-butt.

Kaivan snorts. "Oh my god."

"I know. I could totally go into art if this whole singing thing doesn't work out."

"Thank you." He kisses me on the cheeks. "I don't drink, though."

I blush. "Ah. Sorry."

"Don't be. It was sweet."

He sets the bottle and card down, flops onto his couch, this lumpy monstrosity with heinous green upholstery.

Dressing room couches are really hit-and-miss sometimes.

Kaivan runs both hands over his face and rubs his eyes. I sit down next to him, squeeze his leg. "You tired?"

He nods.

"Was it what you hoped, at least?"

"I guess." Kaivan leans his head back and closes his eyes. "Sorry. I'm kind of in a weird headspace today."

I take his hand and kiss his palm. "You want to talk about it?"

He pulls away. "It's nothing."

This little note of anxiety chimes through my chest. My skin prickles.

"Did I do something?"

He growls and runs his hands through his hair. "You didn't do anything." But he won't look at me.

My mouth goes dry. "What?"

He sighs. "You see the latest gossip?"

"No. Which?"

He hands me his phone, shows me the article.

"'The Battle for Hunter's Heart'?" I skim it. "Just the usual bullshit."

"Yeah, but it's trending. That's all they wanted to talk about at my interview this morning. You."

"I'm sorry. They do that sometimes."

Kaivan grunts and stands. He scratches at the back of his neck. "Yeah, but this was supposed to be my day. Our day, me and my brothers. I worked so hard on it, and all anyone wants to talk about is whether you've dumped me."

"I wouldn't do that," I say. More notes join the anxiety in my chest, dread and worry combining into a minor chord. "Nothing is going on with Aidan. You said you trusted me."

"That's not the point!" he shouts. "I don't know what is. It just sucks is all."

"I know." I get up and try to wrap my arms around him, but he steps away. "Kaivan?"

"Sorry," he says. "I just need a minute. I need some space."

I clamp my throat shut until I'm sure I'm not going to let out any of the sadness inside me.

"Okay. I'll give you some, then." I sniff and blink. "Let me know if you want to talk, I guess."

I close the door behind me, take a deep breath. I'm not going to cry about this. Kaivan isn't even mad at me, he's just mad at the business. He's going to get over it.

It's not about me.

LH: It's been quite a year for PAR-K, hasn't it? A surprise hit LP, a great new single, not to mention you're opening for Kiss & Tell! And you're even dating one of the members!

KP: Yeah, it's been wild. I don't think any of us expected the kind of reception for our album that we ended up getting. I mean, we're just three guys from Ohio. But we're all really proud of what we've accomplished, and we hope people really like "Memories."

LH: Speaking of memories, you've been making plenty with Hunter Drake lately, haven't you?

KP: Yeah, definitely. He's a great guy, talented and brave. But—

LH: Do you ever get jealous?

KP: Jealous?

LH: Of the reports about him and Aidan. They've been spotted together a lot lately.

KP: Oh, no. It's hard to avoid each other when you're on tour, you know? And Aidan's been traveling with his brother, so it is what it is. But no, we're good. Actually—

LH: Have you ever felt like a rebound, with Hunter coming off such a high-profile relationship before you?

KP: No. I felt like we had a genuine connection.

LH: Hunter wrote quite a few songs about his ex. Is he working on new songs about you?

KP: Hah, I can't really say. But you know, it's funny, I wrote "Memories" before I even met Hunter, but now, it's like it fits so perfectly.

LH: It must be fate! What's next for you two?

KP: Uh, I mean, we're both touring for a while yet.

LH: Any more romantic gondola rides planned?

KP: Hah, we try to take things as they come.

LH: Well, we can't wait to see what you have in store for us!

29

I keep it together as best I can.

After sound check, Ashton asks me if I'm okay. I tell him I'm just tired.

At intermission, Ethan wraps an arm around my neck. "Your throat okay? Need some honey-ginger-lemon?"

"Yeah. Thanks."

Before the meet and greet, Ian pats me on my shoulder. "Good show," he says. "You feeling all right?"

I hate it when people ask me if I'm okay. It's like they're poking at the cracks in my walls. If they'd just leave me alone, I'd be fine.

I catch Kaivan's eye as we're boarding our buses. He gives a little nod and half a smile before he turns and boards. That's it.

While the guys crowd in the lounge to play more *Over-cooked* (seriously, I think it might be an addiction), I hide in the studio.

Owen's made another two demos with fucking Gregg. They sound good, but not as good as "Over & Out." I promised I'd give him some notes and ideas. Gregg's not that bad, he seems really keen to collaborate and make sure he's helping us execute our vision and not his, but he's still an outsider.

I listen, over and over, notebook in hand, but nothing.

I'm useless.

And I still haven't written anything of my own to share.

"Fuck," I groan, and pull my headphones off. I stare at the computer screen, all my markers and changes. I highlight everything and hit delete.

"Hunter?" Aidan's at the door. "You working?"

"No." I close the session without saving. "Just messing around."

He leans against the door frame. "What's going on with you?"

"Nothing."

Aidan gets this funny smile. "Liar. You're doing that thing with your jaw."

I bring my hand to my jaw and massage it. I have been clenching my teeth. "Have not."

"I get it," he says. "I didn't mean to make you uncomfortable."

"You didn't. You just know me too well is all."

He laughs. "Yeah, well. You know me too."

"Yeah." I sigh. "Yeah, I do. We've been through a lot, huh?"

"That's an understatement."

The bus hits a pothole, and Aidan staggers to the stool next to me.

"Look. I know you don't want to be friends with me. But, I mean, we've known each other forever. I can listen, if you want to talk."

"It's . . ." I don't even know if I want to be friends with Aidan or not.

But Aidan went through the same kind of stuff that Kaivan did. Maybe he knows how I can make it better.

"I think Kaivan and I had a fight. Or at least, he was upset. I mean, I don't blame him, I get why he was upset and all. You know?"

Aidan's eyes widen. "Uh, no. Can you tell me what actually happened?"

"Just, he had a new single drop today, but I guess he was doing an interview and all the interviewer wanted to know was about me, and about you and me, and about Kaivan and me, and he just felt kind of . . . eclipsed?"

"I get that."

"Yeah. I guess that happened to you too?"

He nods. "Yeah. It sucked, being in your shadow."

"I didn't want you to be."

"I know, Hunt. I don't blame you for being talented. But it was rough, sometimes, always feeling left behind. Always feeling like I had to remind people I existed."

"And you think Kaivan's feeling like he doesn't exist?"

Aidan puffs up his cheeks and upper lip and slowly sighs. "I think he cares a lot about his career. And he's having to figure some stuff out."

"Like what?"

Aidan's lips twist back and forth. "How much did you know about him, before you started seeing him?"

"Not much, I guess. I knew some of PAR-K's songs. But I didn't even know he was queer until he told me."

Aidan's tongue darts out to worry at a chapped spot on his lower lip. He won't meet my eyes.

"What?"

"Just, some of the interviews and stuff he did. Some of the stuff he said about you guys."

"Stuff like what?"

"I shouldn't have said anything," he says, sitting up straighter. "I don't want to get in between you guys."

"Aidan." I rest my hand on his knee to stop him standing. "What stuff?"

"Hunter . . ."

I let go of him and turn to the computer. "Show me."

He bites his lip for a second. I scoot aside for him and gesture to the keyboard.

He sighs and starts pulling up sites for me, articles and interviews from last year. It doesn't take much skimming for a pattern to emerge.

My eyes start burning as I read, but Aidan's seen me cry before, so I don't even bother wiping the tears away.

Kaivan thinks we suck.

He thinks we're safe and vapid.

Fuck.

All those things he said to me—being surprised I could play guitar, or thinking dancers can't sing—they weren't just jokes. He really thinks all that.

He thinks I'm talentless.

I rub my knee. I feel like I've been checked against the boards again.

"Wow," I finally say.

"I'm sorry, Hunt."

"It's fine." I use my shoulder to wipe my eyes and nose. I want to curl into a ball.

He said he liked me. But how can that be true, if this is what he thinks of me, of my friends, of the music we make?

I feel so fucking used.

Aidan rests a hand on my shoulder as I cry. "It's okay," he says, and pulls me into a hug.

Aidan was always a really good hugger. I miss that more than anything, I think.

I relax and let him hug me, cry onto his shoulder, but then

he leans back and looks at me. He's got this look in his eyes, one I've seen before, as he starts leaning into me.

"What are you doing?"

Aidan blanches and leans away. "I don't know. I'm sorry."

"We're not . . . I'm not going to kiss you."

"I know. I know."

"Shit." I stand, hug myself, retreat to the corner of the studio. "Did you show me all that stuff just because you thought I'd be easier to hook up with if I was a mess? Is that what all this is?"

"No. I promise." Aidan gets up too, runs a hand through his hair, pulls on the back of it. "I'm just a fuck-up. I'm sorry. I don't know." He's crying now too. "I'm a mess, Hunt. I'm a disaster. And you're the only thing that still feels right. Or at least familiar."

"I can't fix you, Aidan," I say. "Only you can do that."

"I know. I'm sorry. I'm sorry." Aidan's eyes dart around the studio, like he's trapped, like he's utterly lost. "I just, shit, I should go. I'm sorry, Hunt. Really. I'm sorry."

He does, closing the door behind him.

And then I'm alone again.

INTERVIEW WITH KAIVAN PARVANI

Ohio State Radio
November 7, 2021

HOST: And we are back, and we are live with Kaivan Parvani of hometown band PAR-K, whose first album made a big splash on the charts this summer. Kaivan, welcome to the show.

KAIVAN PARVANI: Thanks for having me. I can't believe I'm on. I always listen to your show.

HOST: Flattery will get you everywhere, my man. So tell me, what's it been like, seeing your first album take off like this?

KAIVAN PARVANI: It's pretty amazing, not gonna lie. Some days it doesn't feel real.

HOST: Now, you're only seventeen, are you still in school?

KAIVAN PARVANI: I've had to switch to home-schooling, and working toward my GED, but I was up until recently.

HOST: What did your classmates think of all this?

KAIVAN PARVANI: To be honest, I don't think anyone noticed, not until we did *America's Best Band*. After that, though, people thought we were pretty cool. For the most part.

HOST: Only for the most part?

KAIVAN PARVANI: Well, not everyone at school likes Iranians, no matter what we do.

HOST: But you never thought about toning all that down?

KAIVAN PARVANI: Not really. We wanted to be authentic, you know? We're proud of our heritage. Iran has a rich musical history and some of the world's best poetry, going back hundreds or even thousands of years. So we wanted to honor that.

HOST: Well, I think you've done that. So what's next? Working on another album?

KAIVAN PARVANI: We are, we're taking our time with it. We're still kind of figuring this all out, what we want our sound to be, how we want to grow. We don't want to be a flash in the pan, popcorn-music-type band, like some of these boy bands out there whose only "talent" is being white and conventionally attractive.

HOST: Wow, sounds like you've got some strong feelings about the whole boy band thing. Doesn't PAR-K count as one, though?

KAIVAN PARVANI: No. We're three guys, but, you know, we're making music with depth. We play our own instruments, write our own songs. We want people to remember our music in five years, which means getting at deep truths about life, not just appealing to the lowest common denominator.

HOST: Well, I can't wait to see what you pull off next. Coming up, off their debut album, it's PAR-K's "Knocking from the Inside."

30

I don't sleep. I just stare at the bottom of Ian's bunk and replay every interaction Kaivan and I have ever had, trying to figure out how I got everything so wrong. Was he using me? Was he just going along with things because that's what The Label wanted?

I guess I did that too. But I thought he meant it when he said it was real. That we were real.

My anger is cold and brassy, a tuba resting against my diaphragm. And the worst thing is, I can't figure out if I'm madder at him or myself.

It's raining when we pull up to the hotel in Chicago, the sort of gray morning haze that makes me miss home. I wish I was home. I wish I was pulling up to our condo, and Mom was there with some cinnamon buns she picked up from that little bakery on Dunbar.

But instead I just lug my suitcase and Hummingbird to my suite overlooking Lake Michigan, which goes on forever and ever before vanishing into gray. It's almost peaceful. But kind of scary too.

I'd give anything to disappear right now. Not be Hunter Drake for a day, for an hour.

But I can't. I've got a show tonight.

Always another show.

There's a single sharp rap on the door. My stomach knots up.

I roll out of bed. I still haven't slept any, but I made it to that weird half-asleep place. It's nearly noon.

I pad through the suite and open the door.

It's Kaivan. Of course. He holds up a brown paper bag, and the smell of fried dough makes my stomach growl.

"Hey," he says. "Sorry, I know it's early. Can I come in?"

I let him in. I don't know why.

"I brought doughnuts." He sits on the couch and pulls out the little paper tray. There's four doughnuts, one glazed, one chocolate, one pink-frosted, and one that's either jelly- or lemon-filled. "I hope that's okay."

I stay standing. "What's all this for?"

Kaivan sighs. "I was a jerk yesterday. I wanted to apologize. I was in a weird space and I shouldn't have taken it out on you. I thought maybe we could just have some doughnuts and chill. If you like?"

"Are you sure that's not just 'appealing to the lowest common denominator'?"

Kaivan scrunches up his eyebrows. "What?"

"I'm just a conventionally attractive white boy who writes vapid songs, what does it matter? Why do you even care?"

"Hunter, what . . ." Memory flickers in Kaivan's eyes. He looks down at the doughnuts, his cheeks darkening. "That's not . . ."

"Not what? You said it. And lots of other shit too."

"I was out of line. Listen—"

I'm not in the mood to listen. I'm in the mood to shout, to scream until my throat is sandpaper and I can't perform tonight. But instead, my voice turns cold and dark.

"Why did you do it? Why say you liked me, why date me, if I was a joke to you?" I clear my throat. "We said we were going to be real with each other. Honest. But all this time, you were . . . what? Just using me?"

Kaivan sets his jaw. "Using you? Okay, you're the one who needed to rehab your image. You're the one who was worried because everyone thought you were a slut." That was the whole point of all of this.

I'm not a slut. Fuck him for saying so.

"That was the whole point of all of this."

"No, the point was that I liked you, and you said you liked me. And we weren't going to give in to The Label deciding we should date just because we're gay. We were going to be the ones in control."

Kaivan runs his hands through his hair. "You're so fucking white sometimes. Maybe you actually do have some control over your career. Everything gets handed to you. Everything is easy. Hunter Drake, Gay Savior."

"That's not fair." I don't understand why this is suddenly about me.

"No, what's not fair is having your name mispronounced by every single person on The Label's marketing team. What's not fair is having people shout 'go back where you came from, terrorist' at you during a gig. What's not fair is the way people find me threatening, just because I'm Iranian, but change their minds once they find out I'm gay. I mean, look at this fucking suite. It's three times the size of my room."

My face is on fire.

"What, so it's my fault? I can't help being white."

"No, it's not your fault. But you benefit from it all, don't you? You do your little charity stuff, give out your shelter tickets, and act like you're fucking saving the world. But we don't need you to save us."

"That's not . . . that's not what I'm doing. I don't know what else to do. I'm trying to do good. I'm trying to learn and be better."

"I'm not a fucking lesson, Hunter. I'm a person. I have feelings. Not some token you can date to prove how woke you are. Not some rebound for you to get over your ex."

"I never thought that." My eyes are burning but no tears

are coming. I'm too mad to cry. Every word out of Kaivan's mouth is a Puck to the chest.

How the fuck did I end up being the bad guy in this?

"You never think of anything except yourself," Kaivan says. "That's the worst part. You think you care about other people. But all you care about is you."

"You're wrong," I want to say. He's wrong about me. That's not who I am.

But instead all that comes out is "Fuck you."

And all Kaivan says is "You wish I would."

That hurts more than anything else. That really does make the tears come.

"Shit. That was . . . Hunter . . ."

"Get out," I say. "We're done."

"I didn't mean it."

I shake my head. "I don't care. I want you to go."

"I'm sorry."

"I don't care!" I shout. "Get the fuck out!"

Kaivan looks close to tears himself.

I want to hug him.

I want to check him.

I want to throw myself out the window, into the lake, swim away and disappear.

"Just go," I say.

And he finally does.

KISS & TELL DOCUMENTARY

Footage transcription
061/01:02:48;00

OWEN: Something people don't really get is that the schedule is so intense. Like, we got on the bus in Minneapolis around midnight, got to Chicago close to nine in the morning, we've got a few hours to get some recording done before we leave for United Center. Trying to put an album out every year, while we also do a tour, it's a lot. Sleep's hard to come by. Sometimes it's on the bus, if you're lucky it's in a hotel, but sometimes it's tucked in a corner backstage.

(elevator dings; ADR required)

OWEN: So, yeah, you use the time you have. Especially me and Hunter, since we're writing a lot of the songs, we keep longer hours than the other guys, working on demos and stuff. Don't get me wrong, Ethan and Ian and Ashton are all working hard too. But like, we've got some new recordings to review today and send back to Gregg, who's helping us produce our next album. 1624, right? This is it.

(Owen knocks on Hunter's door.)

OWEN: He might be asleep, it was kind of a weird bus ride last night, plus he's got some stuff going on.

(Owen knocks again.)

HUNTER (O/S): Yeah?

OWEN: Hey, Hunter. Did you see Gregg's email? He's got some stuff for us to look over this morning.

HUNTER (O/S): I'm not in the mood.

OWEN: Come on, Hunter, we've got a deadline.

(Hunter opens door, audio questionable)

HUNTER: Just leave me alone, Owen. God. Can't I have just one day where people don't want things from me?

OWEN: Whoa, dude, are you okay?

HUNTER: I'm fine! I'm just fucking exhausted of everyone needing things from Hunter Fucking

Drake. Thinking that I'm some sort of . . . some sort of machine that doesn't have any feelings, just churns out shitty music that no one will remember in five years, just a stepping-stone on their path to success, just . . .

(Hunter cries, audio unusable)

OWEN: What happened? Hunter, what's going on? Uh, stop, cut, can we turn the cameras off?

From: Janet Lundgren (janet@kissandtellmusic.com)
To: Ryan Silva (ryansilvamanager@gmail.com),
Bill Holt (b.holt@thelabel.com)
Subject: BREAKUP NEWS?!?!
4/16/22 12:05 P.M.

What the maple-flavoured fuck? A little warning would've
been nice before Kaivan broke up with Hunter. He's got
shows to do.

Janet
Sent from my iPhone

From: Ryan Silva (ryansilvamanager@gmail.com)
To: Janet Lundgren (janet@kissandtellmusic.com),
Bill Holt (b.holt@thelabel.com)
Subject: Re: BREAKUP NEWS?!?!
4/16/22 12:14 P.M.

The way Kaivan tells it Hunter broke up with him. Either way
its a mess.

-Ryan

From: Bill Holt (b.holt@thelabel.com)
To: Ryan Silva (ryansilvamanager@gmail.com),
Janet Lundgren (janet@kissandtellmusic.com)
Subject: Re: BREAKUP NEWS?!?!
4/16/22 1:08 P.M.

Not ideal but we'll manage.

-BH

From: Bill Holt (b.holt@thelabel.com)
To: Janet Lundgren (janet@kissandtellmusic.com)
Subject: Re: BREAKUP NEWS?!?!
4/16/22 1:10 P.M.

Any chance we can spin this as Hunter getting back with Aidan? Might be decent PR.

-BH

From: Janet Lundgren (janet@kissandtellmusic.com)
To: Bill Holt (b.holt@thelabel.com)
Subject: Re: BREAKUP NEWS?!?!
4/16/22 1:38 P.M.

Absolutely not. Hunter's miserable right now. If we push him I don't think he'll be able to perform. I was worried things would turn out this way.

Janet
Sent from my iPhone

From: Ryan Silva (ryansilvamanager@gmail.com)
To: Bill Holt (b.holt@thelabel.com)
Subject: Re: BREAKUP NEWS?!?!

4/16/22 2:01 P.M.

It sukcs, but we want to keep focus on the single drop.
Heartbreak sells rite?

-Ryan

HUNTER DRAKE & KAVIAM PARVANI
CALL IT QUITS

TRS (The Real Scoop)
Date: April 16, 2022

Hunter Drake has split with Kaviam Parvani, TRS has learned.

Sources close to the couple have confirmed the breakup, which comes just weeks after the couple announced their relationship publicly. No reason has been given for the split, though Drake has recently been spotted with ex Aidan Nightingale.

PAR-K's latest single, "Memories," dropped yesterday; Kiss & Tell is currently touring North America, with PAR-K opening. Both bands play Chicago's United Center tonight and tomorrow.

<u>Owen Jogia and Mira Dillon Deny Dating Rumors</u>

<u>Hunter Drake and Kaivan Parvani's Escape Room Escapade</u>

TRENDING: HUNTER DRAKE
Trending: Kaivan Parvani
Trending: KAVIAM

@wkxapologist: they can't even spell @kaivanandon name right!!

@tissandkell03: noooooooooooo 😭 i loved Kaivan and Hunter together!!!

@hunterdr4kesgirl: no no no no no Hunter and Kaivan were so good

@samalicious: do you think @hunterdrake forgot to clean out again?

@lillybean14: hope Kaivan is taking care of himself!

@hashtaghashton: 💔 💔 💔 💔 💔 💔 hunter

@huntergreeneyes: can't stop crying, @hunterdrake deserves better!!!

@xiyaotroll: @kaivanandon should go back where he came from, heartless asshole

PRE-ROLL SCRIPT FOR KISS & TELL
SEGMENT ON *AMERICA TONIGHT*

DANIEL (V/O): They're the hottest ticket in the country right now, five friends from north of the border who've taken the world by storm with their charm, good looks, clever lyrics, and sweet harmonies.

Ashton Nightingale, Ethan Nguyen, Ian Souza, Owen Jogia, and Hunter Drake have been touring America for their second album, *Come Say Hello*, and they're here to say a big "Hello!" to us in the *America Tonight* studio. Kiss & Tell is coming right up, after the break.

31

I can't stop fidgeting. Ashton grabs my knee to stop it jiggling.

I don't want to do this interview. I don't want to do any interviews. I want to crawl into a hole and hide.

But this is the job. Screw on my smile and act like everything's fine, while everyone in the world weighs in on what I did wrong this time, and just how slutty I really am, and whether Kaivan and I had sex. Weighing in on everything except whether I'm okay.

I'm not okay. But I have to be.

My face feels painted on, and I've been powdered to within an inch of my life, but the worst part is my wardrobe. I'm in a white cable-knit sweater with a literal rainbow across the chest.

It's heinous, and it's not me, but what's the point in fighting it anymore. In being the real me. No one wants the real Hunter Drake anyway.

Ian's with me and Ashton on the couch, while Owen and Ethan sit behind us on high stools. The host of *America Tonight*, Daniel Swenson, sits behind a dark wood desk with nothing on it except an iPad and a few note cards.

"Sixty seconds," someone calls over the speaker. Instinct makes me sit up straighter, which is hard to do while also looking relaxed. Ashton's nailed the posture, though: legs crossed, an arm resting on the back of the couch behind Ian's head. He's wearing a pair of black jeans and a white Henley that's unbuttoned all the way to let his tattoo peek through. Ian, on his other side, is wearing a yellow button-up and white chinos. And behind us, Ethan and Owen look good too. It's not like they made Owen wear a kurta or something like that.

Daniel double-checks the button on his suit jacket as the stage manager counts us in. Janet's standing beside them, arms crossed, her phone still clutched in her hand.

Everything goes like it's supposed to. Ashton is charming and talks about how New York is so amazing and big. I mean, it is amazing and big, but Vancouver's not exactly a small town.

Ethan is funny and coy. He's wearing these black plastic fashion glasses, and he pushes them up the bridge of his nose as he answers easy questions about the pranks we've played on tour. His smile turns more thoughtful when Daniel asks if he's going to get back together with Kelly K, but he doesn't mention any of the stuff he told me, the real stuff. He just fakes it all.

Ian is earnest and excited about our tour, talking about how cool the venues have been, how great our fans are, the moments of connection we've had at our meet and greets.

Owen runs a hand through his hair as he talks about our new album, how hard we've been working on it, how excited we all are.

We've become a bunch of talking points.

Kaivan was right about us.

The audience is eating it up, though: laughing at the corny jokes, clapping in all the right spots. But there's a pressure building in my ears, a buzzing amp with a blown tube.

"Last but not least, Hunter Drake. You've been in the news a lot lately, haven't you? It seems like your latest relationship was over almost as soon as it began."

"Yeah. It sucks," I say.

Daniel blinks at me.

I wasn't supposed to say that. I don't remember what else I'm supposed to say.

The buzz between my ears is getting worse.

"It sucks, having my love life posted all over the Internet. Having my sexuality examined and dissected by strangers. How everyone wanted to know if me and Aidan were having sex but no one was happy with the answer. There's no part of me that I get to keep for myself anymore. Every piece is up for public consumption. You know I get like twenty dick pics a day?"

"Hunter," Ashton says, a warning, but I keep going, even though Janet's waving at me off-camera and Daniel's eyes look like they're about to burst.

"Not to mention all the shit we get for being in a boy band. No one takes us seriously. Not even our peers. Not even our openers! People act like we're talentless hacks, just because we write songs that appeal to teen girls. People act like our fans are crazy. Did you know the Whisper Network raised over a million dollars to wildfire relief last summer? But no, none of that matters. All that matters is whether I'm a fucking bottom!"

"Hunter!" Ashton says, grabbing my knee. "We're on live TV!"

"Oh, excuse me for being tired of being treated like I'm not a real human being. Sorry if I'm going through some things. You guys don't even know what it's like."

Ashton's nostrils flare. "We're the only ones who know what it's like. If you'd give us a break and think about someone else, you'd realize we're all going through stuff. You know how often Owen and Ethan and even Ian get racist insults? You think you're the only one who has it rough. We all do. And none of us are taking it out on each other, so why are you taking it out on us?"

It's like he's skated right into my knee again. Asshole.

Maybe we're all assholes.

I'm a grenade, about to explode into a cacophony of air and sound and brass shrapnel. I get up and try to pull my mic off, but the wire has somehow made it into one of my sleeves, so I end up pulling the whole hideous sweater off and throwing it on the studio floor.

"I can't take this anymore."

No one tries to stop me as I storm off the set.

TRENDING: HUNTER DRAKE
Trending: Kiss & Tell
Trending: America Tonight

@maccattacc: My kids stayed up late to watch. Hunter should be ashamed of himself.

@haidanfan12: YAS QUEEN @hunterdrake

@straightpridenews: Kiss & Tell's Hunter Drake embarrasses himself on live tv, watch the video below

@singing_toad: CAN'T WAIT FOR THE AUTO-TUNE VERSION OF THIS, IT'S WHAT WE DESERVE

@samalicious: don't they say shite in canada tho

@maggs_rt: Never thought I'd find myself agreeing with @hunterdrake but he's right: society chronically undervalues teen girls.

@hdidi04: Pour one out for whoever was supposed to be manning the bleeper for that interview.

@xiyaotroll: their music still sucks though

32

I find the nearest exit and yank the door open. It leads to an orange-lit stairwell, and I head down, down, footsteps echoing off the brick walls. I don't know where I'm going, I just want to get away: from the guys, from the cameras, from everything.

Away from being Hunter Fucking Drake.

"Hunter!" someone calls from above, but I keep going, taking the stairs as fast as I can. The next landing has heavy gray doors with an exit sign above. I don't know if it's going to set off any alarms, and I don't really care.

I push out onto a crowded street. Cold wind whips me right away, and I blink at all the lights. I'm just in my white undershirt, and a light drizzle falls against my arms and the back of my neck.

I get maybe five meters before the screaming starts.

Shit.

We were supposed to greet our fans after the show. They've been camped outside the studio all day, in the rain even, hoping to see us. And I've stepped right into them.

The closest people, a trio of girls, burst into happy tears when they see me, but they're quickly shoved out of the way by the crush of people behind them.

I should've thought this through.

I don't even have time to find a smile before I'm surrounded. People are shoving posters and albums at me. Strange fingers run through my hair. Gentle hands press against mine. Rude ones grab my ass.

Someone yanks the back of my shirt, but their friend tries to pry them off, which leads to me getting choked by my collar. I cough, and more hands pat my back.

I get drawn closer to the center of the crowd, a swirling, hungry mass of people. I'm not human anymore: I'm a slab of meat. A cinnamon roll to get pulled apart and consumed.

I think I hear Nazeer's voice, but it's impossible to make out over the noise. More hands press against me. There are phones everywhere, flashes bursting in my face, others with the light steady for video, as I try to make it to the barricade, where a bunch of local security folks are trying to figure out what to do.

Two of them finally make their way into the crowd and force a little bubble of space around me. I try to thank them over the din, but I'm not sure they can even hear me. They get me out, over the barricade. One of them, who's shorter, with blond hair up in a short ponytail, gets on the radio, while the other tries to get the crowd to calm down.

My shirt is ripped in the armpit. I'm not sure when it happened. Cold rain trickles down my shoulder blade, turns the powder on my face to paste. I wipe it off on the hem of my ruined shirt.

Cars crawl by on the street, which I'm pretty sure is Broadway, and the sidewalk is full of regular people on their way to who knows where.

As soon as the security officer lets go of my arm, I slip into the tide of humanity and start walking, hiding behind a tall gentleman in a puffy coat. I shiver and let the foot traffic take me down the block until the roar of the crowd finally fades.

Then I'm free.

I hug myself as I walk. My nipples could cut glass right now.

No one looks at me, except an occasional raised eyebrow at my torn, dirty shirt. I'm invisible, some random kid walking through Times Square at night, staring at the lights and video walls, enjoying the occasional bursts of warm air that rise from the subway grates.

I don't really know where I'm going. I thought I was on Broadway, but somehow I've ended up on Seventh Avenue. It's nearly midnight, but the sidewalks are still crowded, and everyone's walking at straight-pace. I make myself slow down and take in the city.

New York is supposed to be a rite of passage for gay guys.

It's the dream: Stonewall and Broadway and pizza and hot dog carts.

Last time we came through, we were only here for a day, just enough time for some carefully orchestrated publicity photos at the Empire State Building. I didn't get to see anything.

Now, I pass shops and restaurants, subway stations and food carts. No one looks twice at me, except when I actually stop at a crosswalk instead of weaving through the traffic.

I can't remember the last time I got to just wander. Be a regular person. Every minute of the last two years has been filled with Kiss & Tell. With my friends.

Hot guilt bubbles in my guts. Ashton's right, I shouldn't take out my frustrations on the guys. But they just don't get it. And I'm so tired.

Maybe I've ruined everything. Maybe this is the end.

I don't even care anymore.

The rainbow flags start popping up so slowly, it takes me a solid couple blocks before I realize I've found the gayborhood. It reminds me of Davie Street back home. People line up on the sidewalks outside what must be clubs, because as I get closer the thrumming bass permeates the air. I bob my head to the beat and let out a laugh.

I've never been to a gay club before.

I wonder if I could get in. I'm probably too young, but I'm famous, right?

So I take a spot in the line trailing from an awning that says *BOIZ* in sparkling letters. Everyone's dressed for the club, in tight shirts and tighter jeans, some in crop tops despite the night's chill. I'm rubbing my arms and clenching my jaw when the couple in front of me turn around to glance at me. They turn forward again, and then spin around. Their eyes go wide.

"Oh my god," the first one, a skinny blond with a buzz cut, says.

"Are you . . ." starts the other, whose dark skin shines under the streetlights.

"Yeah," I say, because these are my people, and also I'm really fucking cold, and maybe being famous will get me into the club faster.

"Oh my god!" the blond shouts again. They take me by the arm, and their date (I think?) places a guiding hand between my shoulder blades as we step out of the line and make our way to the bouncer.

I say bouncer, but they don't look anything like the kind of bouncers they have in movies, the buff guys with dark sunglasses and too-tight black T-shirts. This bouncer is young, with light brown skin, curly hair colored vivid blue, and black jeans tucked into knee-high boots.

"Look who we found!" the blond says.

I put on my best Media Smile. "Hey."

The bouncer blinks at me. Behind me, the people we cut in front of are taking photos of us. I turn back to them and say "Sorry," then turn back to the bouncer.

"Honey, they're going to eat you alive in there," they say.

"I'll be fine."

"Aren't you still seventeen?"

"Only for two more months," I say, like that matters.

The bouncer blinks again, then holds up their index finger for me to give them a second as they turn away and talk into their earpiece.

"Excuse me," the person behind me says. "Can I get a picture?"

"Sure!" I lean back and smile.

"Can we do a silly one?"

"Of course!"

I stick out my tongue and bite it, while they kiss my cheek.

"Hey," the bouncer says, and I turn back around. "You can get in, but you have to wear this." They wrap an orange wristband around my left wrist.

"Is this so they don't booze me?"

"Be careful in there," they say quietly as they open the door.

"Cheers." I step inside and wait for the couple that got me in while the bouncer checks their IDs. They eventually follow me in.

"That was awesome," the dark-skinned one says. "Thanks,

honey." And then they both take off down the dark, narrow hallway, leaving me alone.

Pretty sure I just got used, but weirdly, I don't mind.

I make my way down the hall, and the bass thrums a familiar beat beneath my feet. One more door and then I'm in.

I have to laugh.

There's actual go-go boys dancing on the bar, and on raised platforms that look like they probably wouldn't pass a safety inspection. People dance and kiss and grind on the dance floor. The scents of vodka and sweat and too many kinds of cologne fill the air.

A remix of "Heartbeat Fever" is pounding out of the speakers.

I can't believe it. I close my eyes for a second, feel the bass vibrating my every cell, until someone tugs my arm to get around me.

"Sorry." My heart tremolos as I wind my way onto the dance floor and lose myself.

It's dark, so no one pays me any special attention. We're just a bunch of queer people, reveling in our community, laughing and dancing and existing.

Euphoria. There's no other word for it.

Someone bumps against me. Another runs their hands down my arm as they pass, on the way to the bar. It's casual and it's loaded. A guy presses up against my butt for a second, but I don't feel dirty. I don't feel like a slut.

I feel sexy and alive and at home.

I dance harder, push my wet hair off my face, smile at the people around me, who finally recognize me. Phones start flashing, people elbow their friends, their dates, but I don't care.

The guy closest to me shouts "Sing it!" at the top of his lungs, and I do. There's no way anyone can hear me, but still, soon the whole club is singing along, off-key and vibrant and gay and beautiful.

These are my people.

A dancer in a mesh crop top (I didn't know people really wore those) steps closer, matches their feet to mine. Another stands behind, grinning at me, or maybe ogling me. I feel the press of skin against my arms as I let another dancer twirl me. Someone's grinding against my back; I can feel their erection pressed up against me.

"Your shirt is ripped," a voice shouts in my ear. "What happened?"

"Nothing," I say, and peel it off, because between the dancing and the bodies all around me, I'm not cold anymore.

A hand appears to pass me a drink. I'm certain it's not allowed but equally certain I don't care. It doesn't taste like much, except for the squeeze of lime, but the bubbles tingle my tongue and the alcohol warms my throat, my stomach, my fingertips.

I drain the whole thing before anyone can stop me; another dancer laughs, takes the empty glass out of my hand.

I swivel my hips as the song changes, something darker

and moodier. There's this guy a few feet away, and he's looking at my bare chest. I clench my stomach as subtly as I can and study him too: He's white but tanned, with brown hair that's had highlights bleached in, and a cute, upturned nose. He's not wearing a shirt either. His chest is smooth and dewy and contoured. He's even got a single vein visible above his Adonis belt.

Damn.

I look back at his face, and our eyes lock. He caught me looking. But he smiles, and I smile back, and I'm blushing because I was so obviously checking him out and he was definitely checking me out too. He starts toward me, head bobbing, dipping through the crowd, and I back up a little to make space for him. He rests his hands on my hips.

"You're even hotter in person," he says. I can barely hear him over the music.

"You too," I say, because my brain isn't working and my mouth has gone dry.

He laughs and presses his skin against mine. Our hearts beat in time to the music. Hot Guy's hands reach lower so they're cradling my butt. He doesn't squeeze or anything but I wouldn't mind if he did.

Someone presses another drink into my hands, another fizzy thing with limes, and I take this one slower as I dance. Hot Guy's cologne is subtle and fresh and citrusy, unless that's just the lime wedge from my drink. His cheeks are flushed, and they dimple up as he smiles.

I take another swig of my drink, press the cup against the pulse point on my wrist to feel the cold, because I'm sweaty all over, and the warmth in my belly is spreading lower. My boner is trapped against my jeans, and the dancing is not helping.

"What's your name?"

"What?" he asks. He's holding me from behind now, his chin resting against the crook of my neck, his chest pressed against my back.

"What's your name?" I shout, turning a little so he can hear me better, but that brings his lips in range of my ear and he nibbles it a little bit.

My knee gives out for a second.

"Jared," he says.

"I'm—"

"I know who you are. I love your music."

"Thanks."

Another nibble. I giggle and try to finish my drink, but I spill it down my front.

"Oh no." I think it was vodka. It's definitely stronger than the shitty beers I'm used to. "I spilled."

"It's cool." He rubs his hand across my stomach, where the drink is trickling down toward my waistband.

"I'm thirsty."

He chuckles. "Yeah?"

"Yeah. I need some water."

"Come on." He takes my hand and pulls me off the dance floor toward a side hall, where there's a water fountain next to the washroom. I lean over and take a couple gulps.

"Better?"

It's quieter now and I can hear Jared's voice better. It's kind of raspy, in a cool way.

I nod and wipe my mouth with the back of my hand, but Jared steps closer and runs his thumb under my lip. "Missed a spot."

"Oops," I say, because my brain has gone soft and fuzzy. I'm definitely buzzed, but I don't care.

Jared's hand keeps moving until he's cradling the back of my neck. I know what he wants. I lean in and he leans in and then we're kissing.

We're kissing and it's hot and amazing, his breath in my lungs, my tongue against his teeth, my hands tracing the valley of his spine, his dipping below my waistband to squeeze my ass through my underwear.

I know what's happening and I am here for it.

"You want to . . . ?" His voice trails against my collarbone.

"I don't have any condoms."

"There's a bowl in the bathroom."

"Okay."

He takes my hands and smiles at me.

And pulls me toward the washroom door.

GROUP CHAT

Ashton, Ethan, Ian, Owen
Tue, Apr 19, 2022, 1:18 AM

ASHTON

I heard from Nazeer. Still no word

Ethan has changed the group name to
"H. Middle Initial Drake Search Party"

OWEN

You don't think that was him quitting was it?
On live tv?

ASHTON

I shouldn't have argued with him

ETHAN

Dude your the only one he listens to!!

IAN

I think he was just overwhelmed. He's never been
good at reaching out for help. Sometimes it's like he
thinks he has to carry the whole band on his
shoulders, just because he started it.

OWEN
That's fair
I saw Kaivan at the hotel, he seemed worried too

ETHAN
Oh dip!
Spotted at a club lol!!
Go Hunter!!

         ASHTON
         Really?
         Link??

ETHAN
<u>Kiss & Tell's Hunter Drake Spotted Dancing at BOIZ</u>

         ASHTON
         I'll call Nazeer

OWEN
It's a gay bar dude, you should send Aidan

IAN
You said Kaivan was worried. Maybe he'll go.

KISS & TELL'S HUNTER DRAKE
SPOTTED DANCING AT BOIZ

Rainbow News Now—News that Slays
April 19, 2022

After a contentious appearance on *America Tonight* with Daniel Swenson, Hunter Drake, Kiss & Tell's rebellious twink, was spotted popping into BOIZ, a club in Chelsea that opened last summer. Drake took time to pose for photos outside before being granted VIP access and hitting the floor to show off his moves. Check out the video below. (WARNING: Contains flashing lights.)

33

I've seen enough TV shows (and porn) to know what a club's washroom is supposed to be like: dimly lit, kind of gross, maybe one of the stall doors broken or something.

This one is dimly lit, but it's actually pretty clean. There's one of those light-up scent diffusers on the counter next to the sink, and it smells like chocolate chip cookies, which is half-heinous and half-hilarious. Next to that is the bowl of condoms. There's a bunch of different kinds: flavored ones and ribbed ones, ones with desensitizing gel or tingly gel or warming gel. Aidan and I only ever used the regular ones, which Aidan ordered online from Shoppers since neither of us wanted to be spotted buying condoms at the store. I shake the memory out of my head.

Forget Aidan.

Forget everyone.

Jared reaches into the bowl, pulls out a gold-foil Magnum, and winks at me.

I swallow.

"Just kidding." He drops it and grabs two flavored ones and two warming ones.

I don't care. I just want to go back to kissing him, feeling him.

"Doesn't matter," I say, and mash my lips against his.

He pulls me into the corner between the urinals and the counter, which feels sleazy and excellent. The light casts a rosy glow across his flush cheeks. Our breaths echo off the tiles.

I kiss along his jaw, down his neck, hit that little spot between his collarbones with my tongue. He laughs and squeezes my butt again, starts to pull my pants down a little bit to expose my underwear.

"Is it okay to block the sink?" I ask. "What if someone needs to wash their hands?"

If we're going to hook up in a washroom, we can't be dicks about it.

Jared laughs. His fingers have slipped under the waistband of my underwear again, warm and insistent against my skin.

"Come on." Without letting go, he maneuvers us into one of the stalls, walking me backward until my legs hits the toilet and I fall over laughing.

He helps me up and I plant my face into his chest. It's firm and hot.

"You okay?" he asks as I giggle.

"I'm fine," I say. "I'm not drunk. Promise. Just buzzed."

"You sure?"

My everything feels warm, and I'm annoyed that he's stopped kissing me, so I mash my face against his, relishing the scratch of stubble against my chin.

He wants me.

And I don't even care anymore if he wants me because he likes my ass or because he thinks I'm cute or because he thinks it'd be cool to fuck someone famous.

It doesn't matter.

He wants me, and sex is fun, and I like to do it, and fuck Aidan and fuck the world for making me feel bad about that. Fuck Kaivan too, for making me feel bad about . . . I'm not even sure. Just, fuck him too.

Fuck everyone.

I kiss Jared's chest, do a little exploratory nipple-biting, but that doesn't seem to do anything for him, so I move to the valley of his chest, keep kissing lower.

The door to the washroom opens but we both ignore it. Jared plants his feet a little firmer as I keep kissing down, down, kneeling to get a better angle on his zipper. He runs a hand through my hair and lets out a shaky breath.

"Hunter? You in here?"

I snap back and somehow hit my funny bone right on the rim of the toilet bowl. I grab my arm to massage the spot, but knock Jared against the stall.

"Shit," I hiss.

"Hunter?"

It's Kaivan.

What the fuck is he doing here?

The stall door shakes, but Jared keeps it closed.

"Hunter? Is that you? Are you okay?"

"I'm fine," I say, and use the toilet paper holder to pull myself up.

"You know him?" Jared says.

"Who's in there with you?" Kaivan's voice is low and flinty.

I clear my throat and reach around Jared to hold the door closed.

"That's my business. Go away."

"Have you been drinking?"

"No," I say, but then I start giggling.

Kaivan pushes against the door. He's strong but I'm stubborn. He lets up.

"Hey," Jared says. "We're in here."

"Let him out," Kaivan growls.

"We're busy."

"He's seventeen, asshole. That's statutory."

Jared studies me for a second. "Point taken."

And just like that, every bit of warmth is gone. He pulls open the door and squeezes out past Kaivan, leaving me shivering and shirtless as I fall back onto the toilet.

Maybe I can flush myself and disappear into the plumbing.

"Did he hurt you?"

"No. I'm fine. Why do you care?" I try to stand and succeed on the second try.

"You are drunk."

"Am not." I push past him to the sink to wash my hands. Habit. "Why are you here?"

"I was worried. We all were."

"Whatever." I turn around and stare at him. "Worried I was going to hook up with that guy. Jealous much?"

"No. I mean, I'm glad you didn't, but—"

"You're just mad I didn't give you a blowjob," I say. "You should be. I give amazing blowjobs."

"Hunter . . ."

"Go away. I'm having fun."

"Nazeer is outside looking for you." He reaches for me but I pull away. "Hunter, please."

"No. Just leave me alone. You didn't care about me before. Don't act like you do now."

"Fine. Then should I go tell Nazeer you're in here and have him carry you out?"

"You wouldn't dare."

"He'd probably do one of those bodyguard carries too."

I pinch my lips. If anything, Nazeer would throw me over his shoulder and lecture me on the way out.

I laugh at the mental image, because it would be pretty

funny, but laughing makes the room spin. I hold on to the counter to stay upright.

Maybe I'm drunker than I thought.

Shit.

I clear my throat. "Fine," I say, and move toward the door, but I start leaning to the side. Kaivan starts to catch me, but I correct myself. "Don't touch me."

"Okay." He opens the door for me. "But let's at least get out of here."

Nazeer's parked halfway on the curb with his hazards on, which I'm pretty sure is illegal. New York parking is even worse than Vancouver.

He doesn't say anything as we get in the car. Just opens my door, makes sure I'm buckled, and starts driving. It's two in the morning, according to the little clock in the dash. I shiver against the leather seat. My flush from earlier is giving way to chills.

I close my eyes, but the stopping and starting of the car makes me dizzy. The quiet is smothering.

"How'd you find me anyway?" I mutter.

"You're all over the Internet dancing with that creeper," Kaivan says next to me. The sad-drunk part of me wants to lean against him and soak up his warmth. The angry-drunk part of me wants to push him out of the car.

"He wasn't a creeper. He was . . ." But I don't know. Now

that I'm not in the club anymore, Jared doesn't seem so cool and hot anymore.

"He had no business touching you," Nazeer says from the front. His voice is flat, no anger in it at all, which is how I know he's truly pissed.

I didn't ask him to come get me. I didn't ask Kaivan either.

"I would've been fine."

Kaivan scoffs. "You've been drinking. What if someone slipped you something? How do you know that guy wasn't going to hurt you? He was at least twenty-five. Maybe thirty. That's gross."

"You're gross. He wasn't that old."

Kaivan rolls his eyes at me.

"Why were you so worried anyway? You don't want anything to do with me."

"I still care about you."

I scoff.

"I know I hurt you, but it's true. You act like everything is all black and white."

"I do not."

"Yes you do. You alone are capable of nuance. The rest of us are all either good or bad. We can't ever make mistakes, or say things we don't really mean, or . . ." Kaivan trails off.

Or what?

I don't know if it's the vodka or the car ride, but I get this swooping sensation in my stomach, like I'm going to vom.

"I don't feel good."

"Water," Nazeer says. Kaivan hands me one of the little bottles.

I chug it and wipe my mouth with my forearm. "Am I in trouble?"

"A world of it. But not with me. I'm just glad you're okay."

"Why not? You should be pissed at me."

"Because you're young. Because I remember all the stupid shit my kids did when they were your age. And sometimes they didn't need to be yelled at. They needed someone to listen to them."

I shake my head.

Nazeer pulls up to the gate for the hotel's loading dock and swipes a badge. The gate swings up and he pulls in.

"Here we are."

I open the door and immediately retch at the smell of trash.

"Not in the car," Nazeer warns.

I stagger out of the car and make it to a corner before my stomach tries very hard to invert itself. Nothing comes up except bile. I spit a couple times to get the taste out of my mouth.

"You know," Nazeer says, resting a warm, callused hand on my back, "I always thought Ethan was going to end up being the problem child. Not you."

That does make me feel kind of shitty.

"Sorry."

"Good. Then don't pull a stunt like this again."

I look up at him. He doesn't look mad, but he does look stern.

"I worry about you."

"I'll be okay," I say, but I can't meet his eyes.

"I know you will. Come on. Let's get out of this stink."

Nazeer leads the way to the elevator and Kaivan keeps behind me, like they're not sure if I'm going to take off again or what. But I'm not going anywhere. I want to crawl into bed and hide.

"I don't have my key," I say when we get to my door.

Nazeer holds up the backpack I left back at the studio.

"Thanks."

"Sure. Get some sleep, Hunter. We'll talk in the morning."

"Okay." I step inside and start to close the door, but then I turn back. Kaivan is still there.

"Thanks for coming to get me," I say.

"Sure."

For a second, I think he's going to ask to come in.

I don't know if I want him to.

Maybe I should invite him, though.

But then he says, "Good night, Hunter."

H. MIDDLE INITIAL DRAKE SEARCH PARTY

Ashton, Ethan, Ian, Owen
Tue, Apr 19, 2022, 2:25 A.M.

> **ASHTON**
> He's back now
> They found him in a washroom with that creeper
> Nothing happened

Ethan has changed the group name to
"MISSION ACCOMPLISHED"

IAN
Damn, really?

ETHAN
He owes us so much pizza for this!!

OWEN
Glad he's ok

IAN
Same.

> **ASHTON**
> I'm gonna go talk to him

34

My armpits smell rank. I don't know if it's the club or the alcohol seeping out of my skin. My face is a pizza.

I hop in the shower and then wrap myself in the puffy white hotel towel as I dry off. I'm shivering, even though my room's not that cold. I pull on my favorite leggings, the gray camo ones, and my softest Canucks hoodie.

I dig through my backpack and pull my phone out. I've got about a million missed messages, but I ignore them all except for the ones from Mom. I send her a quick message letting her know I'm safe and I'll call her in the morning.

I flop onto the bed on my stomach, grab the little chocolate off the pillow and stuff it in my mouth. I think I'm hungry, but maybe that's just the adrenaline leaving my system. Now that I'm sobering up, it kind of scares me what I did. Kaivan was right. What if someone had spiked my drink? What if . . .

353

There's a knock on my door. I groan into my bed. I don't want anyone to see me.

"Hunt?" Ashton's voice is quiet, muffled. "You awake?"

I definitely don't want Ashton to see me. But better to get it over with.

I crack the door.

"Hey."

"Hey, Hunt." He runs a hand through his messy hair. "Can I come in?"

I should say no. After what he said to me, I should be pissed at him.

But what Kaivan said, about me seeing everything in black and white, keeps rattling around in my head. So I nod and let him in.

I flop back on my bed, facedown, and after a second, Ashton flops down next to me.

"You really scared us, Hunt."

"Sorry," I say to my pillow.

I am sorry. I was a dick to everyone. I didn't want them worrying.

I just wanted to be alone for a while.

"I'm sorry too. I shouldn't have gone off on you like that."

"Well." The silence stretches between us until I think it's going to snap.

"I guess you kind of had a point," I finally say. "You all did. The guys all tried to tell me. Kaivan too. I just . . ."

I sigh into my pillow.

"You guys all act like it doesn't bother you. The shows, the interviews, the life. You act like you love it all."

"I do love it, Hunt. But I get tired too. I get hurt sometimes. We all do."

"You never told me."

"Huh?"

I turn my head to look at Ashton. He's on his back, with his hands behind his head. "You never told me you were hurting."

Ashton nods. "I guess we're all kind of bad at talking about it."

"You could've talked to me, though. I'm your best friend."

"Yeah." He toys with the hem of his T-shirt. "You know why I quit hockey, Hunt?"

"No. I mean, Aidan always said it was because you felt guilty."

"I did feel guilty, and probably always will."

"It was a freak accident."

"But still. I destroyed your dream."

"I don't blame you, though. I never have." I've told him that a million times, but I don't know if he's ever going to believe me.

"I guess. But that's not why I quit."

"Then why?"

"I quit hockey because I knew you. And I knew that if you couldn't play hockey, you'd find something else to be amazing at. And I wanted to be part of it."

My eyes start to burn.

"And you're my best friend too. After what happened with hockey, I wasn't going to let anything get in the way of your new dream. So maybe I didn't always tell you when things were hard for me. But it's not because things weren't hard. It's because I didn't want you to think I wasn't all in. Because I am, for as long as you want."

He chews his lip. I roll all the way over onto my back, so our shoulders are butted up together.

"So if you don't want to do all this anymore? I'll support you. If you want to quit, if you want to disband the whole thing, I'll go with you. Because it's not worth being miserable. It's not worth . . . whatever happened tonight."

"In the biz, I think they call this a 'meltdown.'"

Ashton chuckles.

"But for real. I've got your back. Always."

"Thanks."

Do I want to quit?

I don't know what else I'd do.

And it's not all bad. I love seeing our fans' faces light up at concerts. I love being able to support Mom and Haley. And give to so many charities. And feel like I'm making a difference.

"I think I want to keep going, though. I think maybe this is what I have to give. And I should try my best to give it."

"You don't owe anyone anything, Hunter. You don't have to give anything you don't want to give. Not your love life, not your sexuality, not your music. Not anything."

"I know. But this makes me happy. I think I just couldn't see it."

"Okay."

"I guess I should apologize to the guys too."

"Yeah. You probably owe about a month's worth of pizza."

"I figured."

"But that can wait for tomorrow. You should get some sleep."

"Yeah."

"Sleepover?"

"You don't mind?"

"Nah." Ashton burrows under the covers. He's such a blanket hog.

"Leave some for me."

"You've got your hoodie!"

"I still get cold, though!"

Finally we get situated.

"Night, Hunt."

"Night, Ashton. And thanks. For everything."

ONLINE PETITION CALLS FOR FIRING OF HUNTER DRAKE

NewzList

Date: April 19, 2022

A petition is circulating online asking The Label to fire Hunter Drake from Kiss & Tell.

Last night, Drake appeared with Kiss & Tell on *America Tonight* with Daniel Swenson in connection with their *Come Say Hello* tour. During the brief segment, an agitated Drake lashed out at his band-mates, went on a profanity-laden tirade about the pressures of celebrity, and stormed off set, leaving the band to perform without him.

Later that night, despite being a minor, Drake was spotted drinking and dancing at a gay nightclub, before disappearing into the bathroom with an older man.

Kiss & Tell's management has released a statement affirming Drake's commitment to the band, which is performing the first of three nights at New York's famous Madison Square Garden tonight.

18 Best Tweets About That Hunter Drake Club Video

How Popular Are Your Kiss & Tell Opinions?

35

wake up cold. Ashton stole the blankets in the middle of the night.

I think about yanking them back, but that feels like a shitty thanks for keeping me company. For putting up with me.

It's past noon. I've missed a call from Mom plus two texts from Janet and one from Nazeer.

"Shit. Ashton. Wake up."

He groans and pulls the blankets over his head.

"The presser."

He throws the blankets off. "Shit!"

He rolls out of bed, stuffs his feet into his shoes, and ducks out, while I go to the washroom to get ready.

Nazeer knocks on my door while I'm talking to Mom.

"I've gotta go, Mom," I say as he taps his wristwatch.

"Okay, Hunter," she says. "Talk soon. Love you."

359

"Yeah. Love you. Bye." I hang up and turn to Nazeer. "Sorry. I'm ready."

"You're wearing that?"

I'm in a faded Pink Floyd T-shirt and jeans. I'm going to do this as myself.

"Yeah."

"You ready, then?"

"Just . . . sorry for being such a pain in the ass. I promise not to run off ever again."

Nazeer laughs. "Thanks."

"And thanks for always looking out for me."

"You're welcome."

The guys are quiet as we pile into the car. I wait until we're on the road before I clear my throat.

"Hey guys." I swallow away my dread. "Uh. I'd like to apologize for my behavior yesterday. I'm sorry for the stuff I said, and I'm sorry for walking off like that and leaving you all high and dry. And I'm sorry for being a disaster lately. I've been having a hard time, but you all don't deserve me taking it out on you. So. Sorry. I won't do it again."

"Thanks, Hunt," Ashton says. But the other guys are quiet. My freckles start tingling.

But then Ian says, "To be honest, I'm just surprised you didn't try to bleach your hair."

"Or get a neck tattoo," Owen muses.

Ethan squeezes my shoulder. "You still owe us pizza, though."

"Thanks, guys."

"You should probably order it now, in case Janet murders you."

"Don't worry, I'll put it in my will."

Ethan musses my hair. "Good thinking."

Janet doesn't murder me, thankfully.

"I'm pissed as hell at you, Hunter," she tells me as I'm getting my hair done. "But I appreciate your apology. And at the end of the day, I'm not your boss. I'm your manager. So if you're struggling, we need to talk things out and make changes."

"Really?"

"Really," she says. "You're the talent."

"Okay." I look down at my T-shirt. "I want The Label to back off on how I dress. And no more messing with my dating life."

"Anything else?"

I think about what Kaivan said about not being a lesson. About Masha Patriarki, and how they made me feel like I could do better.

About who I want to be.

"I want to do more good. With my platform. I'm not sure how yet, but . . ."

"How about expanding the inclusion rider?" Owen asks next to me. "Or, like, mentorships?"

"That would be cool," I say.

"Great. Anything else?"

"I don't know," I admit. "I'm still trying to figure this stuff out. And I know there's lots of problems to solve out there. Like, for people of color and stuff. Like, the other guys probably have better ideas than mine." I meet Ethan's eyes and he gives me a nod.

"You don't have to fight our battles for us," he says. "Just take a backseat sometimes."

"Yeah," I say.

"We'll figure it out together," Ian says. "But I was thinking about food banks. You know, there's so much food wasted at all these shows."

Ethan nods. "And drinks too."

Ashton says, "We could do something for making sports more queer-inclusive. Maybe?"

Owen runs a hand through his hair. "Yeah, that would be cool too."

Janet makes a few notes on her phone as the guys all talk over each other, listing off one idea after another.

I have the most amazing friends. I can't believe I didn't see it before.

Eventually Janet holds up her hand. "All right, let's pause here so I can do some research. And I'll talk to The Label, Hunter. We'll get things changed."

"Just like that?"

"Just like that." Janet smirks. "I'm pretty good at making things happen, you know. Now get ready. You're on in five."

**TRANSCRIPT OF KISS & TELL
PRESS CONFERENCE**

April 19, 2022–1:00 P.M. Eastern Daylight Time

ASHTON NIGHTINGALE: Thank you all so much for coming today. Before we get started, Hunter wanted to say a few things.

HUNTER DRAKE: Yeah, thanks for putting me on the spot, dude.

ASHTON NIGHTINGALE: Anytime.

HUNTER DRAKE: I'd just like to apologize for my behavior last night, on *America Tonight*, and after at the club. It was selfish and very uncool, and I'm sorry to anyone I've disappointed. But we're making some changes and I'm going to try to be better about articulating when I'm struggling, instead of bottling things up and then melting down. So, just, sorry.

ETHAN NGUYEN: Right, that was awkward. Anyway, rumors of Hunter leaving or getting kicked out have been greatly exaggerated. We're stuck with him. And so are all of you.

IAN SOUZA: So, we're here today to share some exciting news. The first item of which is that . . . Owen, why don't you tell them?

OWEN JOGIA: We have officially begun recording our third studio album. We're exploring new horizons with this one, working with an amazing producer named Gregg G. Jones, to expand our sound. Hunter and I have loved working on the first two albums, but we're all excited to learn and grow and evolve as artists.

ETHAN NGUYEN: It's going to be awesome.

IAN SOUZA: It is. And now, the second piece of news . . . Ashton?

ASHTON NIGHTINGALE: All right. Well. We are thrilled to announce that we are adding dates to our *Come Say Hello* tour. We'll be taking a brief break in May, and then, starting in June, we'll be playing arenas in South America, Europe, Africa, Asia, and Australia.

ETHAN NYUGEN: WORLD TOUR, BABY!

OWEN JOGIA: We tried to figure out a show in Antarctica, but it didn't work out.

IAN SOUZA: The whole schedule is going up this afternoon, and tickets will be going on sale next week. We're so grateful to our fans all over the world, and hope you'll come and say hello!

HUNTER DRAKE: Thank you!

36

NEW YORK, NY • APRIL 19, 2022

After sound check, Owen comes back to my dressing room to go over the latest demos—including one from Ashton.

"When did he even record it?"

"He's been working on it for a while. I thought he told you."

I shake my head. "No. I've had my head up my ass too much."

Owen gives me a playful shove. "Well, you finally managed to extricate it."

"Yeah."

I listen along. It's a good start, but it's missing something.

"What if we add in a second bridge?" I pull my Strat onto my lap and play a riff, scat along. "Something like that?"

Owen bobs his head. "Yeah."

366

"Ashton give it a name?"

"Crossover."

I laugh and sing, "The way your pillow smells like your shampoo, Oh I wanna crossover to you . . ."

Owen cocks his head. "Actually that's really good."

"I was just joking."

"Yeah, your best stuff comes when you don't take yourself too seriously."

"You think?"

"Yeah. What else?"

I write out some more lyrics. They're unrefined and don't always rhyme, but they're a start.

"Yeah. Good. Lemme show Ashton."

"Don't tell him I wrote them, okay? He'll just go along with it if he knows. I want him to be honest."

Owen purses his lips. "That's fair. But they're good, Hunter."

"I thought maybe I didn't know how to make anything good anymore."

"I think that every time I sit down to write. Maybe that's just part of it."

"Maybe. I wish it wasn't so hard, though."

There's a knock on the door frame. Aidan asks, "Hey. You got a minute?"

Owen shuts his laptop. "I need to grab a snack anyway. You good?"

"Yeah. Thanks, Owen."

Aidan and I study each other for a long moment. He's wearing a crooked I ♥ NEW YORK cap, and he's got a huge pair of sunglasses tucked into his shirt collar.

"You go sightseeing?"

"Yeah, me and Mom. I wanted to do it before I headed home."

"What do you mean?"

"I fly out on Thursday."

"Oh."

Aidan glances at the spot on the couch Owen vacated; I scoot aside so he can sit.

"I thought you'd be glad."

"I don't hate you, Aidan."

"Even after the whole, uh, thing in the studio?"

I shake my head. "No. I mean, I've been kind of a mess myself."

"I'm sorry. I promise, I didn't come to try and, like, get back together."

"Why did you?"

"Well, Dad really was pissed at me, so that was a big part of it. But." He sighs. "Growing up, it was me and Ashton. And then it was all three of us. And then it was just you and me. And then it was just me. I didn't know how to handle it."

"I get that."

"But that's not very fair, to you or to Ashton. I think I need to figure out how to be Aidan again. I've spent so long being your boyfriend, being your ex, being a disaster . . . I think

I need to just be, for a while. Does that make any sense?"

"It does." I pat his knee in return. "Maybe I need to figure out how to be Hunter again."

"I don't think you've ever had a problem with that," Aidan says. "You've always known exactly who you want to be."

The muffled sounds of PAR-K's sound check crackle over the speakers as Kaivan tunes his tom-toms.

"And you've always known what you wanted."

"What's that supposed to mean?" I say.

"You still like him, don't you? I saw the way you two were together."

"It was all fake."

"I don't think it was. I, uh, talked to him some, last night, while we were trying to figure out where you went. He was freaking out. He cares about you. Why else would he go along with Nazeer to come get you?"

"Lost a rock-paper-scissors tourney?"

"Hunt."

I sigh. Everything's so messed up. With The Label, with our careers. How are we supposed to be together now?

Should we even try?

"At least talk to him."

"I guess." I study Aidan's face. There's a tiny bit of light in his eyes again. "I missed being friends. Everything was different once we started dating. But we were good at being friends, weren't we?"

He squeezes my shoulder and stands. "Yeah. We were."

The label on Kaivan's dressing room is misspelled: K-H-A-I-V-A-N, printed in block letters over a blue silhouette of Madison Square Garden. I shake my head and knock on his door.

Time for one last stop on the Hunter Drake Apology Tour.

"Oh. Hey, Hunter."

"Hey." I hold up a brown paper bag. "Peace offering?"

Kaivan snorts and lets me in. His dressing room is basically identical to mine, except the washroom is on the left instead of the right.

I set the bag on the coffee table. "The lady at the store told me these were good."

He pulls out the little box of diamond-shaped cakes and gasps. "You found loz?"

"She said they were almond cakes."

"Loz badoom." Kaivan pops one into his mouth and smiles.

"Cool." I swallow. He's still standing over the table, so I can't just sit. I lean against the wall, but that seems too casual, so I straighten up. "Listen. I wanted to thank you. For coming to get me. I don't think I ever said it properly, but. Well. Thanks."

Kaivan nods. I stare at his neck muscles instead of his eyes, because I don't know what I'll see. I don't know what I want to see.

"You didn't have to do it. I wouldn't blame you if you didn't."

"I wanted to," he mutters.

"Why?"

I meet his eyes then. Dark brown, filled with warmth, but his eyebrows are furrowed.

"Do you really have to ask?"

"Yeah," I say. "I don't understand. I thought . . . I don't know what to think."

Kaivan finally sits, rests his elbows on his knees. "I'm sorry. I was a dick."

I step closer, balance on the armrest of his couch. "I'm sorry too."

"Wait. Let me finish. Okay?"

I nod.

"I had honestly forgotten about all those old interviews. They were before I came out, and I was trying to read as straight, you know? And it was easy to shit on you, and music like yours, because that's what all the straight guys at school did."

"Kaivan . . ."

He holds up his hand. "You know the first time I got called a fag?"

I close my eyes. I hate that word.

I've always felt comfortable reclaiming queer, but the f-word always felt . . . I don't know. More violent.

"I was ten, and I was on the bus home from school, and one of the girls was singing along to One Direction, and so I joined in. And my best friend at the time turned and asked me if I was a fag."

My face is on fire. "I'm so . . ."

"You don't need to apologize. I just want you to understand. I haven't always been as brave as you. I've had to do things and say things because at the time I thought that was the only way to survive."

"It's okay." I reach for his hand, and when he doesn't pull away, I rest mine on top of his. "I get it."

"How can you?"

"I mean, I played hockey for ten years. I've said and done things to survive too. So I get it. Maybe not the same way as you, or as bad as you, but . . ."

"Okay." He relaxes his hand a bit underneath mine, gently twines our fingers, and I let him.

"I'm sorry for not listening better. For not getting what it was like."

"It's okay. It wasn't fair of me to take everything out on you, either. I was more mad at the system, you know? Racism, capitalism, all that shit. You didn't build it. But you benefit from it. And it was easier to be mad at you."

"I can take it," I say, and I'm kind of surprised at myself how much I mean it. How much I want to mean it.

"You shouldn't have to."

I focus on Kaivan's jaw, because his eyes are too intense. "You still didn't tell me why you came. To the club."

Kaivan snorts. "Because I still care about you. I still like you. And not because I think you're good for my career or anything."

He rests his free hand against my cheek.

"You're sweet. You're funny. You're brave. You're kind of a disaster. But I like that about you. Not to mention your hockey butt."

I blush.

"I still like you too. You make me want to be better than I am."

Kaivan's expression softens.

"So what now?"

"I don't know," I say. "What do you want?"

"I want you." Kaivan's eyes are shining. "You make me want to be better than I am too."

"So, what? We just decide to be boyfriends again?"

Kaivan pulls my hand to his chest and holds it over his heart, but then he smirks. "Unless you want to see if The Label will do a press release?"

I groan, and laugh, and hide my blushing face against his shoulder. "No. They are not allowed to mess with my dating life anymore."

"Okay, then." Kaivan shifts, places his hand beneath my chin, and suddenly we're nose-to-nose.

My breath hitches.

He leans in, slowly, so slowly.

Fuck that.

I press my lips against his, feel him laugh and smile against me.

I kiss him. I hold him. I hum as he wraps his arms around me and pulls me down on top of him. He breaks the kiss, cheeks flushed.

"So. World tour, huh?"

"Yeah. Is that okay? It's not for a couple months. We've got time to figure us out."

"Yeah. I'm happy for you. You've earned this."

I shake my head.

"You have. I know I said some shitty things. But you work hard and you're talented. And maybe there was luck and timing involved too. But that doesn't mean you don't deserve it."

"Thanks." I rest my head against his chest.

"Hunter?" He asks.

"Yeah?"

"You sure I can't call you baby?"

"Absolutely not."

"But—"

I shut him up with another kiss.

SET LIST

Ginásio do Ibirapuera—June 11, 2022

Heartbreak Fever

Found You First

Young & Free

By Ourselves

Find Me Waiting

Competition

No Restraint

Kiss & Tell

INTERMISSION

Come Say Hello

Missing You

Wish You Were Here

Prodigy

Euphoria

Your Room

Crossover

Over & Out

ENCORE

Poutine

EPILOGUE

"**O**brigado, amamos vocês!" Ian shouts, and the crowd screams. They adore him. He's in a Brazilian national team soccer jersey, canary yellow and loud, and he looks right at home even though he's never been to Brazil before. "We are so happy to be here tonight!"

Ethan steps up next to Ian. He's wearing his fashion glasses tonight, though he has to keep pushing them up his nose as he sweats. "All this is because of you. Our beautiful fans."

Another scream.

Owen comes up on Ian's other side, throws his arm over Ian's shoulder. "We've got just a few more songs for you tonight. This next one is brand! New!"

This time, the scream is so loud I actually wince, because it starts bleeding through my in-ears.

Owen waits for the crowd to settle. "It was written by our very own Ashton Nightingale."

A spotlight picks up Ashton, who's literally blushing.

Ashton never blushes.

"I only did the music. Hunter did the words."

My spotlight picks me up too, at my pedal board, and I give a wave. "I can't believe we never actually wrote a song together before. We've been friends for, what? Nine years?"

"Nearly ten," Ashton says.

I pop my mic back into its stand, sling my Strat over my shoulders. "Well, it's pretty amazing being up here, with all of you. Getting to sing together with my friends. Being gay and doing crimes."

Laughter ripples through the audience.

"Yeah, same," Ethan says.

"You've got the crimes down, all right," Ian says, shoving Ethan away.

"Hey!" Ethan and Ian pretend to wrestle until Ian gets Ethan in a headlock.

"Don't mind them," Owen says.

Ashton clears his throat. "Anyway! This one is for all of you. It's called 'Crossover.'"

The crowd applauds. The lights shift. The drums kick in.

I check the presets on my pedal board.

Spotlights pick us up, one by one: Ashton and Ethan and Ian and Owen and then me.

I hit a chord, let it ring.

Across the stage, Ashton catches my eye and smiles, before he brings his mic to his lips and starts to sing.

My skin crackles. My heart sparks.

The crowd screams, waves Brazilian flags, Canadian flags, rainbow flags, signboards to let us know how much they love us.

I love them too. I love getting to do this.

I love getting to be with my friends.

There's no other word for it.

Euphoria.

KISS & TELL
COME SAY HELLO TOUR 2022

THE AUTHOR WOULD LIKE TO THANK...

AGENT	MOLLY O'NEILL & THE ROOT LITERARY TEAM
EDITORS	DANA CHIDIAC ELLEN CORMIER
PUBLICIST	KAITLIN KNEAFSEY
PUBLISHER	LAURI HORNIK
EDITORIAL DIRECTOR	NANCY MERCADO
COVER DESIGN	SAMIRA IRAVANI KAITLIN YANG THERESE EVANGELISTA
COVER ILLUSTRATION	SUNSHEINE
INTERIOR DESIGN	JASON HENRY
COPYEDITING	REGINA CASTILLO
MANAGING EDITOR	TABITHA DULLA
MARKETING	BRI LOCKHART EMILY ROMERO CHRISTINA COLANGELO KARA BRAMMER
DIGITAL MARKETING	ALEX GARBER FELICITY VALLENCE JAMES AKINAKA SHANNON SPANNER
PUBLICITY	SHANTA NEWLIN ELYSE MARSHALL
SCHOOL & LIBRARY	SUMMER OGATA VENESSA CARSON CARMELA IARIA TREVOR INGERSON

SALES	DEBRA POLANSKY
	JOE ENGLISH
	TODD JONES
	MARY MCGRATH
SUBRIGHTS TEAM	HELEN BOOMER
	KIM RYAN
	SIAU RUI GOH
	MICAH HECHT
FILM & TV AGENT	DEBBIE DEUBLE HILL
TITLING	NATALIE C. PARKER
EARLY READERS	TESSA GRATTON
	LANA WOOD JOHNSON
	JULIAN WINTERS
EMOTIONAL SUPPORT	THE GROUP CHAT
	THE SLACK
	THE UNTAMED
	WORD OF HONOR
	TED LASSO
GUITAR LESSONS	MICHAEL JUDD
SKATING LESSONS	CHRISTY TURNER
SPECIAL THANKS	TARA HUDSON
	ALEX LONDON
	JULIE MURPHY
	SIERRA SIMONE
	JANDY NELSON
	& THE MAGIC HOUR MUSES
	MADCAP RETREATS
	MY FRIENDS
	MY FAMILY
SUPPORTERS & FANS	BOOKSELLERS
	LIBRARIANS
	EDUCATORS
	INFLUENCERS
	READERS LIKE YOU